I0588230

Quake at Candlestick

Quake at Candlestick

Jacki Rush Warych

A Novel

This book is dedicated to
my supportive husband, Michael.

Quake at Candlestick

ACKNOWLEDGMENTS

I am grateful to all of my friends and family members who have listened to my ideas about this novel through the years and have been extremely supportive.

My wholehearted appreciation goes out to all of those who read my manuscript and helped with proofreading and suggestions: Jan Bullard, Velma Choury, Karen Corral, Shirley Genetin, Terri Robertson, Kristen Rush, Richard Rush and Michael Warych.

A big thank you to my niece, Barbara Genetin, for all of her support and help on early cover design ideas, and to my fellow writer and sister-in-law, Mary Vosika, for her encouragement and support.

My amazing Mendocino County friends inspired many of the characters and events that took place in my book, especially Mary Korte and Cindy Morninglight. Heartfelt thanks to you.

Thank you to the staff at Next Century Publishing Company, especially my project manager, Tiffany Harelik, who was a great help throughout the process of publishing this book.

CHAPTER 1

October 17, 1989

10:30 a.m.

As Katie drove across the Golden Gate Bridge toward downtown San Francisco, she looked over at her son Sam next to her in the shotgun spot. Sam was thirteen, had short, brown, curly hair, and bright blue eyes like his mother. He was wearing a San Francisco Giants hat pulled over his eyes, as he was reading a Sports Illustrated magazine. He was tall for his age and had a lanky build like his father. It was hard for Katie to fathom that her first born was a teenager already. She glanced in her rearview mirror at her eight-year-old son Max in the back seat of her car. His blonde collar-length hair peeked out of the bottom of his baseball cap and he was starting to wake up. "Are we almost there, Mom?" he said, rubbing his emerald green eyes.

"Yeah, we are on Van Ness Avenue now. Watch for Tommy's Joynt. It's on the corner of Geary and Van Ness."

"There it is!" Max yelled out. He recognized the bright blue building with big red letters that spelled out the name of the famous Hof Brau. "Do you think Nonno is there already?" They had always called their mother's dad Nonno, the Italian word for grandfather.

"I'm sure he is. He planned to get here early to make sure we got a spot, since it's sure to be crowded today with the World Series.

It's hard to believe that the Giants are finally in the World Series, and if that wasn't enough, they are playing Oakland. Lots of people will be staking out a place to watch the game at Tommy's. Help me look for a parking spot." Miraculously, a car pulled out of a spot only a couple blocks from the restaurant, and Katie was able to pull in. It was a two-hour spot, but that was plenty of time.

As Sam opened his door he said, "It's really warm today. I don't think I need my jacket."

While giving Max quarters to put in the parking meter, Katie said, "It is pretty warm and a little humid, too, but you need to take your jacket along. You know how Candlestick is; it could be extremely cold there, especially when the sun goes down and the wind and fog come in."

Katie locked the doors of her small, yellow Datsun station wagon as the boys stuffed their jackets in their backpacks and headed down the street toward Tommy's Joynt. Max ran down the sidewalk ahead of them as Katie yelled to him, "Wait at the corner."

Sam ran ahead to catch up with him and yelled, "Watch out for cars, stupid, this is the city and cars go fast here—you don't want to get run over."

Max reluctantly took his brother's hand, and about that time Katie caught up with them. "Max, I know you are very excited about going to the World Series game with your grandfather, but you need to slow down and pay attention. Thanks, Sam, I appreciate you running ahead like you did; will you keep an eye on him at the game, too?"

"Aw, Mom, I don't want to be worrying about him, I just want to watch the game." When he saw his mom's serious expression he relented. "Okay, but tell him not to be a pain."

"He called me stupid," Max complained. Katie rolled her eyes and changed the subject, "Let's go in, and I need the two of you to get along. This is a big deal that you get to go to this game, and you need to be on your best behavior for your grandfathers. And Max, you need to listen to your big brother." Max nodded reluctantly.

They could smell the delicious aroma of garlic and roasted meat wafting from the restaurant before they even walked in the door. When they walked into Tommy's Joynt, their grandfather Gino, sixty-four years old with short salt-and-pepper hair and wire-rimmed glasses, immediately spotted them and waved them over to one of the long tables where he had saved seats. Lots of people were milling around and standing in line to order the delicious sandwiches and buffalo stew that Tommy's was known for. Max ran over and yelled, "Nonno!" and gave him a big hug, which Gino returned by swinging him through the air and giving him a kiss on the top of the head. Sam, who was now 5 '11, towered over his 5' 6 grandfather, and offered him a handshake. He had recently become self conscious about public displays of affection, which his Nonno understood, shaking his hand and patting his shoulder.

Gino said, "Are you guys ready for the big game? Oakland may have beaten us the last two games, but we will be on our own turf today and our luck is bound to turn around. Let's get you guys some chow." He looked at his daughter and smiled. At 38, she looked prettier than ever with her brown, curly hair pulled back in a pony tail, her beautiful blue eyes sparkling under her long, dark eye lashes, and her gorgeous smile. She had always been a natural beauty, and wore very little makeup. More importantly, he was proud of what a good mother she was to his grandchildren.

Sam ordered a roast beef sandwich on a French roll, Gino chose the Buffalo Stew, and Katie and Max decided to share a turkey sandwich. The steam off the freshly cooked food permeated the air as they walked down the counter, and the men with their large white hats who were carving the huge pieces of meat smiled at the big-eyed boys as they piled it on their plates.

As they sat down at a long wooden table, the manager came by, patted Gino on the back, and said, "Gino Pulli, my favorite cop, this town just isn't the same since you retired. Are these your grandsons?"

Gino nodded proudly, and the man continued, "Your grandfather is a legend around here. We always knew we could count on him to keep the neighborhood safe."

"Thanks. Well, it helped that I had a good place like this to eat and all the free coffee I could drink. You know, this restaurant opened the same year I became a cop, in 1947; this area was my first beat, and I was here at least ten years. Even when I worked other places in the city, this was always my go-to place for lunch. This is my daughter, Katie; I used to bring her in here a lot when she was young. These are her sons Max and Sam. I'm taking them to the game. Looks like you are going to have quite a crowd here to watch the game."

"You boys are very lucky! Yeah, I better get back to work; it is going to be a busy night. It's a few hours before the game even starts and we already have a full house," the man said as he quickly wiped the nearby table and picked up some large glass beer mugs.

They all enjoyed their meal, and the boys were stuffed. Gino said, "How about if we get dessert at the ballpark? I know you boys like those malted ice cream cups; does that sound good?" The boys nodded eagerly and then Gino continued, "Let's get going. Traffic is going to be bad, and so is finding a place to park. We want to get there early so we can watch batting practice."

Sam said, "We both brought our mitts; I sure hope I catch a foul ball!"

"Yeah, wouldn't that be a keepsake?" Gino continued, "So what are your plans, Katie?"

"I am going to do a little shopping and then I am going to go over to Oakland. I am supposed to meet my friend Rosemary for dinner at 5:30 at her sister's house. I'll spend the night there and then head back tomorrow."

Max piped in, "Our dad is going to meet us at your house, Nonno, after the game."

"Yeah, I talked to him, so he knows where I hide the spare key, and if he gets there before us he's just going to hang out and wait. He may come early and watch the game on TV."

The guys walked Katie to her car to see her off. They then walked further up Geary near St. Mary's Cathedral where Gino had parked his car. Sam yelled, "Shotgun!" and received the coveted spot in his grandfather's light blue Ford Taurus sedan.

3:30 p.m.

As Gino predicted, traffic toward Candlestick Park was very congested, and when they arrived there they had to go to a couple of parking lots before they found one that had space available. The boys grabbed their backpacks and Gino got his trusty red plaid picnic bag which contained his thermos and worn plaid blanket. Max took his grandfather's hand as they headed to the crowded entrance of the park. The smell of hot dogs, popcorn, garlic fries, and stale beer permeated the air.

Gino gave the boys their tickets to hand to the man at the turnstile entrance and said, "Make sure you hold onto the stub. It will be worth some money someday. Stay close to me, boys. Be prepared that Candlestick Park is going to be rocking tonight and electrified with all the excitement like you have never experienced. This crowd could get totally carried away."

They made their way to the seats that were right up from first base. Gino had had season tickets since 1960 when they had opened the Park. They were prime seats, and Gino especially appreciated them now that he was retired and could go to more games. For many years, he had shared the tickets with some of his police friends. They would take turns going depending on their days off and shifts, but now one of them had died and the other retired to Palm Springs, so Gino was sole owner of the tickets.

As they headed down the steps to their seats Sam asked, "Grandpa Bill is supposed to meet us at the seats, right?"

"Right," said Gino abruptly. Bill was the boys' dad's father and he had also had season tickets next to Gino's since 1960. He was a retired, wealthy investment broker who had a very expensive house in the exclusive Woodside community of the Bay Area. He and Gino had taken an instant disliking to each other when they met in 1960, but neither of them wanted to give up their prime seats. Much to their chagrin, Bill's son Eric had fallen in love with Gino's daughter Katie, and their lives had become entwined.

As they sat down, Max asked, "Nonno, how come you and Grandpa Bill don't like each other?"

Taken aback, Gino said, "Well, I don't know if it's that. I guess we are just different in a lot of ways. What we have in common is that we love the two of you and are lucky to be your grandpas. That's truly special."

4:45 p.m.

Max exclaimed, "I see Grandpa Bill!" A tall, slim, good-looking man with silver hair was heading down the aisle to their row and waved casually at the boys. He then squeezed past Gino and his grandsons to get to his seat, shaking Sam's hand as he passed and awkwardly accepted Max's exuberant hug.

Gino wished that he didn't have to share his grandchildren and this special event with cold, snobbish Bill Smith. He realized the boys were Bill's grandsons too, but Bill never seemed that excited to see them and he had totally ignored Gino, which was typical.

Gino thought that taking a little walk and taking a break from the situation would be a good idea, so he announced, "It's still forty-five minutes before the game starts; I think I'll go to the snack bar and get that ice cream." He stood up and started to walk down the aisle.

The boys looked at the programs, and Sam and Bill commented on the batting order and the potential pitchers. "Too bad Dave Dravecky can't pitch for us anymore, huh? Having cancer of the bone must really suck. Will Clark is definitely my favorite player," said Sam and then added, "Mom said she thought that Stevie Wonder was going to sing the Star-Spangled Banner and she was right. It's right here in the program."

Out of the blue, Max announced, "Grandpa, I've gotta pee."

"For God's sake, Max, the third game of the World Series is going to start in a little while," Bill said sharply. "They are warming up now. It's the first time the Giants have been in it in over twenty-five years and I sure as hell don't want to get stuck in this crowd and miss the first pitch. Your Nonno just left to go to the snack bar ten minutes ago. Why didn't you say you needed to go then?"

Max shrugged and his eyes welled up with tears. Trying to appease his grandfather's aggravation, Sam looked up from his program and piped in, "I'll take him."

"Okay. Thanks, Sam, I guess that is all right. You are thirteen after all, but make sure to go to the one right by the snack bar near our aisle. Go directly there, don't get separated, and do not talk to anyone!"

As the boys scooted down the row toward the aisle, Bill noticed what good-looking young men they were becoming. He thought, "But I'm not one to gush over them and spoil them like their other grandfather, the wop cop. He is so overboard with affection. Why does he go by that Italian word for grandfather, anyway, for God's sake, the guy was born in America? I sure dread spending the next three hours or more with him. I disliked him the first time I met him in 1960 when I went to the opening game and discovered I had season tickets next to him, and I still can't stand him. If these seats weren't so prime, at field level and on the first baseline, I would have changed my seats twenty-nine years ago. It's damned ironic that we ended up having grandkids in common."

Some of the people who had neighboring season seats started arriving, and Bill started talking to them. It was interesting having lives cross here at the games throughout the years, watching families growing up and their parents growing old. Gino made his way through the row and, noticing the empty seats, he asked sharply, "Bill, where are the boys?"

"Max had to go to the bathroom, so Sam took him."

"What the hell were you thinking to let them go to the bathroom by themselves? Do you have any idea how many perverts lurk in ballparks? Besides, there are 60,000 people here today—they could easily get lost!" Gino shouted.

Bill argued, "For God's sake, Gino, I was riding around on streetcars going to games at Seal Stadium when I was Max's age. You are such an old woman, worrying all the time. You coddle those boys."

Gino yelled, "Bill, you dumb ass, the world is damn different now!"

At that moment, there was a loud cracking noise, and the stadium started shaking. Gino grabbed the seat in front of him, and he watched the light stanchions swaying back and forth. The concrete on the upper deck moved apart and he could see the sky on the other side and then it moved back into place. Pieces of Section 53 broke loose. He looked out at the field and saw the grass roll as if it were waves on the ocean. Gino screamed in panic, "Oh, my God, the boys!" Although the quake only lasted about fifteen seconds, it felt much longer as he worried about his grandsons. The announcer at the ballpark croaked, "Everyone on the upper deck of the stadium, please calmly evacuate the stands." Then the public-address system went dead because of a power outage.

A stunned and shaken Gino took a deep breath and yelled to Bill, "I'm going to find the boys!"

Bill yelled over the frantic noise of the crowd to Gino, "No, you stay here in case they find their way back here. I'm a lot taller than you and will be able to see them over the crowd. Talk to the security guards down by the field and find out where they might take lost kids. See if they have radio communication with other security guys, and if they can track the boys down."

The players fled the dugouts and were standing in clusters on the field. They called for their loved ones to come and stand with them on the grass on the edge of the infield. The players were hugging their wives and holding their little children. Team members, coaches and their families paced. Someone from the crowd yelled, "An Omen, that's what it is! The Giants will rock this series." Someone else had made a hasty sign out of cardboard that said, "That's nothing, wait till the Giants bat!"

Gino headed toward the security guard while he scanned the crowd for the boys. He said a frantic prayer for their safety, "God, please, let the boys be safe, and Katie, too, wherever she is."

CHAPTER 2

October 16, 1962

10:00 a.m.

"Katie, are you ready for the big game? This World Series is the longest one since 1911, and it's the thirteenth day today. First, it got rained out in New York and then got rained out here for a few days. The series is tied 3 to 3 and the Giants sure let them have it yesterday; they won 5–2 and the game before that 5–3. Our boys just need to win one more time and we will be world champs!" exclaimed 5-foot 6-inch, muscular, dark-haired Gino. He and his eleven-year-old daughter climbed into his blue and white 1955 Oldsmobile.

Katie said, "Oh, Daddy, thanks for taking me to the game. All the boys in my class are so jealous of me. They couldn't believe that my dad would take me to the World Series to see the Giants play the Yankees. They said it was a waste that a girl got to see Willie Mays and Willie McCovey play against Mickey Mantle and Yogi Berra."

"What did Sister Mary have to say about that?"

"She said, 'You are blessed, Katie Pulli, those tickets are worth a fortune, and girls can appreciate the World Series just as much as the boys; I wish I could go myself. And because this is such a special event I will let the class listen to the game on the radio.' The class cheered when she said that because we have never listened to the radio in class before."

Gino smiled and said, "Sister Mary has always been a baseball fan. Did you know that she went to high school with your Aunt Katherine and that she was quite a softball pitcher in her day? Unfortunately, girls still don't get to compete in leagues like the boys do, but someday, hopefully that will change."

"She plays baseball with the boys sometimes. You should see her run from base to base holding up her long black habit and trying to keep her veil from flying up. One time the wind was blowing very hard and we saw her hair! The kids were all surprised that she had hair because they thought all nuns were bald. I said that they usually just had short hair because that's what Aunt Katherine told me when I asked her if she was bald, remember, Daddy?"

"Yes, I remember. You were about five. She had just taken her final vows, and you asked her in front of Mother Superior and all of the other sisters. I was worried you had embarrassed her, but she just started laughing and then the other sisters joined in."

"I miss her, Daddy. Can we stop at the convent and see her on the way home?"

"We'll see what time it is when the game is over. We are almost to the Golden Gate Bridge. Look in the glove compartment and get me a quarter. Looks like we have time to stop at the Round House diner on the other side of the bridge and get ourselves a banana split."

"Thanks, Daddy, a banana split and the World Series; I am so lucky!" Katie said as her shiny, long, brown, curly hair bobbed as she nodded her approval. She had inherited her mother's beautiful Irish blue eyes, creamy complexion, and her father's dark hair and long eyelashes. Her big smile revealed a mouth full of metal braces that she had recently acquired.

"Yeah, we were so lucky to get these tickets. You know I share the two season tickets with Joe and Bob who work with me at the San Francisco Police Department. We drew straws on who would get first pick of the games. I got the long straw and I chose this game. I thought about taking your mom since she loves baseball so much, but

I just couldn't see how I could manage her wheelchair in the stands. Someday I hope they make it so people in wheelchairs can have access to places like ballparks."

"Dad, do you think Mama will ever be out of her wheelchair? I pray every day for a miracle for her."

Gino choked up, cleared his throat and said,"I don't know, honey. Multiple sclerosis is a terrible disease. Of course, we can pray for a miracle, but I don't want you to get your hopes up." He found a parking place in the crowded lot of the diner and said, "Ready to go in and get that banana split?" As he walked into the diner with his daughter, he marveled how he could be a tough cop in the worst of circumstances, and yet could choke up so easily when talking about his precious wife.

1:00 p.m. - Candlestick Park

Katie and Gino stood in line at the gate of Candlestick Park and made their way through the excited crowd. Ticket scalpers were trying to hawk their seats for outrageous prices, and vendors of souvenirs were calling out their goods. It was a carnival atmosphere full of banners and flags, and the familiar smell of popcorn and hot dogs permeated the air.

Gino said, "Hold onto my hand, Katie, and don't let go. This crowd is crazy. I have never seen this place pumped up like this. I don't want you to get trampled."

Katie replied, "So, Daddy, whoever wins this game wins the World Series? Is that why everyone is so excited?"

"That's right. It's tied now three games for the Yankees and three for the Giants, and that doesn't happen very often in the World Series. The Yankees have won nine out of the last twelve years, so they have been quite smug. They have been saying that they would easily take this series, and for it to be tied is truly amazing. You know that the Giants used to be a New York team. They just moved out here four years ago. There is nothing like the rivalry between two teams that are from the same town. And it is very exciting for SF because up until the Giants came there has never been a Major League Baseball team in Northern California. We had a Minor League team, the Seals, but they left when the Giants moved here.

"Got your ticket ready? We are about to go through the turnstile. Make sure to hold onto that ticket stub, it might be worth some money someday."

Gino and Katie made their way through the crowd. They got to their row and sat next to Bill Smith, a tall, good-looking man, and his thirteen- year-old son, Eric. Katie was caught off guard by how cute Eric was, and she thought "Wow! He looks like a surfer with that great tan and blonde hair sweeping over his eyebrow. There are no guys in my school who are nearly that good looking. Why am I even thinking about this? I want to be a nun. That isn't what future nuns are supposed to be thinking about. And the boy's father, isn't that the man my dad is always complaining about—the stuck-up, wealthy broker who lives in the rich town of Woodside?"

Gino interrupted her thoughts by saying, "Alvin Dark, the Giants' manager, has a lot riding on this game, so the starting line-up is downright important. Juan Marichal pitched Game Four and they creamed the Yankees 7–3, but it looks like they have Jack Sanford pitching today, and of course, Willie McCovey in left field, and Willie Mays in center field. Orlando Cepeda is on first base and Felipe Alou is in right field."

Katie was following along in her program and said, "The Yankees starting pitcher is Ralph Terry. Mickey Mantle is playing center field, Roger Maris is in right field, but I don't see Yogi Berra on the starting line-up."

The teams were announced and then went to their positions. Gino said, "Of course, the Yankees will be up first because they are the visiting team."

Standing for the Star-Spangled Banner, Gino put his arm around Katie as they held their hands over their hearts, and enthusiastically sang along with the crowd and joined in the thunderous applause when the umpire yelled "PLAY BALL!"

The first four innings of the game were scoreless, and then in the top of the fifth inning, Yankee first baseman Bill Skowron got to third base, shortstop Tony Kubek grounded into a double play, and Skowron scored the first run of the game.

Gino pulled out his red plaid picnic bag that contained a matching big thermos of hot chocolate and poured a cup for himself and Katie. She loved the aroma of the Ghirardelli chocolate that her father always used to make the hot chocolate. He unwrapped the wax paper that contained the delicious salami and cheese sandwiches that he had made for them.

Eric was engrossed in the game and said very little to Katie. At one point, she offered him some of the hot chocolate, but he declined. The wind really picked up and Gino offered his red plaid stadium blanket to Katie, and she gratefully tucked it around herself.

The innings ticked away with the score 1–0 until it was time for the seventh inning stretch, and the crowd all stood to sing "Take Me Out to the Ball Game." She loved to sing this song with her dad, swaying and exaggerating the words. They laughed and sat down. Gino bought her some cracker jacks and a Giants pennant from one of the vendors. She opened her cracker jacks to find a tiny compass.

At the bottom of the ninth inning, the Giants were sweating it. They needed to score two runs to win the game and at least one run to tie it. Matty Alou was up first, batting for Giants' relief pitcher Billy O'Dell. He hit a foul ball and then hit a bunt and made it to first base. The Yankees' pitcher struck out the next two batters, Felipe Alou and Chuck Hiller.

"Look, Daddy, Willie Mays is up. He'll save the day!" Katie exclaimed. Mays hit a double into the right field corner, but Alou stayed at third base because he knew how hard Roger Maris could throw, and he wanted to play it safe. Next up was Willie McCovey, known as a great hitter, but he hit a line drive that was caught by second baseman Bobby Richardson. The game was over.

Gino said, "Can you believe that we lost this World Series by one point, what a heartbreaker!"

The crowd somberly trailed out of their seats as they lamented their team's loss of the World Series. The Smiths had exited out the other side of the row without saying anything. After they left, Katie said, "Daddy, I was expecting that Mr. Smith to be a lot worse; he didn't seem stuck-up and his son seemed pretty nice."

"Well, he was probably on his best behavior because he had his son with him. He usually has one of his bank clients with him and he is constantly name-dropping about living on the Peninsula and golfing with Bing Crosby or sailing his yacht. He is definitely full of himself and that son of his is probably spoiled rotten. Let's get to our car and get over to Tommy's Joynt for dinner. I can't wait to have some of their buffalo stew and to warm up after that game."

As they drove to the restaurant and her dad replayed the game in his mind, Katie thought of something else. She was reconsidering her plan of becoming a nun. Would her mom and dad be disappointed? Until she saw Eric, she didn't know what it felt like to have a crush on a boy—and he was so cute. Well, she had plenty of time to figure that out!

6:30 p.m. - Tommy's Joynt

"Daddy, that dinner was so good here; I think that was the best hamburger I ever had. And did you know that in the women's bathroom when you sit on the toilet a siren goes off? And so many of the people in the restaurant know you," Katie chatted excitedly as they got up from their seats.

"Yeah, there is nothing like their buffalo stew. This area used to be my beat, and I ate many meals in here, and it is like family still."

After paying the bill and leaving a generous tip, Gino stopped to use the payphone to make two calls. After getting off the phone he said, "I called your mom and she is doing fine and said to take our time. I called the convent and talked to Mother Superior about seeing Sister Katherine and she said we could come from 7:30 to 8:00 and visit with her in the parlor, so we will head over there right now." Gino and Katie walked out the front door as staff and some customers yelled their farewells to Gino. They climbed into Gino's Oldsmobile, and he started up the car and cranked the heat up.

As they drove along Katie said, "I sure wish that Sister Katherine could come and stay with us sometime, Dad. The only time we see her is in her convent parlor. I know she came for your mother's funeral, but that is the only time I can remember her coming and that was just for the day. And she hardly ever gets to call us, she just can write us."

"The rules do seem strict, but there must be good reasons. I am so proud of my little sister; it is such an honor. Did you know that my mother always prayed that one of us would become a priest or nun? And from what I understand, she is an excellent teacher as well. OK, here we are."

Katie and Gino walked up the brick steps of the convent. Katie rang the bell, and a little elderly nun opened the peephole. "I am Gino Pulli, and this is my daughter, Katie. We are here to see Sister Katherine." She opened the heavy oak door and led them down a shiny waxed hardwood floor entryway into a parlor that had a brown brocade sofa, three wooden chairs, several shelves filled with books, a large crucifix, and two beautiful paintings of Jesus and His Blessed Mother on adjacent walls.

A few minutes later, Sister Katherine dressed in a full-length habit and veil glided into the room with the rosary beads around her waist making a jingling noise. Katie hugged her aunt and excitedly told her that they had just come back from the game. Gino wanted to throw his arms around her and give her a kiss, but thought better of it and took her hand and squeezed it instead. "Sis, I mean Sister; it is so good to see you." It was always awkward to know what would be considered appropriate.

Sister Katherine was smiling from ear to ear, "It is such a blessing to see both of you. And Katie, you have grown up so much since I saw you last; I have missed you so. I know I haven't written as often as I should, but you are always in my thoughts and prayers, especially Maggie. How is she doing?"

"Mama needs to use a wheelchair now most of the time. Sometimes she can walk a little bit if she has something to hold onto. Our neighbor Mrs. Williams is staying with her today while we have been in the city. We called her after the game, and she had listened to it on the radio and was sad that the Giants didn't win, but she was glad that they made it this far and maybe next year they will go all the way!"

Gino could see the sympathy in his sister's eyes and, trying to keep from getting emotional, he added, "Multiple sclerosis is so darn unpredictable. We sure have been hoping it will go into remission, but so far it keeps progressing. I am so proud of Katie; she is such a big help to her mom. I try to work the swing shift, and that way I am there in the mornings and Katie is there after school. "

"Your mom is a beautiful woman and has such a great attitude, and you seem to be taking after her, in looks and in your outlook." Lowering her voice Sister Katherine continued, "I would love to come and visit her, but my request was denied because she is not in critical condition and she is not an immediate family member. I know I have taken a vow of obedience, but sometimes it is very difficult. With Vatican II in session right now, there is talk that Pope John XXIII is going to push for orders to become less rigid and become more modern. Hopefully, this will include more flexibility in visiting privileges; after all, we aren't criminals! I hear that they may even encourage updating our habits; can you imagine showing my legs or my hair again?" she giggled.

The bell started chiming softly from the convent chapel. "It is time for evening prayers. God bless you and know that I pray for you all each day," Sister Katherine said gently as she led them to the heavy dark oak doors and hugged them as they exited into the cold, foggy night.

8:00 p.m.

Gino and Katie left the convent bundled in their hats and coats, but they could hardly see the blue and white '58 Oldsmobile across the street through the thick fog. Some kids were running down the street, and Gino yelled at them as he got close to the car and noticed two of his hubcaps were missing. He would probably have chased after them if he hadn't had Katie with him. "Damn it anyway. What is this world coming to when you can't park your car across from a convent for a half hour without getting ripped off? This neighborhood was a good one when I was growing up, but it has really gone downhill like a lot of others in the city. No wonder so many people have moved into the suburbs."

"Is that why we moved to San Rafael, Dad?'

"Yeah, part of it. You know your mom and I lived here in the city from the time we got married until you were about a year old, but we were in a small apartment and we wanted to buy a house we could afford with a yard and a safe neighborhood. At that time, there were a lot of subdivisions being developed in Marin County that were reasonably priced. My folks weren't happy about our moving. They expected us to live in the old neighborhood in North Beach near their restaurant. They gave me a hard time at first until I pointed out that they moved thousands of miles away from their parents in Tuscany to build their lives, and I was only moving twenty miles away. They had a hard time arguing with that. You were their first grandchild, so it broke their heart that they couldn't see their bambina every day. We still saw them frequently, though," Gino answered. He immensely missed his mother who passed away two years previously, and his father who had died four years before that.

"I miss Nonna so much; she was such a super grandma," Katie said. "I loved the way she made me feel so special; she always seemed excited when I came, and I loved helping her make her delicious biscotti and pizzelle cookies. Remember how she loved for me to read to her? She would always say, 'Caterina, maka sure to bringa book to read.' I would take Bobbsey Twins and read to her while she crocheted and embroidered."

Gino said, "Yes, she was so proud of how well you did in school. Your nonna did not get to go to school. Her father sent her brothers to school, but she never had the opportunity because he thought it wasn't important for girls to be educated, that they should just help out at home and learn domestic duties. I don't think she ever forgave her dad for that. You know that shortly after your nonna and nonno were married they came to this country and they never returned."

"You mean they never saw their parents ever again?" Katie asked.

"That's right. Well, shortly after they immigrated, World War I started, then the Depression, and World War II. It was expensive and a long trip, and I also think they worried if they left they might not be able to get back in the country. Those were tough times. Your nonno worked long hours in restaurants, they took in boarders, and they skimped and saved until they could buy the restaurant with my uncle Guido. The brothers ran that restaurant together until my father died. Guido retired about that time, and that is when my cousin Frank took over the restaurant. He is an excellent chef and a great guy. We grew up together and he is like a brother to me."

"I'm so glad that they are going to move to San Rafael, too. It's going to be so great to have Laura and her brothers and sisters nearby."

"Yeah, it's good for you to have all those cousins to grow up with."

"Dad, did you work in the restaurant?"

"Oh, yes, from the time I was a little boy I would go with my father and do whatever I could. I started setting tables and peeling potatoes, then washing dishes and bussing tables. Eventually, when I got to high school I was a waiter. My pa would have liked me to take over the restaurant, but it just wasn't what I wanted to do with my life. After high school graduation, I went to City College, studying criminal justice while I worked part time at the restaurant. When I was nineteen, Pearl Harbor was bombed. Well, I knew I was going to get drafted, so I decided to join the Navy. I was sent to the Pacific because first generation Italians were not considered a good match for the war in Europe. Well, at least our families weren't sent to relocation camps like the Japanese families. There was a lot of suspicion of the Italian community and those who had not become citizens were often on house arrest except for going to work."

"Tell me again how you met Mama; I love that story."

"The atomic bombs in Hiroshima and Nagasaki ended the war in the Pacific in August 1945. I was on a supply ship, so we continued to transport supplies for several months after the war was over. I can't even describe how overjoyed I was to sail through those golden gates and disembark at Treasure Island just in time for Thanksgiving in 1945. All my family was there to meet me, and my mother was crying tears of joy; she had continually prayed the rosary the entire time I was gone. She always said she was going to get drunk when the war was over, but she wasn't much of a drinker and I think she had a glass of my pa's strong homemade wine and that was the extent of it. You know, until I was a father, I had no understanding of how much my parents loved me or how heart-wrenching it must have been for them to send me off to war when I was nineteen years old," Gino reminisced.

"San Francisco was in turmoil at the end of the war; a lot of the returning servicemen ended up being released in the area, and of course, everyone loved San Francisco and didn't want to leave. There was a three-day period where the city actually had riots because of drunken, rowdy servicemen and it took a while for things to get back to normal. It didn't help that the police force was shorthanded because so many of the policemen were drafted, and some didn't survive the war to reclaim their positions.

"After I got back, I applied for the police academy, and while I was waiting to find out about whether I was accepted or not, I worked in the restaurant. We had our Russian River cabin right outside Guerneville even back then, so the women and kids would stay up there all summer to get out of the city and swim and play along the river, and we men would go up there on the weekends during the summer.

"Some of my fondest childhood memories are going to the cabin with my mom, back in the thirties. Our cousins also had cabins right next to us and we always had such a wonderful time. Of course, the Golden Gate Bridge was not there yet, so we would go over on the ferry and head up on the train through Santa Rosa and west to the

Russian River. It seemed like half of the Italian families in SF had a place at the Russian River. It was very rustic, no indoor plumbing like we have now. We slept under the stars. Besides spending long, lazy days, splashing in the river with my cousins, there were horse stables nearby, and I would get free riding lessons for mucking out the stalls."

At this point, they had reached the Golden Gate Bridge. Gino fished a quarter out of his pocket and gave it to the toll taker.

As they drove across the bridge in the dense fog, he continued, "I found out that I had been accepted by the police academy just before the Fourth of July weekend. I was so excited, and our whole family was headed up to our cabin for the long weekend. After we arrived, my mom realized that she needed some first aid supplies, so I went to the little drug store in town. Behind the counter at the soda fountain, there was the prettiest girl I had ever seen. She had freckles and a blonde ponytail with a red ribbon and was wearing a red checkered blouse, blue skirt, bobby socks and oxfords, and when she smiled and asked if she could help me, I was speechless. I actually hadn't planned to get an ice cream soda, but I sat down and ordered one anyway. I lingered drinking that soda and talked to her between her waiting on other customers.

"I found out that she was a local girl, her uncle owned the drugstore, and that she had just graduated from high school. She was planning on going to nursing school in the fall. I explained that my family had a cabin and that I had just gotten out of the Navy and would be entering the police academy soon. About that time, her uncle came over scowling and clearing his throat said curtly, 'Maggie, it is time for you to close up the soda fountain.'

"I had been so distracted that I almost forgot the bandages and ointment, so I asked her where I could find them and she directed me to the First Aid aisle. You know, back then we didn't have band-aids. You had to make your own with gauze and tape. She asked me if someone was injured, and I said, 'No, but I have an Italian mother who always needs to be prepared for the worst.' She laughed and rang up the total on the old fashioned register with the round buttons, and when she gave me the change and when my hand brushed hers, I could feel the electricity.

"As I walked out the door, and the bell on the handle rang, I turned around and she smiled at me. My heart melted and I couldn't wait to find an excuse to see her again!"

"And then what happened, Daddy? Get to the good part," Katie insisted.

"The next night, they were having a dance at nearby Monte Rio, which was a very popular resort at the time. Monte Rio was known for its huge outdoor dance floor pavilion surrounded by majestic redwoods and couples could dance under the stars while listening to a full orchestra playing the latest big band songs. After a day on the river, no one else in the family wanted to go to the dance. However, I knew that a lot of the young people in the area went to the Saturday night dances, and I thought there was a possibility that I would see your mom there.

"I looked across the crowd that night, and there she was. She was wearing a pretty blue dress and her hair was down past her shoulders in a pageboy hairstyle and I caught sight of those snappy Irish blue eyes and I was mesmerized. Just as I was going to head over to her, a boy about her age pulled her out to the dance floor and they started to do the jitterbug. Your mom could sure jitterbug with her petticoats swirling and her hair swinging. It was very difficult for me to watch her dance with him, I was so smitten, and it hadn't occurred to me that she might have a boyfriend. I asked another girl to dance, and I started dancing toward her direction and acted surprised when she noticed me.

"Later in the evening, the orchestra was taking a break and I noticed that your mom was talking to another girl and the guy she had been dancing with wasn't around, so I walked over and introduced myself to the two girls and asked if any of them wanted some punch.

Your mom and her friend Marie said yes, so I went over to the punch bowl and brought them back small glass cups of pink punch. After we talked about the orchestra and the weather, the Orchestra started playing a Frank Sinatra song. I had the worst case of butterflies, and I asked your mom to dance, and my heart skipped a beat when she said yes. It was a slow dance and I felt so self-conscious, I hadn't danced for a long time. I worried about my sweaty palms and whether my breath was okay. We went out to the dance floor, and I was entranced with her beautiful blue eyes and great smile. About half way through the song, the guy I had seen her dancing with before staggered up from behind me, tapped me on the shoulder and said, 'Hey, this is my girl. I will take over from here.'

"Your mom said, 'Eddie, you are drunk and I have told you before, I just want to be friends. Please leave me alone and quit acting like you own me.'

"Eddie slurred, 'Are you telling me you would rather dance with this greasy dago than me? You dagos come from the city and are trying to take over our town buying up the cattle land to build those shacks and driving up the cost of property probably with Mafia money. Why don't you go back to where you belong?' About then he grabbed your mom's arm and jerked her away, and I lost my temper. I took a swing at him and before you knew it, we were in a full-blown fight. Before I knew it, two other guys jumped in and started swinging at me, too. I ended up getting knocked off the dance floor platform and was out cold.'

"When I came to, a couple of Sonoma County Sheriff's Deputies were standing there as well as your mom and a whole crowd of people. Your mom was trying to explain how Eddie had been harassing her and that I had just come to her defense, but all they were interested in was who threw the first punch. Before I knew it they were arresting me and taking me to the Sonoma County Jail in Santa Rosa. I was so humiliated; I had just been accepted to the police academy and here I was being arrested. Would this prevent me from fulfilling my dream? Also, how would my family react? My mother felt her children's behavior was a reflection of her, and besides that they had no phone at the cabins, so there was no way to even get a hold of them. Would I ever be able to face your mom again?

"On the way to the jail, I told the sheriff's deputies about my recent naval service and my acceptance to the police academy. They asked me about what happened regarding the fight and I explained. One of them said, 'Yeah, that Eddie is a real spoiled brat. His daddy is a rich cattle rancher in the area, and he has always gotten everything he has ever wanted. He was driving drunk while heading over to the coast a couple of years ago, had a bad wreck and a girl was killed, but daddy got a high priced lawyer and got him off all the charges. He stands to inherit a lot of land and so he thinks he's a big shot. We needed to arrest you because you threw the first punch, but it was obvious that he was drunker than a skunk. Probably he was out drinking with his buddies in the parking lot during the break and then was looking for trouble when he came in and did whatever he could to provoke you. Maggie O'Brien confirmed that. We will let the judge know that and maybe the charges will be dropped. Unfortunately, Eddie's dad has a lot of land, money, and power so lots of people are afraid to stand up to him.'

"They put me in a jail cell, but before sunrise, I heard the deputy call my name. My dad was there to bail me out. Someone from the dance had gone by the cabin and told them that I had been arrested. Talk about a walk of shame; I couldn't even look at my dad as we walked to the car that he had borrowed from a neighbor. On the way back to pick up the family car in the Monte Rio parking lot, I explained to him in Italian about the altercation at the dance and that I liked your mom. He frowned and said, 'Gino, you needa to find a nice Italian Catholic girl. Stay with your own kind, otherwise, lotsa trouble. Capisce?'

"After picking up the car in Monte Rio, we headed back to the cabin. My mother was standing at the door wringing her hands and gave me a big kiss when I came through the door. She examined my black eye and the bruises and cuts on my face and arms and then sighed, 'I think you safe now you return from the war, but you get in a fight on the vacation? Whatsa matta wit you? Letsa fix your face—good thing we gotta the bandages. And then I will maka you some breakfast.' That was your nonna; she thought any problem could be fixed with food!

"Luckily, the charges were dropped. I found out the address of the drug store and wrote your mom a couple of letters there, apologizing and asking her if we could get together, but I never heard back from her. I didn't go back to Russian River that summer. My father kept me busy at the restaurant and any time I even hinted about going to the cabin, he scowled and told me that he needed me at the restaurant. I figured she wasn't interested, and I was disappointed.

"Although the Police Academy never mentioned my Guerneville arrest, I was on pins and needles that it would come up. In September I started my training at the academy, which was located near Golden Gate Park. They used some old barracks and it was like I was in the Navy again. I was only a couple of miles from my home and couldn't even drop by the restaurant. It was a thirty-two-week program starting after Labor Day. I had to stay at the academy and the first time I got to go home was Thanksgiving. Your Aunt Katherine was about twelve at the time, and she always loved to see the lighting of the big, three-story Christmas tree at the City of Paris department store, so the day after Thanksgiving, we were on the third floor looking over the balcony when I spotted your mom on the second floor. I was ecstatic. I grabbed Katherine by the hand and I raced to the stairs, but I was going against the flow of people and by the time I got there she had disappeared, and I was so disappointed. Later though, we were walking through the front door, and I saw her outside talking to her friend. With my heart pounding, I went and said hello. Looking really surprised, she introduced her friend Betty to us. I asked if the two of them would like to go have coffee. She smiled and nodded. I asked, 'What are you doing in the city, Maggie?'

"She replied, 'I am in Nursing School. I am in a two year program and I am staying in a boarding house. Betty is my roommate.'

"I said, 'Maggie, like I said in the letters, I am so sorry about what happened at Monte Rio. It must have been embarrassing for you and—'

"'What letters, Gino?'

"'I wrote two letters to you apologizing and asking if we could get together. Didn't you get them?'

"'No, I bet my Uncle Bob intercepted those letters! He has always been overly protective. He and my Aunt Alice raised me after my parents died.'

"We all went to a little diner nearby, and Katherine had hot chocolate and pie, and the rest of us had coffee. We talked for a long time, and your mom gave me her phone number before we left the restaurant. Your mother and Katherine took an instant liking to each other.

"Well, after that, I saw your mom every chance I got. It was hard because we both had busy schedules. The first time I brought her home for Sunday dinner, my parents knew we were crazy about each other. I had never brought a girl home before, so they knew it was serious. Although they would have preferred that she was Italian, they were happy that she was Catholic and we would often go to Mass together at Saints Peter and Paul in North Beach. We were madly in love, and we wanted to get married. My family knew this, but we had not broken the news to your mom's family. So at Easter that year, I went to Guerneville with your mom, and we told her Uncle Bill and Aunt Alice that we were planning on getting married as soon as I finished the police academy.

"They did not approve of our impending 'mixed marriage' (Italian and Irish), and they said that if we did proceed, not to expect them to put on a wedding or even attend. This was very hard for your mom, so we decided to get married quietly in a little church in Bodega Bay and honeymooned in that area. My family would have loved for us to have had a big wedding, but it was just too hard for your mom with her family not wanting to attend."

Katie chimed in, "Is that the same church where Alfred Hitchcock filmed the movie about the birds? It was so cool going by there when they were filming that."

"Yeah, that's right. My buddy and your mom's friend Betty stood up for us. After spending the night at Jenner by the Sea, we settled in a little apartment in the North Beach area of San Francisco near the restaurant. I started out as a rookie policeman and she continued her nursing studies. About two years later, our greatest joy was born—you, my princess."

"Daddy, I wish I wasn't an only child. Sometimes it's so boring. I think everybody else at my school has brothers and sisters. My friend Elizabeth is from a family of twelve children and she always has someone to play with. I hate always hearing how spoiled I am because I have my own room."

"I know, Katie, I wish we could have given you brothers and sisters. It was our intention to have a big family, but your mom was unable to have more children, and we are so grateful that we have you. You are our sunshine and the joy of our lives. Thanks for all you do to help out with your mom. I know she appreciates it and I sure do. I hope it isn't too much for you."

"It's okay, Daddy. I like to spend time with Mama and she always lets me have my friends come over and she tells us stories about when she was a little girl and lived on the ranch and rode horses. She plays board games and colors with us, which none of the other moms do."

"Yeah. She is a great wife and mother, that is for sure. Well, we are almost home. I bet you are tired." They rounded the corner to their suburban one-story tract home, which had big picture windows along the front. They drove past their well-manicured lawn bordered by beautiful rose bushes. Gino parked the car in his one-car garage, and they jumped out and headed into the house, excited to tell Maggie about their big day.

CHAPTER 3

August 29, 1966

"Eric, you ready for something to eat?" the family's housekeeper asked him with a heavy Spanish accent.

"Maria, I am leaving pretty soon; I am going to a concert with some friends and then I am going to spend the night at my friend's house."

"What friend you spend the night with? What kind of concert? Does your papa know that? Did you talk to him before his go play golf?" she quizzed him.

"Um, my friend John. I don't think you know him. It is a music concert, Maria."

"He know John and his parents? You think it okay with him?" Maria asked.

"Oh, I'm sure he would think it's fine. He probably won't even notice I am gone; he is so busy. I think he has plans to go sailing with a client tomorrow morning. What do I smell? Maria thanks so much for making enchiladas, and you know how I love them. . ."

"Yes, Eric, I make it special for you. You know you are like my own son, maybe more like grandson. I take care of you since you were a baby and you and your brother grow up so fast. Seem like yesterday you were little boy out in the corral riding your pony."

"Yeah, Maria, you have always been like a mama to us. What

would we have done without you, especially when my mom left and moved to Sedona?"

"Yes, you were only ten, and your brother fifteen, too young to be without your mother."

As Maria served Eric the enchiladas and rice she said, "I worry so much about your brother Stephen. I hope we get a letter from him soon. I worry so much about him being in war in Vietnam. Every night on news they say how many soldiers die. I hope you not go to war like your brother."

Eric couldn't help but grimace. Little did Maria know that every chance Eric got, he protested the Vietnam War. He was much more likely to go to Canada as a draft dodger than head to Vietnam. "I know you worry a lot about Stephen, but he will be home in less than four months, and then we will all have enchiladas together. As for me, I am not a military type of guy. I will let my brother be the war hero and make his father proud."

"Your papa proud of you too, Eric. You are a good boy and you are smart. He just wants you to work hard in school, get in a good college and get a haircut," she said as she glanced at his blonde, curly hair, hanging over his eyebrows and his ears.

Eric answered defensively, "Yeah, well, I know appearances are everything for my dad and that there is nothing more important to him than me getting into some big-name school, but it's not going to happen, and he needs to get used to that. Thanks for the delicious meal, Maria. I need to get going. My friend is expecting me." He gave her a hug as he rushed out the door.

As he headed toward his blue '64 convertible VW bug, he waved at the Japanese gardener who was trimming the hedges in front of their huge two-story colonial home. Eric felt uncomfortable in this rich, horsey community. He could see why his mother had wanted to leave this place. She was never comfortable here as a wife or a mother. The only things she seemed to connect with were her horses and her beatnik friends whom his dad hated.

He picked up his friends at the neighborhood market. As Melissa got in the car she squealed, "I can't believe that we are really going to get to see the Beatles, this is so groovy. I brought a big basket of food. If you pop the front, I can put it in there. Thanks for giving us a ride, Eric!"

"Sure, Melissa. Thanks for bringing the food. Hey, John, you got the tickets?"

"Yeah, they cost $4.50 each. I was worried that they would be sold out, but it wasn't. Surprised me because I thought for sure all the seats in Candlestick would be full. I also got some beer, but I couldn't score any weed. If you want we can stop at the Haight, I think I can find some there," John replied.

Eric replied, "Okay, let's all figure out what we spent and settle up later. I'm fine without the weed. How about you guys?"

"Yeah, if we really want some pot I'm sure we could find some at the concert," John said.

When they arrived at Candlestick, they remembered why the park was nicknamed Windlestick. It was foggy, windy, and freezing cold. They sat bundled up next to each other in seats near home plate and had a clear view of the stage behind second base, which had an eight foot wire fence surrounding it. First of all, the Ronettes took the stage to headline for the Beatles. The trio, who were the only girls' band that toured with the Beatles, sang many of their popular songs, including, "Be My Baby." However, the crowd was restless with anticipation for the Beatles' appearance. There was a heavily guarded trailer on the ball field that everyone assumed was their dressing room. At 9:27 pm, after much chanting from the crowd, the Beatles made their way out of the dugout and onto the caged stage. The sound system was poor, and combined with the wind and the screaming fans, it was virtually impossible for most people to hear the performance.

As they played their first song, "Rock and Roll Music," Melissa looked through her mom's bird-watching binoculars and reported what the Beatles were wearing: matching green suits, white shirts with a design on them, and signature Beatle boots—except George Harrison, who was wearing loafers and white socks. That surprised her.

The Beatles played nine more of their songs: "She's a Woman," "If I Needed Someone," "Day Tripper," "I Feel Fine," "Baby's In Black," "Yesterday," "I Wanna Be Your Man," "Nowhere Man," and "Paperback Writer." Several boys scaled the fence and jumped onto the stage, and the security police removed them. McCartney clowned and waved to the crowd and quipped, "It's a bit chilly out here. Sorry about the weather," and then he announced, "This is our last song. We want you to join in or whatever—clap or such with us." They started playing "Long Tall Sally," and the crowd went wild. At the end of the song, and in spite of the crowd's protest of their performance coming to a close after only thirty minutes, the Beatles were escorted offstage and left in a waiting armored car.

As Eric, Melissa, and John fought the crowd through the dense fog to get back to the VW, Eric felt energized by the excitement of the crowd. And he was glad that he didn't have to take anything mind-altering to enjoy it. It was great to be part of this exciting, new time in music and changes in the world. He was seriously considering the Peace Corps, but hadn't brought that up with his dad. Even as a little boy, he had wanted to become a doctor, and so his father had latched onto that. Bill had been pushing Eric to get into some big-name school like Stanford or Harvard to do pre-med so he would have a better chance of getting into good medical schools. Although he did very well in his classes, he just was not willing to go through some of the hoops that his high school teachers required of him. He got A's on his tests but lacked the willingness to do all of the homework assignments and therefore was not getting the high grade point average that he needed to get into any big-name colleges. He wanted to help people—but did not want to spend nine more years in school before he could do it. Well, he didn't need to figure it all out tonight. In about a week, his senior year would be starting and he'd start thinking about it then.

1:45 p.m.

Gino grumbled, "What a mess this traffic is! I thought it would have cleared up by now. Can you believe that all these people spent money to freeze their asses off in that windy stadium, sat through a bunch of girls screaming and fainting to see those long-haired English guys? What is this world coming to? When they were on Ed Sullivan a couple of years ago, I thought that it was just a fad. Beatles, what kind of stupid name is that anyway? Remember, Ron, when music was truly music, like the big bands, and couples actually danced, but now they just twist around making a fool of themselves. I remember how much I loved dancing with Maggie at the Winterland Ballroom. It's been a lot of years since we hit the dance floor. I know she really misses it."

Ron, Gino's SFPD partner, asked, "How is Maggie doing?"

"Her multiple sclerosis has really progressed, and the one thing we do know is that she is never going to get better. She is completely paralyzed, except for one hand, and it has affected her speech and sight as well. Katie keeps praying for a miracle, but to tell you the truth, Ron, I don't know if she will live through the year. Maggie told me if she gets pneumonia or something like that to just let her go, but God, I don't know if I can do that. I can't even imagine living without her."

"Gino, you have been a great husband to her. A lot of guys would have just put their wives in a convalescent home or somewhere. I know keeping her at home has been hard and you have had to put in a lot of overtime to afford the extra help."

"Oh, I could never put her in one of those places. Yeah, these overtime security jobs like tonight at the performance have helped me get some extra nursing care that comes in. But I never could have done it without the help of the family. Katie helps out a lot and family and friends pitch in a lot so I can work extra shifts, and even my sister Katherine comes and helps out, too, on the weekends."

"Is that your sister who is a nun?"

"Yeah. You know there are some changes in the Catholic Church since Vatican II that I don't like, such as not having the Mass in Latin anymore. However, it has helped immensely that Katherine's order is so much more lenient about letting her come to visit us and help out. Even a few years ago, that would have never happened. And no more full-length habits or full veils. I hadn't seen Katherine's legs or hair since she went into the convent. It was kind of a shock to see her pretty, curly dark brown hair peaking out of their shorter more modern veils—and of course their habits are shorter and they even wear regular shoes and hose. She teaches history at a Catholic high school in the city. Katie absolutely adores her. They get along great and Katie loves to help her grade papers."

"Is Katie still thinking about being a nun?"

"I don't think so. I think that was a passing phase. You know it would have been an honor to have her go into the convent, but to tell you the truth, since she is my only child, there is nothing that would make me happier than having grandchildren someday."

"I pity the poor guy who comes around your house, Gino. You probably have your service revolver ready for anyone who knocks at your door. She is a beautiful girl, so you are lucky if you haven't had anyone knocking on your door."

"She is going to a challenging Catholic girls' high school and she is getting straight A's. She thinks she wants to be a nurse like her mother. She just turned fifteen a few months ago, and she is way too young to be dating. But I tell you she better be selective when the time comes. She knows not to bring around any greasers or long-haired hippie type guys. Clean cut boys from good Catholic families, boys that have manners, play sports—that will be the only kind of young man I will be letting her go out with."

Ron smiled and changed the subject. "Hey, Gino, should I take the next turn-off?"

"Yeah, take the Marinwood exit and then go over the freeway and turn right."

"How do you like living here?"

"You know this part of San Rafael is called Terra Linda and

most of the homes have been built in the last fifteen years. It's a very family-oriented and a safe community, so it has been a great place to raise Katie."

Gino continued, "Hey, thanks, Ron, I sure appreciate your driving tonight. It gave me a chance to close my eyes for a few minutes. You know I need to set the clock to wake up every few hours and move Maggie to her other side to prevent bed sores, so I can use the extra shut-eye."

"No problem, Gino, it is right on my way home to Petaluma. You know being your partner for these last two years has been really great. Thanks for taking me under your wing and showing me the ropes."

"My pleasure, Ron. Things have really changed on our beat even since we were partners there. Haight-Ashbury used to be just a family neighborhood. But now, it just has a totally different feel. Hippies seem to be all around, sitting on the sidewalk, walking barefoot, smoking marijuana, not working, playing all their hippie music. Hope they move on soon. Here we are—first house on the right. Tell that sweet wife of yours that we said hello."

"My regards to Maggie, too."

"Yeah, I sure wished you had known her before she was sick."

"Yeah, me too."

As Gino got out of Ron's green Chevy pick-up and waved, he took a deep breath and thought, "I'm sure glad to know that Katie is at home, safe with her mom and not with all those crazy kids at the Beatles concert. It's damn hard seeing my sweet wife deteriorate with this damn MS, but I have lots to be grateful for: a steady job, a loving extended family, and most of all a bright and well-behaved daughter." Gino unlocked his front door, turned off the porch light, and quietly closed the door.

October 17, 1989

4:30 p.m.

Katie enjoyed looking at the consignment shops on San Francisco's Market Street, because she always found great bargains. She was glad that she had time to stop at a couple of them on her way out of San Francisco. She picked up a sweater, a skirt for herself, some pants for the boys, and a book that she thought her old roommate Rosemary would like. Rosemary's sister, Helen, was expecting her for dinner at 5:30 in Oakland, so she had better hurry. She got in her car and headed to Seventh Street to get on the Bay Bridge. Traffic was usually a bear at this time of day, but she was pleasantly surprised that there was not the usual congestion, especially on the day of a World Series at Candlestick. She paid her toll and started across the bottom deck of the bridge. She was listening to oldies on the local radio station, and she was transported back to her teenage years.

CHAPTER 4

June 4, 1967

"We better get going, Katie. Traffic is probably going to be terrible today going across the Golden Gate."

As Katie opened her door of the car she said, "Dad, I am so glad we are going to the Giants game together. Hope the Giants beat the New York Mets today. I can't even remember the last time we went to a game together. I am surprised you even want to go in on your day off, after commuting to the city every day."

"I am so happy to spend the day with you, Katie. It's been a tough year for us, losing your mom after such a long battle with MS. It's hard to believe that she has already been gone for 6 months." His eyes welled up with tears as he continued. "You were such a big help and I always appreciated that you stayed home with her when I went to games."

As she tenderly touched his arm Katie said, "Dad, you were so devoted to Mom and it was the only time you ever took for yourself. I was glad I could do it. Mom would like that we are doing things together, so let's enjoy the day and know that she is smiling down on us and rooting for the Giants, too."

Gino brushed away his tears and glanced over at his beautiful daughter. "You are my sunshine, Katie. Your mom and I have always been so proud of you. My daughter, smart enough to get straight A's in high school while taking all of those hard classes! Keep it up and you will be valedictorian. You will be able to go to any college you want. Have you thought any more about where you want to go to college? There are so many fine Catholic colleges for women."

"There are a lot of girls getting really good grades in my school, so don't count on me being valedictorian. Thank you, Dad, but those private colleges are so expensive, and I don't think we can afford them."

"I have been saving for you your entire life so you can go to an excellent school, so don't worry about that. There is nothing more important than you getting an excellent education." Gino beamed. "I am so glad you are not like those hippie kids who are coming in droves to my beat at Haight-Ashbury. I have never seen anything like it. Boys with long hair, girls barefooted, wearing flowers in their hair, begging for money on the street. I would turn over in my grave if you ever did anything like that. They come from all over—on the Greyhound bus, in cars, hitchhiking. They think they can just camp out in Golden Gate Park and seem surprised when I tell them they can't panhandle or loiter—as if it is their God-given right. I have never seen anything like it."

"Dad, you finally have a day off, so relax and quit talking about work. Your face is getting red just talking about it. You know what the doctor said about your blood pressure. The toll bridge is coming up soon. I would love to stop at the Round House Diner and split a banana split like we used to. Do we have time?"

Gino smiled and said, "Yeah, we have time to do that and then head to the game; the traffic wasn't nearly as bad as I thought it would be. Extra whipped cream and cherries?"

"Sounds fantastic!" Katie replied.

1:00 p.m.

As Bill parked his brand new red corvette in a Candlestick premium parking space, his son Eric said, "Dad, we could have walked a few blocks."

Bill replied, "Are you nuts? This neighborhood is getting worse all the time. I want to get out of the game and have a car that isn't stripped or stolen. Take your jacket, it's going to be freezing out there."

As they were getting out of the car he looked at Eric's collar-length blonde hair, poor boy sweater, and bellbottom pants and shook his head. "You look like a hippie with that damn long hair, when are you—"

Eric interrupted him. "Just stop it—I thought we were going to go to this game to spend some time together, not for you to bitch at me all day. If that's the way it's going to be, let's just go our separate ways and see each other later."

Bill replied, "All right, all right, you don't need to be so damn touchy. Gosh, when was the last time we went to a game together? I think it has been a few years. Remember when you were little, anyone would ask you what you wanted to be when you grew up and you said you wanted to be a Giant. Some people thought you meant a big guy, but no, you wanted to be like Willie Mays. You were always such a hell of a natural athlete, Eric. You were the best pitcher they had in your whole Little League Organization—and then such a star on your JV team—it sure is a shame you gave all that up. . ."

As they walked through the ticket stiles, Eric sighed and scowled at his dad. He just couldn't seem to help himself from being so controlling and negative. As the smells of popcorn wafted through the air and amid the sound of the guys selling programs, he watched as the seagulls swooped down and ate the morsels of a hot dog bun that someone had left behind. "I'll meet you at our seats, Dad."

He loved the feeling of the salty wind on his face. He always had. He loved the games, and he enjoyed the sights, sounds, smells of the ballpark even more. He walked along the edge of the ballpark and looked out of Candlestick Point into the expansive blue-gray ocean. Watching the seagulls swoop through the fog, he envied that they were so free—free from expectations and decisions. Next week he'd be turning eighteen, and he would be required to sign up for "Selective Service." What a euphemism for the draft! He didn't know what he was going to do. His brother Stephen had just left on a tour of duty in Vietnam as a Marine officer. Eric was opposed to the war, but not registering for the draft could land him in jail. What was he going to do about all of that? As he was pondering his future he was brought back to the present moment when he heard the Star-Spangled Banner blasting over the intercom. He decided to walk around the park for a while and then go to his seat.

When he got to their row, it was already the bottom of the first inning. He started to squeeze his way down to his seat when he recognized Gino Pulli, who had the season tickets next to theirs. Sitting next to Pulli was one of the prettiest girls he had ever seen. She had long, brown, wavy hair past the middle of her back tied with a red ribbon, and gorgeous sparkling blue eyes. As he sat down next to her, she gave him a warm smile, which highlighted her beautiful teeth, and he stammered, "Hi, I'm Eric. I'm Bill's son."

"I'm Katie. Gino's my dad. I haven't been to a game in ages, but I think we met before—weren't you here for World Series—the last game?"

"Yeah, I was." However, he didn't remember meeting her—and he certainly would have remembered a beautiful girl like her—wouldn't he? "Yeah, I haven't been to a game for a while either."

Gino, who was sitting on Katie's right, was trying to get her attention. "It's already the bottom of the second inning and look who's up to bat: it's Willie Mays. Haller is on first, so with any luck, Mays will hit a homer and bring them both home." Gino cheered loudly for his team, but he was getting annoyed. He hadn't even thought about the possibility that Bill would bring his long-haired hippie son to the game. Most of the time, Bill brought one of his clients or country club friends to the game, and they showed off their fancy flasks and cigars. All week, he had been looking forward to having this time with Katie, and now she was talking to this loser and not even watching the game.

Katie redirected her attention to the game as Mays cracked a line drive to center field that almost hit the fence. He made it to second base and Haller was held up at third. Next, McCovey was up to bat. The Mets pitcher challenged him with a fastball on the first pitch and McCovey hit it over the right-field fence. The crowd went wild as the runners rounded the bases and returned to the dugout. At times like these, Gino was so grateful that he had kept these great seats behind first base. What a view! The Giants scored another run to end the second inning at four runs, leaving the Mets at zero. There was no score the third inning. The previous year McCovey had thirty-six home runs, Willie had thirty-seven home runs, and they had missed going to the World Series by only one-and-a-half games, behind the Dodgers. There was a lot of talk about the Giants getting to the World Series this year, and it was looking pretty positive.

At the top of the fourth inning, Eric casually asked, "Katie, you want to go to the snack bar with me?"

"Okay. Dad, do you want something at the concession stand?"

Distractedly, Gino answered, "Yeah, maybe some popcorn."

Katie put the hood of her navy-blue wool jacket over her head as they made their way through the row and up the stadium steps and they saw the long line. "I think we can find a shorter line. Let's go down this way," Eric suggested. As they walked out toward the west side of the stadium, a cold wind gust blew into their faces. "It's hard to believe it is June and it is this cold," Eric said.

Katie said, "Wasn't it Mark Twain who said the coldest winter he ever spent was a summer in San Francisco?"

Eric chuckled as they found the other concession stand, and the crowd was just as big. "Well, we might as well stay here. The other line isn't any better. Katie, where do you live?"

"In San Rafael."

Eric smiled. "Next weekend I'm gonna be over in your neck of the woods—in Mill Valley up on Mount Tamalpais for the Fantasy Fair and Magic Mountain Music Festival. Jefferson Airplane, the Byrds, 5th Dimension, Country Joe and the Fish, and a lot of other great bands will be there. Hey, do you want to come? It's going to be outta sight! Tickets are only two bucks and I am pretty sure I could get you one. I'm going with some friends and they would definitely be fine with you coming."

"Oh, thanks for asking, Eric, but I really can't." She was flattered but it was certainly obvious that he didn't know her dad.

Then Eric asked, "Where do you go to school?"

"I'm a sophomore at Dominican High School." She didn't disclose that it was a Catholic girls' school. Instead she asked, "How about you?"

"I'm a senior at Woodside High, you know, down on the Peninsula."

"Well, you are graduating soon then. That must be exciting."

"Yeah, I'll be glad to be done with high school, but I'm not going through the graduation ceremony. Honestly, I don't see the point, and besides, the Monterey Pop Festival is that same weekend and it is going to be so groovy. I wouldn't miss it for the world; the lineup is amazing. It's also my birthday that weekend, so it will be a great way to celebrate. Two weekends in a row of hearing some of the best rock stars in the world."

Katie was surprised and asked, "You are really not going to your own graduation? What do your parents think of that?"

"To tell you the truth, I haven't told my dad yet. My plan was to tell him tonight when we get home. Thought I'd wait until after the game, get home, let him have a few martinis and then break the news. I have my own car, so if he goes ballistic, I can split and go spend the night at a friend's house. I think it is for the best, because I am not winning any awards or scholarships and I'm sure not the valedictorian or even close—so all of this is a real letdown for my dad. He has somehow built up in his mind that I am some kind of genius super-athlete and that I am just not working up to my potential. All that stuff is important to him, but not to me.

"My brother played the game. Good student, star-athlete, ROTC, became a Marine Officer, and serving in Vietnam right now, which scares me to death. By contrast, I'd rather play my guitar and truly figure out what I want to do. I am a real disappointment to my dad. Well, my mom lives in New Mexico and I don't think she was planning on coming anyway. I told her I didn't want to go through with the ceremony and she said whatever makes me happy. Actually, I think she was relieved that she didn't have to come to my graduation and see my dad. She hasn't seen him in years. She left to pursue her life in Sedona when I was about ten and my brother and I flew out to see her once a year or so. My mom is more like an eccentric aunt than a mother. Our housekeeper Maria has really been the one who raised us. How about your mom? I've never seen her at the games."

Katie choked up a little as she said, "My mom died about five months ago from multiple sclerosis. She was in a wheelchair for a long time, so she wasn't able to go to games. She was quite a Giants fan though and would always listen to it on the radio."

"I'm sorry, I shouldn't have asked."

"Don't worry. Oh, it's finally our turn to order."

Back at the seats, Gino was fuming. He had been distracted when Katie said she was going to the snack bar and it certainly hadn't registered that she was going there with that long-haired hippie kid until it was too late to stop them. Although the Giants had scored three more runs in the fifth inning, he hadn't even been able to enjoy it because he was worried about her. Now they had been gone for three innings, almost an hour, and it was the seventh inning stretch. Where the hell could they have gone?

He looked over at Bill and asked, "What do you think happened to the kids?"

Bill seemed oblivious to the situation. No wonder, he'd had a couple of beers and had been nipping at his flask; it was no wonder his kid was turning out the way he was. He decided to get up and look for them. He headed up to the concession stand, and saw no sign of them in the lines. He headed to the right to look for them at the next snack bar.

Heading back to their section Eric asked, "Hey, Katie, would you like to go out to the movies or something?"

"Thanks, Eric, but I can't. My dad is strict and wouldn't allow me."

"Well, do you think it would be okay for me to just call you up and talk sometime?"

"Oh, I don't know. Here's our row, but my dad isn't here."

As they passed Bill, he slurred, "I think your dad is out looking for the two of you."

Katie's heart was in her throat. She had lost all track of time waiting in that line talking to Eric. She looked at the scoreboard. It was already the eighth inning. What should she do? If she went looking for her dad, they would surely miss each other. He had always told her to stay put, so that's what she did. A few minutes later her dad stormed down the steps and his Italian temper was flaring. He looked like a bull ready to charge. Spectators yelled, "Down in front!"

Ignoring the fans screaming at him, Gino yelled at Eric, "What the hell are you doing taking off with my daughter, you long-haired loser? Where were you? What were you doing?"

"Daddy, we were at the concession stand the whole time, and then we came here after."

"The hell you were! I just went to all the damn snack bars and you weren't there!"

"We went to the other one because ours was so crowded and the other one was too but we stayed there and came straight back here after—we must have missed you and, uh, here's your popcorn," Katie explained as she shakily offered it to him.

Gino's face was turning beet red as he bellowed, "I don't want any damn popcorn—and we are getting the hell out of here now!" He grabbed Katie's arm, spilling the popcorn, grabbed his things, and pulled her toward the exit scolding her as they headed out of the stadium and toward their car. "Katie, I am furious with you. I have been looking forward to this time together—and instead of enjoying the game, I spend my time worrying about you and that hairball. You better stay away from him or anyone like him, understand?"

5:20 p.m.

At the end of the game, Bill and Eric exited with a lot of happy Giants fans, celebrating their 7–0 victory over the Mets. When they walked into the parking area, Eric said, "Hey, Dad, let me see your keys." After Bill awkwardly fished through his pocket and got his keys, Eric grabbed them and insisted, "I'm going to drive."

Bill slurred, "I'm ff-fine to drive."

Eric cut him off and said in an angry, low tone, trying not to draw the attention of the parking attendant and fans that were nearby, "You are wasted, Dad and if you insist on driving, I will find another way home, and I will call the highway patrol and give them your license plate number— "

"Who the hell do you think you are to tell me whether I can drive my own car, you snot-nosed brat—I was driving long before you were even born and—" At that point he swung at Eric and missed, falling onto the pavement. Eric grabbed him by the arm and stuffed him into the front seat. Bill took a long swig out of his flask while continuing to curse. Eric ignored him, turning the radio on to the local news to drown out his father's tirade.

Long before they were through the traffic jam, Bill was snoring loudly with his head tilted back and his mouth wide open. Eric changed the radio to the local rock and roll station KFRC and they were playing the song "Feelin' Groovy." How ironic! Looking over at his father, Eric let out a big sigh and thought, "How could such a loser drunk be such a successful businessman? I think you are an alcoholic, Dad, and it is progressing. I always thought alcoholics were just skid-row bums who couldn't hold down a job, but you are a banking investor with lots of money, this brand new sports car, a five-bedroom house. You seem to function pretty well on the weekdays with a few martinis in the evening, but on the weekends you let loose and this is an example of what happens. It scares the hell out of me to think you would have driven if I hadn't intervened. What am I going to do? I'm afraid you are going to kill someone and who can I talk to? It's not like I can count on Mom. She checked out a long time ago and had no control even when she was around I can't bother my brother Stephen about it. He is trudging through the jungles and swamps trying to keep his company from getting blasted by the Vietcong. I sure wish you would go to AA or something."

As the traffic crawled south on Highway 101, Eric's mind switched gears and he flashed to his time talking to Katie. Not only was she one of the cutest girls that he had ever seen, she had such a great personality and that infectious laugh, and he couldn't get her off his mind. He wanted to see her again and he had the feeling that she had been attracted to him, but after that scene with Gino, it would be crazy to pursue her. Wouldn't you know that the girl he liked would have a dad like Gino? What could be worse than a hot-headed, protective Italian policeman? Hey, she's just another girl—or was she? She seemed so different from the girls that he went to high school with—she wasn't full of herself or trying to impress anyone.

His thoughts were interrupted when he realized that he had almost missed his exit. As he down-shifted the high performance sports car, he smiled to himself and said, "At least I got a chance to drive my dad's mid-life obsession—it is a sweet ride. Bet he spent at lot for it. Probably more than most people earn in a year." Driving down the long driveway, Eric was brought back to the present and the next challenging task of getting his dad in the house. He decided to take the keys with him, and just leave his dad in the car to sleep it off. Well, telling him about his non-graduation plans would have to wait.

CHAPTER 5

June 8, 1967

Katie had just finished the delicious lasagna and salad that her dad had made for her before leaving for work. He was such an excellent cook; his years helping in his family's restaurant had paid off. He was always sure to have dinner ready for her when she came home; she just needed to heat it up. As she was finishing up the dishes and listening to the radio, "My Girl" by the Temptations came on, and as she swayed to the music she thought about what it would be like to be someone's girl. What would it be like to be Eric's girl was more like it. "What a stupid thing to even think about because that could never happen. Yeah, he asked me if I wanted to go out and acted like he was interested, but he probably does that with all of the girls. I'm sure that he must be one of the most popular boys at his school. And even if he does like me, there's no way my dad is ever going to let me see him."

She shuddered as her mind traveled back to the ride home from the game a few nights before and she remembered her dad's icy silence; she had never seen him that mad. Since then, they had only exchanged a few words. She saw him in the mornings because he always got up to have breakfast with her. Then she was off to school and when she got home, he had left for work. He had worked the swing shift for many years so that he could take care of her mother.

Now that Maggie had died, he had considered working the day shift, but it would have probably meant changing partners and facing a lot more commute traffic. He worried about Katie being home alone in the evening, but she reassured him that she was fine. They lived in a safe neighborhood and lots of neighbors looked out for her, so she wasn't afraid of being alone.

She looked at the clock and thought, "I better get my essay finished because there are a few things I want to watch on the TV tonight, especially *Laugh-In*. Goldie Hawn is so funny! I sure wish we had a color TV though."

She was putting the finishing touches on her assignment when the doorbell rang. She looked out of the peephole and a woman was standing there; at first she didn't recognize her. Then she realized that it was her Aunt Katherine, but she was not dressed in her nun's habit. Instead, she was wearing long brown pants, a blue sweater, and her short hair was uncovered.

With her mouth gaping open, Katie quickly opened the door, and exclaimed," Sister Katherine, I'm so surprised to see you!"

As her aunt came in, she gave Katie a hug and said, "Probably just call me Aunt Katherine. Your dad's at work, right?"

"Yeah, he won't be home until 11:30 or so. Why?"

As they sat down on the floral print sofa, Katherine said, "I have taken a leave from the convent, Katie. My order has granted me a one-year leave. I had planned to finish out the school year; but Mother Superior thought it was best for me just to go. Maybe she is worried that I will be a bad influence on the other sisters, and I didn't even get to say goodbye to my class. They are going to have a substitute teacher finish out the last two weeks of the school year for me. I know that the family is going to be shocked about this, especially your dad. I'm not ready to tell them yet. But I wanted to let you know, Katie. You and I have always been so close. You are so much like your mother. I always knew I could tell her anything and she wouldn't judge me."

"What happened, Aunt Katherine?"

"Oh, not any one thing, Katie. This has been on my mind for a long time. I just don't know if I want to spend the rest of my life as a nun, and I have been tormented about what to do. There are so many things in the world and in the church that I want to see changed. I haven't wanted to break my vows, but I just feel that I have been living a lie. I wasn't much older than you, Katie, when I entered the convent. Now I am thirty-eight years old and I am so conflicted about whether I made the right decision to go into religious life. I love being part of my spiritual community much of the time—it is what I know, but there is a part of me that wants to be free to express myself, do what I want, stand up for the political causes I believe in and not have to answer to Mother Superior and my order about everything I do."

"What are you going to do?"

"I am going to stay in Berkeley with some people I have met through the peace movement. They have two small children and I will do housework and childcare for them in exchange for room and board, and I will start looking for a job. One of their friends was coming over here to visit his mom at the hospital. I asked if I could get a ride. I figured you would be here. He will be coming back to get me about 9:00. Sorry to lay this all on you, Katie."

"It's okay, Aunt Katherine, but I have no idea what to say. I want to see you happy and if this is what you need to do, I support you, but it is such a shock. I have never even seen you wear clothes before, I mean other than your habit, and you look so different and—"

Just then the black rotary phone on the wall in the kitchen rang. "I better get that, in case it's Dad. He often calls me during his break, but don't worry, I won't tell him you are here."

"Hello, Pulli Residence, Katie speaking."

"Hi, Katie, this is Eric."

Katie's heart skipped a beat and she couldn't respond.

"Katie, are you there? I hope it is okay that I called. Is your dad there?"

"No, he's at work, but how did you get my number? It's unlisted."

"I figured as much with your dad being a policeman, so I called all the Pullis in the Marin County phone book. I reached one of your cousins. I told her we were working on a school project together and that I had lost your number. She believed me."

Katie laughed. "You probably talked to my cousin Laura, but you didn't fool her. You see, I go to an all girls' school."

Eric chuckled and said, "I'm just glad she gave it to me. It's great to hear your voice. I have been thinking of you ever since Saturday and—"

Blushing, Katie interrupted, "Actually, Eric, I have company right now, so it's not a good time for me to talk."

"Oh, yeah, sorry, I should have asked if you were busy. I'll let you go."

Katie stammered, "Well, okay, thanks for calling, Eric."

"Yeah, sure, take care. Bye, Katie."

"Goodbye, Eric."

Katherine smiled and teasingly said, "Who's Eric?"

Katie told her the whole story and her dad's reaction and Katherine simply said, "You sure seem smitten with this Eric. I am not saying that you should go against your dad's wishes, but as much as I love your dad he can be pretty unreasonable about things like this. If you think this Eric is a good guy and you like him, maybe you don't need to give up so quickly."

They could hear a car drive up the driveway, and as Katherine got up to go to the door, she gave Katie a big hug and kiss on the cheek and, pulling a piece of paper out of her purse, she handed it to Katie and said, "Here's my phone number and address. Call me anytime. I'll tell the rest of the family soon. In the meantime, if there is an emergency you will have my contact information. I don't expect you to lie if it comes up, but I would rather tell them myself when the time seems right."

Katie stammered, "I love you, Sister, I mean, Aunt Katherine."

"I love you, too, Katie, and if I had a daughter I would want her to be just like you."

CHAPTER 6

June 9, 1967

As Katie trudged from the bus stop, she grumbled to herself, "It is so blasted hot today and why isn't there a breeze like usual at this time? I hate this stupid blue plaid wool uniform and why do they make them out of wool anyway—especially for California—how ridiculous! And this stack of books I have to drag with me to study for next week's finals. It's bad enough that I have to ride the transit bus unlike my friend Ann Marie who got a brand new Mustang for her sixteenth birthday. Now it's the weekend and what do I have to look forward to besides hanging out with my dad, studying, and going to church. Yippee! And to top it off, I finally have a boy call me and what happens? I cut him off so I can hear about my aunt not being a nun anymore. My life is in the toilet. Eric will probably never call me again. He probably thinks I don't like him. I wonder if I should try to call him back or just wait and see if he calls me back."

And as she unlocked her front door and felt the blast of warm air from inside, she realized it was probably hotter inside because they had no air conditioning and the sun beat into their large picture windows. She fumed as she plopped down her stuff on the dining room table and noticed the note that her dad had left, "Katie girl, hope you had a good day at school. I bought you some spumoni ice cream and it's in the freezer. Let's try to do something fun tomorrow. Maybe the beach? Stay cool! Love, Dad." Well, that was a relief! She was finally out of the doghouse from Sunday night's game incident. That's how her dad made up—through food. It must be the Italian in him.

Katie decided to take advantage of the hot weather and changed into her old pink-flowered, one-piece swimsuit, put on her tortoise-shell sunglasses and reached into the fridge for a cold can of 7-Up. She headed out to the back patio, grabbed the hose, and gave the wilting plants a drink. Then she hosed herself off, took a big swig of her soda, and plunked down on the lounge chair. She closed her eyes and drifted off to sleep until the phone startled her awake. She charged through the back door to answer the phone on the third ring, saying, "Hello."

Her heart leaped as she heard a deep voice say, "Katie, it's Eric. Can you talk?"

She took a deep breath and said, "I'm glad you called back. Sorry that I couldn't talk last night. My aunt dropped by and she was in the middle of telling me some, uh, news and I really needed to talk to her."

Eric laughed with relief, "Your aunt? I thought there was a guy at your house or something. You sound kind of upset. Is your aunt okay? Was it some type of bad news?"

"Well, I'm not sure if you'd call it bad news or not—it's very complicated and well—"

"Oh sure, uh, well the reason I called is that I am going to the Fantasy Fair tomorrow and the next day. I think I told you about it at the game the other night. It is on top of Mount Tam and it's really close to where you live and I wondered if you might be able to—"

Katie cut him off. "Eric, there is no way I can even ask my dad if I can go to that."

"I figured that, and I didn't think you'd be able to. But I was wondering if you might be able to meet me somewhere one of these days—either before or after the festival and we could have a coke or something. . ."

Katie's heart pounded as she said, "Eric, thanks for asking, but honestly, I can't. My dad is home all weekend and we have plans and—"

"Oh, yeah, right, well, um, how's the weather at your house?"

"It is miserably hot. It has been all week and our house is like an oven."

"Actually, it is foggy and cool here. We are pretty close to the ocean."

"That's not fair! I know it's probably lots cooler at the beach here. It is strange that the temperature can be as much as fifty degrees cooler just twenty-five miles from here, and it seems the hotter it is here, the cooler it is there. I think my Dad and I might be going over to Stinson Beach tomorrow to cool off. Maybe I'll take my books with me over there to study for next week's finals."

"Studying at the beach? Sounds like you are a pretty dedicated student, Katie Pulli."

"Well, I don't know. How about you? Did you already have finals?"

"Yeah, senior finals were last week so that they could grade them and let us know if we passed or not—it's all about next week's graduation."

"Did you tell your dad that you are not going through the graduation ceremony?"

"Yeah, I kept trying to tell him in person and I could never seem to find a good time, so on Wednesday afternoon, I called him at work and left a message with his secretary to call me when he had time. So when he called back, I told him. He wasn't happy about it but people were around so he just said, 'Let's talk about this later.' I replied, 'Dad, this is non-negotiable. I'm sorry if you're disappointed, but it's my graduation and I'm not going. You can go if you want, but I won't be there. And I won't be home for a while, so don't worry about me. Bye, Dad.'"

"Yikes, I can't imagine saying anything like that to my dad; he'd kill me."

"Yeah, he came into my work last night and told me he was going to take away my car. I told him that it wasn't in his name—my mom bought it for me out of her dad's trust and she would have to take it away. He left in a huff asking me what he was going to tell the school. I told him I already took my finals and this next week is just stuff like Senior Breakfast, Picnic, signing yearbooks, and I just wasn't going back. I told him he could tell them whatever he wants. What's important to him is what other people think anyway, and if he wants to tell them I'm sick or something, I don't care."

"Do you think he called your mom about it?"

"I doubt he would call her; he hates to talk to her. Anyway, you know when I called her she said, 'Eric, just follow your heart.' To tell you the truth, she sounded stoned. She smokes a lot of pot with her boyfriend, who was her former massage therapist, and he is probably only in his late twenties. Anyway, listen, I have to go because I have to get to work in about half an hour."

Trying to hide her shock about what Eric had revealed about his mother, she stammered, "Oh, okay Eric, thanks for calling. Sorry I can't meet up with you, but I do like to talk to you. If you want to, you could call me next week and tell me about the Fantasy Fair. I hope you have a good time. Just don't call before 2:00 pm on the weekdays or anytime on the weekends; that is when my dad is home."

"Okay, Katie, I'll do that. Bye."

"Bye, Eric," she said, and hung up the black telephone receiver. "My stomach is in knots and my hands are shaking, what's wrong with me?" She realized the cord was all twisted up from pacing around while she was talking. Just then the phone rang again and jolted her out of her giddiness. "Hello."

"Katie, I have been trying to call you for the last twenty minutes! Who the hell have you been talking to? You know I like you to keep the phone free so I can call you when I have a break to make sure that you are all right."

"Oh, I was, uh, talking to Liz about our study guide for our final in history," Katie lied. "Thanks for the spumoni ice cream and the nice note."

"Did you see the tuna casserole for you in the refrigerator? Heat it in the oven for about thirty minutes at 350 degrees."

"Thanks, Dad. I gave the plants in the backyard some extra water because it is so hot here."

"Do you have all the doors dead-bolted?"

"Yes, dad."

"Don't let anyone—"

"I know Dad; don't let anyone in no matter what. I won't."

"Okay, I will be home around midnight and I will come in and tuck you in. Love you, honey."

"Love you, too. Bye, Dad." As she hung up the phone, a wave of guilt came over her. She didn't remember ever lying to her dad before. She then defended herself by thinking, "I wouldn't need to if he weren't so darned overprotective. I mean I am almost sixteen and he still treats me like a baby—'tuck me in' for goodness sake."

CHAPTER 7

June 11, 1967

On Saturday morning, Katie awoke to the aroma of sizzling bacon and Italian dark roast coffee percolating. She looked at the clock and it was about 9:00. After grabbing her robe and slippers, she padded out to the kitchen to see her dad standing at the stove. "Bambina, want pancakes for breakfast? Or should I make French toast?" he asked as he gave her a hug.

"Mmm—I think French toast sounds good." This was their favorite time together—Saturday breakfasts. It had been a long-standing tradition with the two of them ever since she could remember. Saturday was the time to relax and not have to rush like the other days. She noticed that the *San Francisco Chronicle* was spread out on the table. "Dad, looks like you've been up for a while. How do you do it? You work so late at night, and then get up early in the morning."

"Oh, I don't know, Katie; guess I'm just used to it. Still want to go to the beach and then maybe into the city and have dinner at the restaurant after?"

"Gee, Dad, I have a lot of studying to do and—" She saw the smile on his face fade.

"Well, yeah, I understand—I have plenty of yard work to do

around here. . .”

Katie could see how disappointed her father was and quickly added, “I could probably take some of my stuff along to study and put aside tomorrow for studying after church. Yeah, let's go to the beach and then go into the city for dinner.” She knew weekends were especially hard for him since her mom died, and it would probably be good for her not to sit around the hot house thinking of finals and Eric at the Fantasy Fair.

Gino brightened and said, “Great, let's have breakfast and then take off. I was thinking that I should call Sister Katherine and see if she wants us to pick her up at the convent and she could go to dinner with us. I'm so glad that the rules aren't so strict now, and she can go to a restaurant with her family if Mother Superior approves. I think this is early enough for her to ask for permission.”

As Gino got up to use the phone, Katie quickly said, “Oh, Aunt Katherine is not there, uh, today.”

“How do you know? Did you talk to her?”

“Yeah, the other night.”

“Why didn't you tell me she called? Where did she go?”

“Well, I think it's kind of a retreat thing,” she fibbed.

“Okay, well, I guess we can just invite her another time. Listen, I just remembered that there is some big hippie thing going on today on Mount Tam so the traffic might be pretty bad. Let's try to get out of the house in the next hour or so. I'm sure glad I don't have to work that circus. I heard that the Hell's Angels were providing the security. What the hell kind of security is that? A bunch of motorcycle thugs! And what kind of parents let their kids go to something like that? Probably a lot of them will be hopped up on drugs. I have no idea what this world is coming to, and it all started with those Beatle guys and it keeps getting worse. Why the hell did Ed Sullivan ever have them on his show anyway?”

Katie knew that her dad's tirade would continue unless diverted, so she quickly said, “Yeah, let's leave as soon as we can. I'll jump in the shower while you finish making breakfast. I can't wait to have your French toast. It's the best ever!"

CHAPTER 8

June 12, 1967

Katie was sitting on the couch eating ice cream and hoping that Eric would call when the old wall phone rang. She jumped up and ran to get it and then thought about not seeming too eager. She let it ring again and answered.

"Hi, sweetheart, how was your day?" asked a guy with a deep voice, but not the guy she was hoping for.

"It was good, Dad, how about you?"

"It's been pretty tough. Droves of hippies have descended on the Haight-Ashbury area and they have come from all over—on the bus, in loads of cars, hitchhiking. I guess they need somewhere to hang out until the next big music deal down in Monterey. You should see them all just hanging out on the street, barefooted, wearing flowers in their hair and little else. They panhandle and sit on the sidewalk blocking the way. The local residents are going out of their minds and, of course, expect us cops to do something about it. I mean up until recently the neighborhood was a nice family neighborhood, and now it's a zoo. I'm thinking about asking for a transfer to another part of the city. I just can't stand it. I see these young girls about your age hanging out with these long-haired guys and it just makes me sick. I am just not cut out to deal with all this hippie stuff.

"I talked to one girl today who looked about seventeen and she looked about eight months pregnant. I asked her where she was from and she said she was from North Carolina. I asked her if her parents knew where she was and she answered, 'Well, they know I was heading out here, but they said if I did they'd disown me.' Noticing that I had glanced down at her swollen abdomen she added, 'Oh, I'm okay, they're starting a new free clinic here and I'm seeing someone over there.'

"As I left I told her, 'Honey, you need to call your folks and tell them that you're, uh, okay. I know what they said, but I bet they probably just said that in anger and would want to hear from you.' She just shrugged. Anyway, my encounter with her made me want to call you and make sure that you are all right. I just can't imagine if I didn't know where you were and—.'"

"Daddy, I'm fine. Actually I'm sitting here eating a bowl of that delicious spumoni ice cream you got for me. I'm so glad the weather has cooled down; it is very pleasant here right now. You know I had my finals in French and World History and I think I did pretty well."

"I'm sure you did, Katie, you are such a good student and I'm so proud of you and oh, I need to get off the phone—don't forget to—"

"Yep, the doors are locked tight and I won't let anyone in. I saw that pot roast and vegetables that you left for me—thanks, Dad, you must have been cooking all morning! Bye, Dad."

"Bye, honey."

She barely sat down to finish her melting ice cream when the phone rang again. On the second ring she picked it up and taking a breath said, "Hello."

"Hey, Katie, this is Eric. I've been trying to call you and your line's been busy. Can you talk?"

"Yeah, this is a good time. How was the Fantasy Fair?"

"It was out of sight! I don't even know how to put it into words. On Saturday morning we had an amazing ride up Mount Tam from Mill Valley. What an amazingly beautiful area! When we got up there, there was this giant Buddha balloon that was bobbing around the stadium and the place was totally packed. An amazing variety of talent played and I think they all did it for free—Dionne Warwick, the Doors, Spanky and Our Gang, just to mention a few! And then we just crashed at a friend's house and then went back up Sunday and heard Jefferson Airplane, the Byrds, Country Joe and the Fish, and the 5th Dimension. The crowd was totally stoked, but it was really mellow and everyone just really got along. You know, when I heard that the Hell's Angels were going to help with security, I really had my doubts, but they were totally cool and everyone just hung out and enjoyed the music. It was amazing—I've never seen anything like it. I heard that there were over 30,000 people there, and the stadium is set up for about 4,000, so it was just packed, but the place just resonated with peace, love, and joy. The profits go to the Hunter's Point Child Care Center and I know they can really use it. At two dollars a ticket they must have been able to give them a nice donation. How about you, Katie?"

"Nothing as exciting as your weekend, Eric. Let's see. After I talked to you on Friday, I watched TV and went to bed and then on Saturday, my Dad and I went to Stinson Beach in San Francisco and then went out to dinner at our cousin's restaurant, Ristorante Pulli, it's in North Beach. . . My grandfather and his brother started the restaurant back in the late '30s and some of my cousins, who worked with them throughout the years, took it over when he retired. The food is amazing and it is really great to see my cousins. It's a family tradition to eat there whenever we can get together. They serve family style five-course dinners using my grandparents' Tuscan recipes, and using only the freshest of ingredients. The entrée last night was veal scaloppini and it was so tender and delicious served with homemade pasta, and then delicious tiramisu."

"I haven't been there, but I have heard it is really good. You are making me hungry just hearing about it. I am really tired of pizza. The place I work has decent pizza and I can eat here for free but what really makes it a great place is the entertainment. I have to work tonight but tomorrow I'm going down to the Haight to hang out for awhile. There are a lot of people in town because of the festival and I want to connect with some people that I met yesterday."

"Eric, did you know that my dad is a cop and that Haight-Ashbury is his beat?"

"No lie? I knew he was a cop in San Francisco, but I had no idea that Haight-Ashbury was his territory. Wow, what does he think about the whole scene there?"

"You don't even want to know. Believe me. I thought I would give you a heads up to watch out for him."

Eric joked, "Yeah, I'm sure he'd be glad to see me. We could hang out together and maybe have a cup of coffee at the People's Café or something."

Katie laughed and said, "Yeah, I can just see that. Seriously, he's having a tough time with all the changes in the world. He would be happy if the world stayed frozen in 1955. And now there is another big change in our family and I am not sure if I should tell him."

"Yeah, want to tell me about it?"

"Okay, I need to tell someone and get advice on what to do. You see it's about my Aunt Katherine. When she was eighteen, she became a nun and that was about twenty years ago. Remember the other night when I said that I had company when you called and couldn't talk? Well, it was her. She showed up at my door and told me she has taken a leave from the convent and she is living with some family in Berkeley. She says she will tell the rest of the family soon but is waiting for the right time. She wasn't ready but wanted me to know in case of an emergency and gave me a phone number. Saturday, my dad wanted to call her and invite her for dinner. I don't want him to call the convent and find out that way, but I also want to honor Aunt Katherine's request."

"Wow, I don't know what to say. I've never even met a nun before. I guess that's a big deal to leave, huh? Have you tried calling her and seeing when she plans to tell them?"

"Yeah, I called yesterday when my dad was outside working in the yard. A man answered and when I asked for her, he told me that she wasn't there. He said that he'd leave a message for her to call me back. I told him to have her call sometime today after 4:00. So actually, I should get off the phone in case she is trying to call. By the way, where are you staying?"

"I'm couch-surfing, and staying with different friends, but if you ever need to get in touch with me you can call me here at the Pizza Shack. If I can't get to the phone, I'll call you back. I work most weeknights and about half the weekends. I will be around until Friday morning and then I will be leaving for the Monterey Pop Festival with some friends. Sure wish you could go. It is going to be quite the happening. "

"Eric, if we don't talk before you leave for the festival, have fun!"

"Thanks, bye—but I'll call later in the week, for sure, before I leave for Monterey."

"Okay, bye". She hung up the phone reluctantly because she loved talking to him.

She thought to herself, "Maybe I should turn the TV on and get my mind on something else." Then the phone rang again. She sauntered to the phone, grabbed a chair, and sat down before she answered it. "Pulli Residence."

"Hi, Katie, this is Katherine, how are you doing?"

"I am so relieved you called. You have got to tell my dad right away about your leaving the convent. He was going to call you on Saturday. I was able to keep him from doing it, but who knows when he might decide to call you and we can both imagine what his response would be if he heard it from one of the sisters at the convent. I told him that you weren't at the convent because you went to some sort of retreat."

"Quick thinking, Katie, and you are right. In some ways it is kind of like a retreat to figure things out. You know it is a year's leave; it's not like I have left altogether. I'd like to arrange to come to your house and talk to him on Saturday morning around ten. I think I can get a ride then, and if need be, I will take a bus back. I think that is better than meeting him at some restaurant or a public place."

"Yeah, that would probably work; no telling how he will react to your news. I'll leave him a note saying you called and want to come over Saturday morning." Awkwardly changing the subject, Katie spit out, "Well, what have you been doing, Aunt Katherine?"

"I'm looking for a job, but no luck yet. Not a big market for dropout nuns, ha ha! Yesterday I went to a great music festival up on Mount Tam; that's why I wasn't home when you called."

"You went to the Fantasy Fair! I am so jealous. Eric asked me to go and I wanted to go so bad, but I didn't dare ask Dad." Even her aunt, the nun, got to go. That was so unfair!

"Yeah, the crowd was a little overwhelming and the music so different from when I was young, but I had a great time. It was the first time I danced since, uh, I guess 1947, when I was a senior in high school and we danced the jitterbug to big band tunes. Anyway, I just got out there and moved to the music with my friends. Not that there was much room to dance. The place was packed. And no one seemed to care that I had no clue what I was doing. Listen, I have to get off because this is long distance and I'm calling on my friend's phone. I'll plan to be at your house on Saturday morning unless you call and let me know otherwise."

"Okay, Aunt Katherine, goodbye."

"Goodbye, Katie and thank you for—you know—covering for me. I owe you one."

CHAPTER 9

June 13, 1967

As Katie was walking in the door, the phone was ringing. Hoping it was Eric calling her, she ran to the phone and breathlessly said, "Hello?"

Gino yelled, "What the hell is going on?"

Her heart skipped a beat as she wondered if he knew that she had been talking to Eric on the phone. She meekly answered, "What do you mean, Dad?"

"Where is your Aunt Katherine? I decided to go into the city early today. Thought I could drop by at her school at lunch time and bring her some of the cannoli we had left over from Sunday. I went into her classroom and there is some substitute teacher there and when I asked her where Sister Katherine was she said she doesn't know. She only knew that the teacher couldn't finish out the school year, so they had asked her to substitute. I went to the school office and the secretary wouldn't tell me anything, and said that the Mother Superior was busy. I said I would just sit there for as long as it took.

"After about a half hour, Mother Superior called me in and when I asked her what was going on she just said, 'She is on leave. That's all I can tell you.'"

"I asked, 'You mean from teaching?'"

"She tells me, 'She is on leave from her duties as a sister with our order.'

"When I asked her where my sister was, she told me she didn't know am I the last to know? Katie, you said you talked to her. I can't believe you didn't tell me. Is she sick or something? Where is she?"

"Dad, I'm sorry, she did come here about a week ago and told me, but she asked me not to tell anyone because she wanted to tell you yourself. That's why she was coming over on Saturday. She's not sick or hurt or anything. All I know is that she is staying somewhere in Berkeley with some friends."

Gino hollered, "Berkeley with friends! Give me the address and phone number now."

"Dad, I don't have her address, and I am worried about your blood pressure; it's not good for you to be so upset."

"Upset isn't half of it. Give me the damn phone number now!"

CHAPTER 10

June 16, 1967

Katie was sprawled on the couch reading her *Seventeen Magazine*, discovering how Twiggy started her modeling career, when the phone rang. She jumped up and answered the phone, "Pulli residence," in case it was her dad, but was pleasantly surprised to hear Eric's voice on the other end.

"Hi, Katie, how are you doing?"

"It's good to hear from you, Eric. I thought you'd be on your way to the Monterey Pop Festival by now and I didn't expect to hear from you."

"Yeah, well I tried to call around five yesterday and your dad answered, so I hung up. I didn't expect him to answer."

"He took yesterday off because he found out about my Aunt Katherine and he is acting like a maniac. He decided to go over to Berkeley and try to talk her out of her decision to leave the convent and when she refused, he tried to force her to get in the car and to come stay at our house to get her away from the 'hippies who are trying to brainwash her.' I'm sure it was a very ugly scene. I know she is my dad's younger sister, but she is thirty-eight years old and he treats her like she was still a kid! He worries because she has always been sheltered and thinks that people will take advantage of her."

"Wow, sounds like a lot of heavy stuff going on there. Was today your last day of school?"

"I had my last final today. Tomorrow is the last day and it will just be signing yearbooks and stuff like that; we will also have the end-of-the-year Mass to pray for protection for all of us during summer vacation."

"Will you pray for protection from me?" Eric joked.

"Should I?" Katie laughed and changed the subject before he could answer. "When are you heading out?"

"I'm at work now and my friend Pete is going to pick me up in a little while. Wait a minute. I'm on the pay phone, and I need to put more money in." After depositing another quarter he continued, "Yeah, well, four of us are going in his Volkswagen bus. We'll either sleep in the bus or outside, if we can find a spot. It is going to be so far out! All the greats will be there: Jefferson Airplane, the Who, Jimi Hendrix, Janis Joplin, Mamas and the Papas, just to name a few."

"That is so cool, Eric, and I can't wait to hear all about it. I hope you have a great birthday on Saturday. You are so lucky."

"Yeah, I know, the only thing that would make it better is if you were there. I really do want to see you, Katie. How about next week since school is out? I'm off work on Tuesday. Would you meet me somewhere while your dad is at work? How about meeting at that Northgate shopping center near you?" Is there some kind of coffee shop there we could meet?"

"Well, there is one near the Emporium—but I don't know—"

"Hey, I gotta go because Pete just drove up—I'll be there at four on Tuesday. Bye, Katie." He hung up before she could respond.

CHAPTER 11

June 21, 1967

"What are your plans for the rest of the day, Katie?" Gino asked as he gathered his badge and gun and headed to the front door.

"Is it okay if I take the bus to Northgate and go to the Emporium to look at swimsuits?"

"Well, I don't know. Who are you going with and what time will you be home?"

"I would take the 3:10 bus. I'm going to see if my friend Susan can meet me there, and we will probably take the 5:30 home," Katie lied.

Gino hesitated and then said, "I guess that is all right if you make sure to lock up tight before you leave, and I'll call you around 7:00 during my break. And Katie, none of those skimpy two-piece swimsuits, right?"

"Right, Dad, I won't buy anything that Annette Funicello wouldn't wear," joked Katie as she walked him to the door and gave him a big hug and kiss on his familiar, smoothly shaven, Old Spice-scented cheek.

As the door closed behind her dad, Katie took a deep breath and scurried to her room. She grabbed her navy-blue bellbottom pants and burgundy poor boy sweater and slipped them on as she thought, "I can't wait to meet Eric, but I wish I didn't feel so guilty about lying to my dad." As she looked in the mirror she undid her long ponytail and brushed her wavy, cascading brown hair, brushed her teeth, and gargled with cinnamon-flavored Lavoris mouthwash. She was so happy that her braces had been removed a few months before, and she was pleased with her straight teeth. She put a little light pink lip gloss on and wished she wore makeup. It was frowned on by the nuns, and it would probably be an issue with her dad, so she had never pursued it.

Katie grabbed some garden shears, a wax paper bag, and a rubber band from the kitchen drawer and headed out to the rose garden in the backyard. The roses that her mother had planted when Katie was a little girl were in full bloom now. It was sad that her mom wasn't there to see this year's dazzling display. She chose three of the most beautiful variegated red and white roses, which were her mom's favorite, and she clipped them. She raised them to her nostrils and smelled the sweet scents, put them in the wax bag, and twisted the rubber band around the little package. She grabbed her purse and keys and headed out the front door.

The summer fog combined with a slight breeze was rolling in when Katie walked down the sidewalk and saw Mrs. Wilson at her mailbox picking up her mail. As their neighbor caught sight of Katie, she smiled and said, "What are you up to on this fine summer day?"

"I am going to take Golden Gate Transit to Northgate."

Mrs. Wilson noticed the roses in Katie's hand and nodded knowingly, choking back her own emotion. "I miss your mom, too, Katie, and she was such a good friend to me for so many years. I know that it has been very difficult for you, and if you ever need someone to talk to or if you need anything, you know I will always be here for you."

"I know. Thank you, Mrs. Wilson." Katie changed the subject, saying, "Do you need anything at the Northgate Shopping Center?"

"No, thank you, but what a dear for asking."

The big transit bus rounded the corner just as Katie got to the stop. She climbed the steep stairs onto the bus and deposited her coins in the hopper, and said "Northgate." Gary, the driver, nodded and smiled as Katie made her way to one of the front seats. She often took this bus home from school, so they knew each other. There were only a few others on the bus and the ten-minute ride went quickly.

After stepping off the bus, Katie headed left to the Mount Olivet Catholic Cemetery. It was funny that this new shopping center was right next to the cemetery that served as her mom's last resting place. Her mom had loved to shop before she was sick, and she was so glad when this shopping center had been built so close to their home.

Katie walked through the cemetery gate and along the driveway until she came to her mom's section. She trudged up the slope of the hill until she came to the headstone she was looking for. "Margaret Jean Pulli, Loving Wife and Mother, 1929–1966." There were some white lilies in the receptacles, which meant that her dad had probably been there recently. You could see the outline around the grave where the sod had not totally filled in yet.

Katie got down on her knees and tenderly placed the roses in with the lilies. She said a Hail Mary and then burst into tears while whispering, "I miss you so much, Mama. It is so hard without you and I desperately need to talk to you. I want to be a good daughter to Daddy and not cause him any more stress or sadness but you know how overprotective he is. I know I shouldn't be sneaking off to see Eric, but I like him a lot and I don't think Dad will ever think any guy is good enough for me. Mom, should I go ahead and meet him or turn around and go back home?" After hesitating for a minute, Katie got up off her knees and said, "What am I doing? Do I actually think that she is going to talk to me from the grave? I have to decide on my own. Okay, Mom, you taught me to think for myself. I am going to meet with Eric, and if you don't want me to, please ask God to give me a sign." She waited for a couple of minutes, and then brushed off her tears and the cut grass from her pants and started walking toward the shopping center.

She glanced at her watch and noted that it was a few minutes before four. As she was considering whether to change her mind and duck into a store and wait for the next bus to go home, she spotted

Eric standing in front of the coffee shop, giving her his amazing smile and a casual wave. His green eyes twinkled as he walked toward Katie and said, "I didn't know if you would come or not."

"Well, I probably shouldn't have, but you didn't give me a chance to answer, and I thought about you driving over an hour for nothing and—"

"So it is true, that the best way to motivate a Catholic girl is through guilt," he joked.

"Eric, that was a dirty trick," she replied as she looked at his handsome face and her heart melted, reassuring her that she had made the right choice.

"What did you tell your dad?"

"I told him that I was meeting a friend and going shopping for a swimming suit."

"All right, I'd be glad to help you pick out a suit!" Eric teased.

Katie laughed and said, "No, thanks, let's just visit a while and then I can go over to the Emporium to look around. I need to take the 5:30 bus, so we have about an hour."

Disappointment flashed across Eric's face, but he quickly said, "Well I would love to have more time with you, but if an hour is what I get, I'll take it."

They walked inside the '50s-style diner and seated themselves in a back-corner booth, and Katie slid in, so that her back was to any other customers. Katie thought, "Thank God I haven't seen anyone who knows me or my dad, but anyone could come in."

When the waitress approached, Eric said, "Coffee and apple pie a la mode for me. How about you, Katie? Want to see a menu? Get whatever you want."

"Thanks, I'll just have a Cherry Coke." Did he have any idea that her stomach was doing flip flops? There was no way she could have eaten anything. "How was the Monterey Pop Festival? And your birthday?"

"It was out of sight; I don't even know where to begin. My buddy drove his VW bus, and we left around noon and got to the Monterey County Fairgrounds around two. Already there was a long line to get in. It wasn't a beautiful setting like Mount Tam, but it was much more suited to a big crowd of people. They said that it has a capacity of 7,000 and it was definitely overflowing on Saturday night, and there was the amazing array of talent. On Friday night the Association, Lou Rawls and Johnny Rivers, the Animals and Simon and Garfunkel all played. Everyone totally rocked out to all the music and there was a respect for all of the different genres and just loving the music and being together. The concert went till really late and after it was over, we drove to a beach outside of Monterey. We had just gotten to sleep when a cop told us to get out of there, so we found a grocery store parking lot to sleep in and—" Just then the waitress brought their order.

As Katie sipped her cherry coke through the plastic straw, it struck Eric how beautiful Katie was. She could definitely be a model with her creamy complexion accented by the scattering of freckles across her nose, complemented by her bright blue eyes and long dark lashes framed by that beautiful, shiny, wavy hair cascading down her shoulders and a gorgeous smile. He liked her natural look much more than the bouffant hairdos and heavy makeup that a lot of girls wore at his school. Katie interrupted his trance by saying, "The festival sounds cool. Tell me about the rest and how you spent your eighteenth birthday!"

He finished his last bite of pie, which was drenched with melted vanilla ice cream, and then he replied, "Okay, on Saturday we went back to the beach for a while, which was a great way to start my birthday. We met some guys who let us use their surfboards for a while. I am just learning to surf, so I spent more time falling off the board. Was that water freezing! We grabbed some food from the store and then we headed back to the fairgrounds around noon. On Saturday we heard Country Joe and the Fish, Quicksilver Messenger Service, Steve Miller Band, the Byrds, and my favorite band: Jefferson Airplane. Then Booker T. & the MG's and Otis Redding finished out the night. We ended up just sleeping in the parking lot. "

Just then the jukebox started playing Katie's favorite song, "My Girl" by the Temptations, and Katie took another sip of her coke, diverting her attention from Eric. He took another bite of his pie and sipped his coffee and said, "This pie is delicious."

Katie continued, "I heard the crowd got pretty wild."

"For the most part, the crowd was mellow. Of course, a lot of people were drinking and some people were dropping acid and got a little crazy, but most people were smoking pot and were pretty calm. On Sunday, one of the first bands performing was Big Brother and the Holding Company; they have a new lead singer, Janis Joplin, and does that girl have lungs! Buffalo Springfield played after that. Then the British band the Who got on stage and things got really outrageous. At the end of their song, "My Generation," Pete Townsend smashed his guitar on the stage and then a bunch of smoke bombs went off behind the sound system. You should have seen the festival workers scramble to get the expensive microphones off the stage so they didn't get smashed up. After that the Grateful Dead played, which was pretty mellow in comparison; Jerry Garcia is an amazing guitarist. Did you know that he used to come in and play guitar at the pizza place where I work? It was before I worked there, but people still remember that."

Katie added, "My friend Carol heard the Grateful Dead over at the Santa Venetia Armory, which is just across the highway from here near the Marin Civic Center."

"Yeah, they lived in the Haight and have done a lot of stuff around this area, especially charity events. After the Grateful Dead, Jimi Hendrix was on and the last number he played was a crazy rendition of "Wild Thing." He ended the song by kneeling over his guitar, pouring some lighter fluid over it and then he lit his guitar on fire and smashed it a bunch of times. And then threw it into the crowd. I don't know if Jimi thought he had to outdo Pete Townsend or what. At that point, the audience totally erupted, trying to grab Hendrix's guitar pieces that were still hot from the fire. It was quite a spectacle, but I kept thinking that it was such a waste of a world-class guitar. I would have rather seen him give his guitar to someone random in the audience or to charity or something."

"Yeah, my dad read me that in the newspaper yesterday and you can imagine his *shocked* response. I thought the reporter was exaggerating, but I guess he wasn't. Needless to say, it gave my dad one more reason to lecture and forbid me to go to any kind of rock concert."

"The concert ended on a mellow note with the Mamas and the Papas. John Phillips was one of the organizers so I guess that is why they had his band close the festival. They played, "Monday, Monday" and "California Dreaming" as well as some of their new songs. We could hardly hear them since the crowd was so wound up, and it was anticlimactic after all the fireworks."

"You are so lucky, Eric. I would love to see all those bands, especially the Mamas and the Papas. What a variety of music: folk, jazz, rock, country, and all sharing the same stage, which is amazing."

"Yeah, it was so cool, but it would have even been better if you had been there, Katie." He noticed that she blushed and so he quickly went on, "Sunday night we headed home and yesterday I worked and that brings us up to today. That's enough about me; tell me what has been going on for you."

"Not much compared to you. Friday night I just relaxed and watched television, so glad that school is out for the summer. On Saturday, my dad and I went to the movies to see *Camelot*. On Sunday, we went to the family restaurant in the city and then came home and watched Ed Sullivan. My dad loves that show. I have just been trying to keep cool and get some house projects done before I start my job next week, taking care of three children for an attorney and his wife. But you didn't tell me about your birthday—did you have a cake or anything?"

"My mom may have sent me a card with some money, but I haven't been home since I dropped the news about not going to graduation, so I haven't gotten my mail. I don't even know if my father remembered my birthday. Our housekeeper, Maria, always makes me a cake. I have been calling her every few days to reassure her that I'm okay and she always tries to talk me into going back home. Since my brother is in Vietnam and is probably busy dodging bullets and mines, I am not thinking my birthday is on his radar. I will probably go home after I think my dad has cooled off—if for no other reason, for Maria's sake. She is worried sick about my brother and now with me gone, she is having a tough time. She has been with our family since we were tiny and has been like a mom to me, so I owe her a lot. Besides, I'm getting kind of tired of sleeping on the floor at my friend's house." Lifting up his last fork of pie with a glob of melted ice cream on the top, he continued, "So I guess this is my birthday pie, and it couldn't taste better."

"So are you glad that you went to the festival instead of your graduation?"

"Oh, yeah, definitely. Hey, I've been doing all of the talking. Why don't you tell me more about you?"

Katie surprised herself by telling Eric about her life, her mom's illness and death, and taking flowers to the cemetery. As her eyes welled with tears, he reached across the table and took her hand. He seemed interested, and she was pleased that it was getting easier to talk about her mom. The time flew by and Katie glanced at the clock and exclaimed, "It's already 5:20 and I need to get to the bus! No swimsuit shopping today. I'll tell my dad that I didn't see anything I liked."

"Katie, you don't need to take the bus. I can give you a ride home."

"Oh, no thanks, our neighborhood is extremely tight-knit, and if people saw us they would tell my dad."

Eric laughed "I get it. I don't want to tangle with your dad if I can help it. I caught a glimpse of Papa Bear at the game. Hopefully, I will think of a way to win him over. At least, let me walk you to the bus stop."

CHAPTER 12

July 7, 1967

As Katie walked through the front door, the phone was ringing, and she answered it, expecting her dad. "Hello, Pulli Residence."

"Hey, Katie, I have been trying to call you all week," said Eric. "Where have you been?"

"I've been up at Russian River with my cousin Laura and her family at the family cabin. It came up kind of suddenly; I hadn't been up there in a while." She had told herself that the next time Eric called, she would tell him she couldn't talk to him anymore, but when she heard Eric's smooth voice, she just couldn't say it.

"Well, I'm just glad you are okay. I was starting to wonder if your dad changed your number or something. How was Russian River?"

"It was good to hang out with my cousins, swim, play cards, and eat a lot of great food. My Aunt Lena is an excellent cook, and since I don't have siblings, they are more like brothers and sisters to me. I hadn't been there the last couple of summers because my mom was so sick and couldn't travel. My dad came up for the weekend to bring me home. I think it was pretty hard for him to go there since it was where he met my mom and they had so many good times there, but he got through it. How about you? What have you been up to?"

"I did move back home and I'm staying in the pool house. I traded my Volkswagen bug in for a Volkswagen van that needs a lot of work, but will be great to travel in and it will be my back-up if my dad kicks me out. I have been working long hours and saving my money. I plan to move into San Francisco when school starts and go to San Francisco State. I think I finally know what I want to do. You know I have always wanted to do something in the medical field, but being a doctor takes so many years and I just don't want to jump through all of those hoops and spend all those years in school, so I am thinking about becoming a nurse. You know they opened a free clinic in Haight-Ashbury and I went and talked to Dr. Smith, the guy who started it. He said that they have a big need for volunteers. I'd like to just take a year off and work and do some traveling, but with Vietnam going on, if I'm not in school, Uncle Sam will be sending me a draft notice."

"That sounds really great, Eric. Did you know that my mom was a nurse? She didn't work much after she married my dad, but she always was the one that helped out when anyone in the family or neighborhood got sick. My dad has encouraged me to follow in her footsteps, and I think that is the direction that I am heading. On another topic, how's it going with your dad?"

"I haven't talked to him much. We've given each other a wide berth since I've been back. He's usually gone in the morning when I get up and he's asleep when I get home, so it's working out. Maria is so happy that I am home, and my back is appreciating a bed rather than the lumpy couch that I had been sleeping on."

"I just started my job today and I think it's going to work out. I am a summer nanny to three children whose dad is a well-known attorney in San Francisco. They have a gorgeous house and swimming pool and all I have to do is play with the kids all day. The mother doesn't work, but she has a busy social calendar with tennis, bridge, and other country club activities. They have a full-time housekeeper as well as a guy who serves as a combination chauffeur and gardener. I don't have to clean, cook, or anything like that. If I want to take the children anywhere, the chauffeur takes us and picks us up. My dad takes me in the morning and I take the bus home unless they need me in the evening, and then the chauffeur takes me home. It is amazing, and they pay me $1.50 an hour, which is way more than anyone has ever paid me for babysitting. I have never known anyone before who had a chauffeur or housekeeper."

"That sounds great, Katie. Hey, one reason I was calling was to see if maybe we could work something out for us to get together some time soon."

Katie had been dreading this subject, "Eric, I just can't see how I can work that out, and to tell you the truth, I have been feeling so guilty about lying to my dad the last time we got together. I am thinking that we should just—"

"Please don't just brush me off. I like you and want to see you or—"

"I need to go. My dad might be trying to call me and he gets angry when the phone is busy."

"Katie, I'm not giving up this easy because I think you like me, too and—"

She cut him off by saying abruptly, "I'm sorry, but please don't call me anymore. This just isn't going to work. Goodbye, Eric." As Katie hung up the phone, she wiped away the tears rolling down her cheeks and thought, "I really do like Eric, but there is no future for us and it was the right thing to end it. Now I need to do another right thing and go to confession and admit my lying and sneaking behind my dad's back and get focused on school and doing what's right." She had talked extensively to her cousin Laura during her time at Russian River and as hard as it was, she knew she was doing the right thing. But why did she feel so terrible?

CHAPTER 13

September 8, 1967

As Gino and his old patrol partner, Ron, sat down in their seats, inhaling the smells of the ballpark, Ron said loudly over the bustling crowd, "Hey, thanks for inviting me to come to another game. I thought you'd be taking your daughter to the games more and that I would be out of luck."

"It's been a good excuse to take you instead of her and I'll tell you why—it is all about the seat next to you."

"Huh?"

"You know that jerk Bill Smith who has those season seats? When I brought Katie in June, he and his hippie son were here and that long-haired punk was trying really hard to hit on Katie. Can you believe it? It's bad enough that I have had to put up with that rich drunk snob all through the years, but now I've got to deal with that? That kid took off with Katie and went to the snack bar and was gone for about an hour. I was going out of my mind. I forbade her to ever see him again, so I am sure she won't, but I never know when Bill and his kid will be here, so it's just better not to bring her here. It makes me mad, that I am the one missing out, but she hasn't said anything about it, so I guess she doesn't care."

"Gino, I have heard you griping about sitting next to this guy for years. Why don't you just quit being so stubborn and try to exchange your tickets?"

"I looked into that and the seats they have available are really terrible. You know I share these season tickets with two other guys from the department who are retired now, and I really can't ask them to do that. I have told them if they can find someone else who wants to buy my share to go ahead—but in the meantime the good thing is that I haven't seen this Bill guy or his son the last few months. The times I have been here the people who have the tickets seem to be either rich friends or clients of his. One time, a dame was wearing a mink coat. Can you imagine that?"

After they stood and sang the Star-Spangled Banner, they joined in cheering for the Giants as they claimed their positions on the field. As usual, Willie Mays was in center field, Willie McCovey on first base, and Jesús Alou in left field; Ray Sadecki was the pitcher. Chicago Cubs short stop Don Kessinger was up to bat.

As the game began, Gino sighed with relief that Bill's seats were empty, and he hoped that they would stay that way. He pulled out the salami and cheese sandwich on a French roll that Katie had packed for him. The top of the first inning was scoreless, and Cubs pitcher Joe Niekro took the mount. He prevented the Giants from scoring as well.

During the second inning, the Cubs brought in two runs and the Giants scored one. At the top of the third inning, Bill showed up and squeezed past Ben and Gino carrying a beer. He and Gino exchanged dirty looks. It appeared to Gino that he had already been drinking, maybe in the clubhouse bar. Gino had noticed that when Bill had clients with him, he acted the part of a gentleman, and never drank to excess. Today was another story.

Bill flagged down the vendor for another beer, as the Cubs scored another run in the third inning, causing the Giants to trail them 3 to 1. The Giants scored a run at the bottom of the fourth followed by four scoreless innings. Bill continued to drink from his flask and started yelling, "You guys are losers. I don't even know why I even bother to come and see you. When are you going to play decent baseball? You can't even score against the Cubs. You are pathetic."

Gino had been fuming throughout the game at Bill's behavior, but this outburst was uncalled for. After all, the Giants still had a shot at getting to the World Series. St. Louis was their only big contender. He jumped out of his chair and started yelling at Bill, "You know who is a loser? You! You are so drunk that you don't even know what you are saying."

"Who the hell do you think you are, you little dago? So high and mighty because you are a cop. Do I look scared?"

Gino retorted, "No wonder your son is so messed up with you as a dad."

"How dare you say something about my son, you—"

"You better keep that long-haired son away from my daughter if you know what's good for you and him." Ron was motioning to Gino that they needed to leave the stadium before it got more heated.

Bill yelled, "I would disown my son before I'd let him be with anyone who was related to you."

To keep the peace, Ron insisted that they leave "to miss the traffic," and Gino agreed reluctantly. As they headed out of the stadium, Ron and Gino heard the crowd roar. The Giants scored two runs at the bottom of the ninth and had won the game 4 to 3.

CHAPTER 14

Thanksgiving Day, 1967

"What a beautiful day for a walk!" Katherine exclaimed as she and her niece walked around the neighborhood near their cousin's home. "Katie, how are you doing? We haven't had a chance to really talk for a while. I know this has been a tough year for you."

"We are getting by, but it's sure hard having this first Thanksgiving without my mom. I know my Dad is really missing her, even though he tries to be cheerful and friendly. I'm glad we could be with all of you today."

Katherine took Katie's hand and squeezed it. "Yeah, the first holidays are always the most difficult. I haven't talked to your dad at all today. I wanted to offer some consolation, but we haven't spoken since that scene in Berkeley, so I thought it best to give him a wide berth today."

"How are you doing? And what happened with that boy you met at the baseball game? You seemed to be interested in him and then I didn't hear any more about it."

"I decided to cut it off with him. I did meet up with him once, but I had to lie to my dad and sneak around not to get caught. There really wasn't any future in it."

Katherine could sense that Katie was really disappointed that she had cut if off with Eric and didn't want to talk about it anymore, so she went on, "Thanks for passing on your mom's clothes to me. It has really helped me out since I only had two outfits and had to keep washing them by hand. I'll make sure not to wear them around your dad, though, since that might be very strange and sad for him."

"Yeah, I'm glad that my dad finally let me go through her stuff and give most of it away and I'm glad they are being put to good use. She'd like that."

"Katie, I wanted to tell you that I have a new job. A guy is buying a piece of property about ten miles north of here and he is going to start a commune. They need two teachers and I am going to be the one working with the younger students."

"Is that the same place where the Grateful Dead used to live?"

"Yeah, the group is called the Chosen Family, and it is going to be a great situation. People coming together to learn and grow together. It's a beautiful piece of property."

"Are you sure you want to do that, Aunt Katherine? Dad read about that in the *Chronicle* and he did a lot of ranting, saying our county Board of Supervisors shouldn't allow it, and that it sounded like a cult to him."

"I know the name really throws people off, but it's definitely not a cult. They call it the Chosen Family because people have chosen each other as family. It's not that we think we are better than anyone else."

"Aunt Katherine, I just ask one thing of you. Please tell the family your plans, so I am not in the middle of things again, okay?"

"Yes, I will. I am planning on telling the rest of the family when we get back for dessert, but I wanted you to be the first to know."

Katie laughed, "You are full of surprises! Six months ago you were a nun in a convent, and now you are going to live in a hippie commune."

"I'm glad you are amused," Katherine laughed nervously, "but I don't think your dad or Mother Superior will think it's funny. Let's go back to the house; my ride will be picking me up in about half an hour. That will give me just enough time to tell everyone and—"

"I know, and then you make a quick getaway. This is going to be one interesting conversation over the pumpkin pie, "Katie teased.

CHAPTER 15

April 3, 1968

Walking through the front door, Gino yelled, "I'm home, Katie girl! I love not working the swing shift anymore! Just wish that I didn't have to deal with that awful traffic, though. Smells good, what's cooking?"

Katie bounced out of the kitchen, gave her dad a big hug, and replied, "I made stew in the pressure cooker and a salad. It's good to have you home for dinner these days."

As Gino went into his room to put away his badge and service revolver and change out of his uniform, Katie set the table and finished making the salad. When Katie carefully opened the top of the pressure cooker and peered in she realized that she must have cooked it too long. It just looked like a pot of thick gravy; all the meat and vegetables had disintegrated. Katie was horrified and said, "Dad, I don't know what happened to the stew."

Gino looked into the pot and said, "I'm sure it is going to taste great." They sat down at the table together saying the traditional Catholic grace and then started dishing up their plates. When Gino took the first bite of his "stew" he smiled and said, "Mmm, Katie, this stew has the best flavor of any stew I have ever eaten! There just must be something wrong with that pressure cooker. Thank you for coming home from a long day at school and making a nice dinner for us while other kids are probably just hanging out at that Burgie's Drive-In smoking cigarettes and getting into trouble."

Although Katie was disappointed about how the stew turned out, she had to smile at her Dad. He sure loved to eat, and almost every meal was the "best he had ever eaten," which she loved about him. She did enjoy cooking and was grateful that he was so appreciative. At times like this, she was glad she hadn't continued to see Eric because her dad was so trusting and she didn't want to disappoint him.

"I'll do the dishes, since you cooked, and later maybe we can watch the news." Ever since they had purchased a color television at Christmas, Gino had renewed his interest in TV.

When Gino switched on the big console TV, Martin Luther King Jr. was saying, "Well, I don't know what will happen now. We've got some difficult days ahead. But it really doesn't matter with me now, because I've been to the mountaintop. And I don't mind. Like anybody, I would like to live a long life. Longevity has its place. But I'm not concerned about that now. I just want to do God's will. And He's allowed me to go up to the mountain. And I've looked over. And I've seen the Promised Land. I may not get there with you. But I want you to know tonight, that we, as a people, will get to the Promised Land! And so I'm happy, tonight. I'm not worried about anything. I'm not fearing any man! Mine eyes have seen the glory of the coming of the Lord! And so I'm happy, tonight. I'm not worried about anything. I'm not fearing any man! Mine eyes have seen the glory of the coming of the Lord!"

As King finished his speech Katie marveled, "He is such a great speaker, isn't he, Dad?"

"Yeah, he is a good preacher, Katie. But I think going to Memphis right now was a big mistake. That place is a hotbed of racism and unrest. And I heard he is staying in a motel in one of the worst areas of the city. I guess he wants to show his solidarity with the Negro community there, especially the sanitation workers, but he is taking a big chance and I think he's getting things stirred up there which I don't think is helping anything. Just last week the mayor had a mandatory curfew on the city because of all the protests and potential violence."

Katie frowned and said, "I worry about him. It must be tough to be his wife and kids and hearing about all the threats on his life. I know I worry about you, Dad, I don't know what I'd do without you."

"Oh, Bambina, don't worry your little head over me. Now that I have the Golden Gate Park and Haight-Ashbury area, the worst thing I deal with is drugged-up hippies and panhandlers. One thing about them all smoking that marijuana, they generally don't seem to get worked up about too much. Even when they are taking that LSD they mostly just act crazy."

"Promise you'll be careful."

"Of course I will. Let's see if there is something else to watch tonight in color. I'm sure glad you talked me into this color TV set; I guess it was about time."

CHAPTER 16

April 4, 1968

Gino walked through the door as Katie came out of the kitchen and said, "Meatloaf and baked potatoes tonight. I thought that was pretty safe."

Gino laughed and came up and gave her a big hug. "Sounds good, and I'm starving."

As Gino went into the bedroom to change his clothes, the phone rang. He picked it up. "Pulli speaking. Oh my God, when? Yes, I understand. Yes, okay, I will be on standby, just in case you need me." As he hung up the phone he solemnly said, "Turn the news on, Katie. Martin Luther King Jr. has been shot in the neck and is not expected to live. That was police headquarters. They are concerned that this could spark a riot, so I may be called in to go back to work. I guess it happened about an hour ago. I didn't listen to the radio on the way home or I probably would have known."

Katie gasped and ran to the television, and as it warmed up she could hear newscaster Walter Cronkite say, "Good evening. Martin Luther King Jr., the apostle of non violence and the civil rights movement, has been shot to death tonight in Memphis, Tennessee." Tears welled up in her eyes as she watched the broadcast, which explained that King had been on the second floor balcony of his motel room talking to someone when he was shot in the neck. He was transported to the hospital and died about an hour later. Cronkite reported that a well-dressed white man had been seen fleeing the scene and that a hunting rifle had been found about a block away. There was a manhunt underway and a curfew had been initiated by the mayor.

"Katie, this is all so sad, but let's go ahead and have some supper. I need to eat in case they call me in. If you want we can watch this while we eat." They ate silently watching the rest of the news. Just as they were finishing, the phone rang again.

"Pulli residence," her Dad said into the yellow, mounted wall phone. "Just a minute." Katie, this is headquarters again. They do want me to come in for back-up. Will you be okay here if I go in? You could go over to your cousins' if you want."

"No, I'll be okay here, Dad, go ahead."

He returned to the phone, "Yeah, I can come in. I'll be there in about thirty minutes."

After Gino picked up his badge and revolver from the bedroom he headed toward the front door, stopping to give Katie a hug and kiss. "You sure you're okay here? I hate to leave you when you are upset."

"Don't worry about me. I'll call Mrs. Wilson and go over and visit her next door if I need to. I'll lock the door and finish my homework. But just be careful, Daddy."

"I will and I'll call you later on my break," he said as he walked through the door and looked back at his precious daughter. At times like this, he was so glad that he had moved the family out of the city and into this safe neighborhood.

Katie went back to the couch and saw that the news was showing Robert Kennedy getting ready to speak to a big group of people. He was campaigning in Indianapolis, and he looked very grim and asked the crowd to put down their campaign signs and then said solemnly, "Ladies and Gentlemen, I'm only going to talk to you just for a minute or so this evening. Because . . . I have some very sad news for all of you, and I think sad news for all of our fellow citizens and people who love peace all over the world, and that is that Martin Luther King was shot and was killed tonight in Memphis, Tennessee.

"Martin Luther King dedicated his life to love and to justice between fellow human beings. He died in the cause of that effort. In this difficult day, in this difficult time for the United States, it's perhaps well to ask what kind of a nation we are and what direction we want to move in.

"For those of you who are black—considering the evidence evidently is that there were white people who were responsible—you can be filled with bitterness, and with hatred, and a desire for revenge.

"We can move in that direction as a country, in greater polarization—black people amongst blacks, and white amongst whites, filled with hatred toward one another. Or we can make an effort, as Martin Luther King did, to understand and to comprehend, and replace that violence, that stain of bloodshed that has spread across our land, with an effort to understand, compassion and love.

"For those of you who are black and are tempted to be filled with hatred and mistrust of the injustice of such an act, against all white people, I would only say that I can also feel in my own heart the same kind of feeling. I had a member of my family killed, but he was killed by a white man.

"But we have to make an effort in the United States; we have to make an effort to understand, to get beyond these rather difficult times."

At the end of the speech, Katie gathered up the dishes to put them in the sink and the phone rang. It was her Aunt Katherine and Katie could tell that she had been crying. "Did you hear about MLK? Oh, my God, I can't believe it. How could someone do something so awful to someone who was doing so much good?" Katherine said that everyone at the commune is in shock, and that they felt totally devastated. Katie told her that her dad had gone back into the city to do another shift and that she was watching the coverage on TV. "Do you want to come over and watch it? Do they have a TV there at the commune?"

"Thanks, but I think I should stay here, unless you need me, we do have a TV here. But, Katie, on another note, a couple of weeks ago, I met that boy Eric that you told me about and he wanted me to give you his phone number. I have been trying to decide what to do since your dad still isn't speaking to me because of my joining the commune and I did not want to give him something else to be mad at me about."

"How in the world did you meet Eric?"

"About two weeks ago, I was at a workshop on how to passively resist when being arrested at demonstrations. Eric recognized my 'Katherine Pulli' name tag and asked me if we were related. Katie, he is really smitten with you. He told me that you had asked him not to call you, but he was hoping that you might possibly change your mind and that he had never given you his number. He said he'd love to hear from you and that he was really sorry if he had done something to make you upset."

"Oh, Aunt Katherine, Eric must be taking King's assassination so hard. You know he had such admiration for him and really saw him as the hope of the future along with Bobby Kennedy. Did you hear Bobby's amazing speech tonight?"

"No, I missed it, but I am hoping they rebroadcast it or that I can see the text of it in the newspaper tomorrow. Hey, Katie, I need to get off. Others are waiting to use the phone. I'm going to give you Eric's number and you can decide."

Katie clicked her blue pen and carefully wrote down the number on the white message pad, thanked her aunt, and hung up the phone.

CHAPTER 17

April 6, 1968

As Eric walked up three flights of steps to get to his apartment, he thought about all that had happened this week. He was taking a full load of classes at San Francisco State as well as working thirty hours a week at a corner store, and could barely afford this one bedroom apartment that he was sharing with two other guys. He was determined to make it on his own without his parents' help, but he was exhausted. And then Martin Luther King getting assassinated—he could use some good news for a change.

As he walked in the door, his roommate John had just picked up the phone. "It's for you, Eric—a girl." He handed over the phone.

"Hi, Eric, this is Katie. My Aunt Katherine gave me your number and uh—"

"Katie, it's so good to hear from you. Did your aunt tell you where we met?"

"Yeah, and I can't talk long, Eric, I'm at a pay phone and my dad is in the market. He thinks I'm in the car studying. I just had to talk to you. I am just devastated about Martin Luther King and I know you must be too, and I just wanted to tell you that I was sorry and I couldn't think of anyone who would understand more than you and—"

Eric fought back tears, "Yeah, it is the worst—I am still reeling from the shock as so many people are. At State, everyone is just going around like in a stupor. Katie, he was our hope for civil rights and for the end of Vietnam. Our only hope now is for Bobby Kennedy to win the nomination and defeat whoever the Republicans put out there or I just don't know what's going to happen to this country. It's like a powder keg and just gets tenser every day. Did you hear that amazing speech Bobby gave right after King was killed? And to think that he just found out as he was going up to the microphone and did all of that off the cuff. He is such an outstanding speaker."

At that moment, the telephone operator interrupted the conversation saying, "Please deposit thirty cents for three more minutes."

"Please reverse the charges, operator," Eric said in his low voice.

"Thanks, Eric, but I can't talk long. I'm with my Dad and he's in the grocery store. I just wanted to touch bases with you and make sure you were okay."

"How are you doing, Katie? Are you dating anyone?"

"I'm fine. I'm going to the Marin Catholic Junior Prom next Saturday night with a boy I went to grade school with, but we're just friends. How about you?"

"Oh, I've gone out with a few girls this year but none of them… Hey, Katie, can I call you sometime? I know you asked me not to—but could we just talk, you know, just as friends."

"Maybe that would be okay, but my dad is working the day shift now, so don't call in the evening. I get home about 4:00 and he gets home about 5:30 so that would probably be the best time—hey, I gotta go."

"Thanks for calling. Katie, it meant a lot to me. Bye," Eric said as he hung up the phone and sighed as he thought, "Why is that girl so under my skin?"

Katie sat in the front seat of their car, picked up her U.S. History book, and started reading it before her dad came out of the Gala Market smiling. He said, "Got some spumoni ice cream for dessert,

Bambina. Hey, do you have everything you need for the prom? I know you got a dress and shoes, but need anything else like gloves or—"

"Thanks, Dad, I have everything I need."

"I hope I'm making the right decision to let you go to the prom. I do think you are still too young to be dating. But I thought since it was Gary Zucconi, I'd make an exception. He's a nice clean cut Catholic kid, good Italian family, good student, and a heck of a ball player. His dad told me that he has been sweet on you since you were in eighth grade."

"Oh, dad, Gary and I are just old friends, nothing else. We are double dating with Laura and Jay, and we are all just good friends.

"Well, I hope Gary understands that. You know some guys think because they take you on an expensive date you owe them," said Gino as they drove into the driveway.

Katie blushed. "Dad, I can't believe you said that—don't worry. Now let's drop the subject and unload these groceries before the ice cream melts."

CHAPTER 18

June 4, 1968

Katie was putting a chicken casserole in the oven when the phone starting ringing. When she answered the phone and heard his voice, she experienced the familiar butterflies. "Hey, Katie, how you doing?" he asked.

"I'm doing great, Eric. Less than two weeks before school is out, and I can't wait. How were your finals?"

"Took the last one this morning; I think I did OK. I'll be glad when I get beyond the general education classes. My mind has been fixed on the primary election today. Now that Johnson has dropped out of the race, Robert Kennedy's only real Democrat competition is Hubert Humphrey; RFK has gotta win. Did you know that it's the primary election for South Dakota today, too? It would be great if the most populated and the least populated states both chose him—I think it would say something about his overall appeal. Of course, if we didn't have to be twenty-one to vote, RFK would have a huge advantage because most people our age definitely want to see some changes. Isn't it a rip off that guys are old enough to get drafted and die for their country, but they can't even vote for the guys who make those decisions?"

"I sure agree with that, but wonder if it will happen in our lifetime.

The voting age has been the same for 200 years. Did I tell you that my friend Marsha's brother got killed in Vietnam a couple of weeks ago? He just turned nineteen, and the family is so torn apart—I just have no idea what to say."

"You know, there is a group called Youth Power that is promoting changing the voting age to eighteen, and they are having a big rally at the Marin Civic Center next Wednesday before the Board of Supervisors meeting. I'm thinking of coming over for it."

"Eric, I need to go because my dad is due home soon. I'm praying that Bobby wins the primary. I'm going to watch the results on TV, and I will be thinking about you."

"Okay, I'll give you a call tomorrow around 4:00 and we can celebrate his victory—he's just gotta win. It would take lot of pressure off of me if I didn't have to worry about the draft. Bye, Katie."

"Bye, Eric," Katie replied and went into the kitchen to put the casserole in the oven.

After Gino came home, they had a nice dinner together; they watched TV until about 9:30 and then Gino got up to go to bed. "I want to stay up and watch the news, Dad, so I can hear what the poll results are."

"Okay, Katie, but don't stay up too late. Good night," he said lovingly as he gave her a kiss on her forehead.

Gino headed to his bedroom and closed the door, tuning his radio to KGO News Talk. Ever since his wife died, he left his radio on all night; he said it helped distract him and made it easier for him to sleep.

Katie watched the 10:00 news and discovered that the California polls were coming in, in favor of Robert Kennedy. And although it wasn't a landslide, it looked like he was going to win after all. What a relief! And the polls from South Dakota were definitive. He had won there. Katie was elated. Bobby was scheduled to speak from the Ambassador Hotel in about an hour—presumably an acceptance speech. Well, it was already eleven. She had better get to bed. She walked down the hall and could hear the droning of the radio from her dad's room. She put her yellow flannel nightgown on and then slipped under her warm fuzzy blankets and silky purple sheets. She fell asleep immediately.

CHAPTER 19

June 5, 1968

A little while later, she woke up and thought, *what a strange dream.* Someone had repeatedly yelled "Bobby Kennedy has been shot." Reassured that it was just a dream, she rolled over and fell back to sleep. A little while later, her door opened and her dad was standing next to her and said, "Honey, I was called in and I need to go to work early."

Rubbing her eyes, she sleepily said, "Dad, I had the worst nightmare. I dreamed that Bobby Kennedy was shot."

Her father hesitated and then gently said, "Sweetheart, it wasn't a dream, it actually happened. I had the radio on and it got very loud when it happened—you must have heard it in your sleep and thought you were dreaming. They are saying he is critically wounded and don't have much hope that he will survive."

Katie switched on her white bedside lamp and muttered, "No, that can't be. They said on the news that he was winning and he was going to give his victory speech at the headquarters."

"He was shot right after he gave the speech. I know it's a hell of a thing. That family has sure gone through a lot. And listen, I need to go into work. They called from headquarters and they are bracing for potential riots. I need to go in, and I wasn't sure whether to wake you or not. I didn't want to just leave you a note. I may even have to work a double shift, so I'm not sure when I'll be home. Are you okay to get yourself off to school?"

"Yeah, Dad, go ahead, I've got my alarm set and I can take the bus."

"Try to go back to sleep, sweetheart, there is nothing you can do."

"I'll try, Daddy, and please be careful."

CHAPTER 20

June 6, 1968

Katie dropped her books on the coffee table and flopped onto the couch. It had been a grueling day and she so hoped to hear from Eric soon. Her phone rang as she was thinking of this; she ran to the phone and breathlessly said, "Hello."

It was Eric. "Kate, how are you doing?"

"Oh, Eric, I am just sick about Bobby. Are you okay? Is there any word about his condition?"

"He's in critical condition, and I don't think they are giving him any real chance to make it. He was shot in the head so I can't imagine his recovering. How could this all happen? First, JFK four years ago, then King, and now Bobby; I am so stunned. Katie, it's good that we have at least been talking on the phone the last few months, but I just have to see you; life is too short not to see each other. I think you want to see me, too. I am coming to the Marin County Civic Center on Tuesday for that Youth Power demonstration before the Board of Supervisors meeting. Could I please come early and meet you in the library there?"

Katie hesitated and then slowly said, "Okay, I'll try to meet you there at 4:00, but I can only stay until 5:30. I will tell my Dad that I need to do research for my final paper. We have to be discreet, though, since we can easily run into someone who would know me or my Dad."

CHAPTER 21

August 31, 1968

1:00 p.m.

The fog was rolling in as the two men in their heavy jackets, ski hats, and gloves headed toward their Candlestick seats behind home plate. Gino's friend Ron said, "Geez, I can never get used to how damn cold it is in this park this time of year. It was almost one hundred degrees when we left Marin just forty-five minutes ago, and it must be about forty-five degrees here."

Gino answered, "Yeah. But it would really be worth it to see them beat the Dodgers. This is only the third game I've seen all season. It's about time we had a break from all that overtime. The last two summers have been so crazy between the whole hippie thing and then all the riots at the Chicago Democratic Convention, and bracing for anything that might spark riots here. It seems like every time we get a day off, they call us in. I mean, it's been good to have the pay—gives me more money to sock away for Katie's college fund, but I'm not getting any younger."

"Yeah, it's sure been a crazy time. Glad for you that you got that transfer to the Marina District, but I sure as hell will miss having you as my partner."

"You know I always loved working the Golden Gate Park; it was considered one of the most beautiful city parks in the whole world. It used to be such a wonderful place for families and visitors to our great city, and now it's a mess. Kids sleeping all over the place, stoned out of their minds, and when I try to establish some order they call *me* a pig. Go figure."

Sensing his friend's blood pressure was beginning to escalate, Ron said, "Hey, Gino, let's not talk about work anymore. It's gonna be a great line-up today. Willie Mays in center field, Bobby Bonds in right field and McCovey on first base. McCormick is pitching. I guess they needed to give Marichal a day off. Let's head to our seats. At least we have a good view while freezing our asses off. Hey, looks like some young guys are in Smith's seats."

"It better not be that hippie kid of his."

As they sat down, a young man with a military crew cut stood up and said, "Hello, sir, I'm Stephen Smith, Bill's son, and this is my buddy, Frank. We are on leave and are here for a few days so my dad gave me his tickets. I remember you because I used to come to the games with my dad when I was a kid; my brother and I took turns."

Gino was dumbfounded because Stephen looked exactly like Eric except he was clean cut and had military manners. He shook his hand and said, "Thanks for your service, Stephen." He sat down and pulled out his red plaid thermos of steaming hot coffee and poured some into his red cup and took a slow drink as he scanned the field for Willie Mays.

2:30 p.m.

As Eric and Katie hiked through Muir Woods near Mill Valley, Eric put his arm around her and said, "I'm so glad we came here today. This is my favorite park and the redwoods are so beautiful. Isn't it amazing that some of these trees have been here over a thousand years? The stories they could tell, huh?"

"I am just glad they can't tell my dad that—"

"What? That we are in love?" Eric said and then kissed her passionately.

"I wish so much that we didn't have to sneak around like this, always worrying that we are going to run into someone. I hope he's enjoying the Giants game today. It is kind of ironic that I don't think he invites me anymore, because he's worried that you'll be there, and here we are, while he's there."

Eric smiled and said, "Yeah, but seriously, I'm glad we get to see each other, but I wish we weren't always sneaking around at libraries, theaters, and finding places to hike."

"Hey, we went to Salmon Creek Beach at Bodega Bay last week didn't we?"

"Yeah, but you were paranoid the whole time that someone was going to see us."

Katie answered, "But it was nice having that sand dune all to ourselves, wasn't it? You know how guilty I feel about all of this sneaking around."

"Hey, your dad didn't say anything about seeing me on Hippie Hill in Golden Gate Park last Saturday, did he? I was with a few people hanging out, playing music, and your dad came by. You know I've seen him a few times before, always from a distance, but this time he kind of stared at me, shook his head and walked on."

"No, he didn't say anything so I don't know if he recognized you. He doesn't have anything good to say about you guys taking over that part of the park. My Aunt Katherine said she was in the park with some friends and my dad went past her and acted like he didn't know her. You know he hasn't spoken to her since she joined the commune."

"Yeah, I can see that stuff with your aunt would totally throw your dad for a loop, especially with all of that publicity about the nude wedding out at the ranch. Is it true that the groom was one of the teachers there and he used to be a Novato High School teacher who had been married to the nursery school teacher from that little kids TV program?"

"Yeah, that's what I've heard anyway. It all seems kind of weird, but Katherine seems happy. She is the teacher of the younger students and they call their school 'Not School.' She said the kids can choose to come or not and study whatever they want, which is quite a change from having forty-five kids in a parochial school classroom. You know she took a year's leave of absence and that is going to run out. She says she's not sure what she is going to do, but I can't imagine her going back to being a nun."

"Let's stop here and have our picnic." As Eric laid out an old, blue, striped bedspread, Katie pulled out her bag which contained ham sandwiches and homemade chocolate chip cookies. Eric opened the bottles of Orange Crush soda and grabbed some potato chips that he had brought along.

"Have you seen much of your brother while he's been on leave?"

"Yeah, we got together at my dad's for dinner Thursday night, which was a trip, since I hadn't been there since the big blowout about a year ago. My dad called me, though, and said he thought it was important for Stephen's sake for us to have dinner together as a family. Maria, our housekeeper, was so delighted to have us all there. She made an amazing Mexican dinner for us, which is Stephen's favorite. He's been stationed on the East Coast this last year and said it's hard to find good Mexican food in New England. We are supposed to meet tomorrow and show his buddy Frank around the city. I told you he's shipping out for Vietnam next week for his second tour of duty there—volunteered for it. I just don't understand."

"Does he know that you have been protesting against the war?"

"Yeah, I think so, but we don't talk about it. We were so close when we were young and I feel there is a real bond there. We care a lot about each other, yet we see things so differently. I think we are just trying to accept each other's choices."

Eric continued, "Let's start walking back to the van. You know how I've wanted to do something in the medical field, but I am just not sure what. It is great volunteering with Dr. Smith at the Haight Ashbury Free Clinic. I want to make a difference in people's lives. Although I like San Francisco State, this will be my second year and I'm still taking general education classes. I have been thinking of going to City College and doing their paramedic program and just getting on with it. Did you know that in a few months they are going to have a draft lottery? If I get a bad number, I could get drafted whether or not I'm in school."

"Draft lottery? How's that going to work?"

"It will be for all guys born between 1944 and 1950. It seems that they are going to put all the calendar days of the year in some kind of container and then pull them out one at a time. First birth date to get picked would be draft number one, and so on. They are doing that because it seems that most of the guys getting drafted are the ones from poorer areas that can't afford college, and they think this will be a fairer way."

As they got into his Volkswagen, Katie looked at her watch and gasped, "I need to make sure and get home before my dad does. Let's turn on the radio and see if the game is still going!"

The sportscaster bellowed, "The Giants did it. They just beat the Dodgers 5–1, no need for the bottom of the ninth. It's a walk-off win for the Giants!"

"Well, that should give us just enough time to drop you off a few blocks from your house and for you to get home before Papa Bear."

"Yeah, at least he'll be in a good mood, since he loves it when his team wins, especially against the Dodgers."

CHAPTER 22

October 14, 1968

Katie was on the way to San Francisco on the Greyhound bus. Eric had been asking her for months to come into the city so he could show her around, and because she had the day off from school, she had agreed to come in today. Her dad had been transferred to the Marina District, and had to work. She had made a story up about spending the day with her friend Carol, and had arranged for Carol to cover for her if necessary. When she arrived at the San Francisco bus depot it was 10:00. She had told Eric to meet her there at 10:30. She must have looked at the schedule wrong.

She wore a short, navy blue skirt, a light blue turtleneck sweater, a blue cap, and sunglasses. It was a beautiful fall day, but as she stepped off the bus, she was overwhelmed by the stench of urine and trash. There were several guys sitting by the side of the building, dirty and disheveled, asleep or passed out. There were a number of servicemen, mostly sailors, sitting in old stained seats, smoking cigarettes, smiling and winking at her and making comments to each other and laughing. Plump pigeons were eating crumbs and popcorn from the dirty terminal floor. She went across the station and stopped near the ticket booth. There was a mother with a crying baby and two other children speaking in broken English trying to buy tickets and a long line of impatient people behind her waiting. There were a few kids wearing tie dye clothes, no shoes, and playing drums in one of the corners. She found a place to sit, and an old man limped over to her and covered her legs with his newspapers. He said, "You need to cover your legs, otherwise, you will get rheumatism." She wasn't sure what to do, so she just thanked him and then removed the newspapers when he was out of sight.

Another man came up to her and said, "You are a beautiful girl, do you need a job? You could be a movie star, you are so pretty, or at least a model—"

She was scared, so without saying anything, she walked over to the ladies' restroom. She looked at her watch as she went in; it was 10:20. This would be a safe place to stay until Eric arrived. She stood at the sink, next to two girls about her age who were putting on makeup. Katie brushed her hair and applied some lip gloss. Someone else entered the bathroom and headed to the stall furthest from them. The girls looked at each other, and one whispered, "It's a queen." Then she turned to Katie and whispered, "Don't you think that was a queen?"

Katie, thinking that they were trying to pull her leg, answered firmly, "No, of course, a queen would never be taking the bus; they always have chauffeurs and would never be in a bus station." The girls were taken aback by Katie's naiveté and quickly explained to her what a drag queen was.

Right about then, Katie looked in the mirror and saw a tall, thin person in a tight dress, high heels with heavy makeup, which did not hide the stubble, exiting the stall, and leaving the bathroom.

After the door closed, one of the girls asked her, "Girl, where are you from? We are worried about you. Are you here by yourself?"

"Yes, I mean, no. My boyfriend is going to meet me here soon." Katie answered.

"Okay, well, be careful, you seem really innocent to be around here on your own. Watch out for the pimps. They hang out here looking for girls."

The other chimed in, "Yeah, and watch out for those sailors, too. They have been out to sea a long time; need I say more?" They laughed.

Katie glanced at her watch and saw that it was 10:30. She went out the bathroom door and spotted Eric nearby. She ran up to him and gave him a big hug and said, "I am so glad to see you. I got so scared." She told him she had given him the wrong time and explained her experiences in the last thirty minutes, ending with her story about the bathroom. She said, "Can you believe that a man would be dressed like a woman and going in the women's bathroom?"

"Katie, you are so innocent, I think that is one of the things I love about you. I guess the guy needs to use the bathroom and he can't use the guys' bathroom, right—I mean unless he wants to get beat up or something. I can see why all of that would shake you up, though, and I'm sorry I wasn't here. Anyway, let's get out of here because there is so much I want you to see. We'll head over to Haight-Ashbury; I want you to meet some of the people I work with in the clinic. Then I thought we'd go to People's Café and then over to the park for a while. I promise that I will get you back for your 3:00 bus and I will stay here until it leaves." He put his arm around her and they headed out of the bus station.

CHAPTER 23

November 5, 1968

As Katie was unlocking the front door, she heard the phone ringing, and she hoped it was Eric. She dropped her books on the kitchen table and grabbed the phone. Breathlessly, she said, "Pulli Residence."

"How's my girl? Sounds like you are having a hard time catching your breath, are you okay?" Eric said lovingly.

"Yeah, I'm fine but there was a ton of traffic and the bus was running way behind and I knew you would be calling, and I was worried I'd miss you."

"It's cool; I took my dinner break now and still have twenty minutes if my change for the pay phone lasts."

Katie stretched the spiraled yellow cord from the wall phone as she turned on the oven to preheat it for the casserole that her father had left. "Yeah, well my dad will be home in about an hour, so I'm going to need to start getting dinner together as we talk. What do you think is going to happen with the election?" she asked as she pulled the long receiver cord toward the refrigerator to see what she was supposed to get ready.

Eric scoffed, "Well, one thing I know is that Nixon won't win. Kennedy beat him in 1960 and then he came back to California and couldn't even win the election for governor. California has the most electoral votes except for New York, and if we didn't want him for governor there is no way Californians will vote for him for president. You know, just six months ago, I was so hopeful about this election. Bobby Kennedy, George McGovern, and Eugene McCarthy would all have been good Democratic candidates for this election and I was so disappointed when Hubert Humphrey was the one chosen. I mean after serving as Johnson's vice president, I'm concerned he will just continue with President Johnson's agenda, which includes our continued involvement in Vietnam. Do you know that about 1,000 guys die each month and many more are seriously injured and maimed?"

"I know! It breaks my heart to watch the news, and see all of those flag-draped coffins coming back through Travis Air Force Base."

Eric took a deep breath and said, "I am extremely worried about Stephen going over for a second tour of duty. We had a great visit when he was home and I begged him not to go. You know that as an officer he is a prime target. There have been a lot of young officers killed as they disembark the plane after they land in Vietnam, picked off by Viet Cong snipers who can see the bars on their sleeves through their telescopic rifles. Their strategy is to immobilize the troops by killing off their leaders. But other guys are just drafted to take their place or they send guys like Stephen who beat the odds the first time to go back. It's insane. Sorry for getting so worked up. Hey, on another note, did you send your college application in?"

As Katie tucked the phone receiver under her chin and slipped the pan containing chicken cacciatore into the oven, she answered, "Yeah, I applied for the nursing school at University of San Francisco. My counselor at school says that she thinks I have an excellent chance of getting accepted because of my grades, test scores, and my volunteer work at Marin General Hospital. I'm what they call a Candy Striper. I assist patients with non-medical things like filling their water, delivering their mail, and visiting with them."

"Katie, it is going to be so cool to have you in the city and see more of you. Speaking of which, can you meet me at the movies next Saturday afternoon at 2:00 at the Rafael Theater?"

"I'll try; can you call me Friday about this time?"

The operator interrupted. "Put in an additional thirty cents for three minutes, please."

Eric said, "Gotta go. I don't have any more change."

"Okay, talk to you on Friday."

Katie glanced at the clock, and realized it was 4:30 and her dad would be home anytime. She was full of butterflies after talking to Eric and she worried that her dad would be able to tell just by looking at her that she was over the moon in love. She felt so badly lying to him all the time and worrying about getting caught. Carol, who lived on the next block, was her only friend whom she had told about Eric. They made a deal that Katie would cover for Carol when she went to Haight-Ashbury to see her boyfriend, and Carol covered for Katie when she was out with Eric.

As Katie walked into her bedroom to change out of her plaid school uniform, the framed photo of her mom seemed to be looking at her. As she changed her clothes she said to herself, "I wish you were here, Mom, so I could talk to you and that you could convince Dad to let me see Eric. I know you would see what a good guy he is, and you'd look beyond his long hair and liberal viewpoints. I love him, Mom and—" Just then she heard her dad coming through the front door.

CHAPTER 24

November 6, 1968

After turning off her alarm, Katie yawned and stretched as she went out into the living room to join Gino, who was watching the presidential election results on the television. "Did Humphrey win?"

"No, looks like Nixon won. It was pretty close last night, but he got the California electoral votes so that helped him a lot."

Katie was shocked. "What? I thought Nixon had no chance since he didn't even win the California governor race."

Gino answered, "Folks are looking for law and order and think that a conservative Republican can get back on track. It serves those hippies right—all the protesting and riots in Chicago at the Democratic Convention was televised and scared a lot of people. They are sick of all of the riots, draft dodging, drugs, and all that radical stuff, and so am I. I've always voted on the Democratic ticket before, but I voted for Nixon because I think we need to get back on track."

Katie knew better than to argue politics with her dad, because he could not tolerate a viewpoint different from his own. She thought, "If the eighteen-to-twenty year olds could have voted, I bet that would have rocked the vote. We've got to change that."

Just then the newscaster announced, "George Wallace of the American Independent Party won the states of Alabama, Arkansas,

Georgia, and North Carolina, which is the strongest third party effort since 1912."

Katie responded, "I am flabbergasted that he carried so many states. After all, when he was governor he was vicious about blocking integration and has done so many racist things."

"Yeah, I was surprised about that too." Gino glanced at his watch and said, "Honey, you better get ready for school if you want me to drop you off on my way to work. I made some French toast for you. It's in the oven."

"Thanks, Dad." Katie said, still reeling from the shock of the election results.

CHAPTER 25

January 7, 1969

"Good morning, sunshine! Do pancakes and bacon sound good for breakfast?" asked Gino as Katie emerged from her room in her pink, terry cloth bath robe and her white, fuzzy slippers.

"Sounds delicious, Dad."

"Want me to make your pancakes in the shape of Mickey Mouse like I did when you were a little girl?" Gino laughed.

"I always loved that, hey, sure why not? Remember how we'd always eat breakfast and then watch cartoons together on Saturday morning. I bet not many other dads did that with their kids," Katie said as she kissed her dad on his smoothly shaven cheek. "I'll get dressed, Dad, and would you please put the kettle on? I'd love to have tea."

"Sure, Katie, and maybe we can catch some cartoons after breakfast, and we could see if any of our old favorites are still on." Gino was whistling an old Italian song, "Funniculì, Funniculà," frying bacon, and making pancakes when the phone rang. He picked it up on the third ring and said "Pulli Residence." The color drained out of his face as he silently listened to the person on the other side of the line for several minutes. He took a deep breath and croaked, "Yes, sir, thank you for informing me, Captain. If you think it would do any good, I could come down to headquarters. Yes, I understand. Yes, sir,

I would appreciate your keeping me posted."

Katie noticed that Gino's hands were shaking and his face was very pale as he hung up the phone.

"Your Aunt Katherine was arrested early this morning along with the rest of the adults at her commune, on drug charges. She has been booked, but other than that the Captain does not know what is going to happen. He doesn't think it is advisable for me to go to headquarters because it already has turned into media frenzy. Drawing attention to the fact that her brother is a police officer will just give them one more morsel to jump on. It's probably for the best, because I don't know what the hell I would say or do. She got herself into this; maybe she'll learn her lesson and go back to the convent—that is, if they would take her back. How bizarre that a little over a year ago she was a nun in a convent teaching in a parochial school and now she's a hippie being arrested for drugs. How does something like that happen? I'm just glad that my parents aren't here to see all of this because it would have broken their hearts! Have you talked to Katherine recently?"

"This is a shock to me, too, Dad. She called here a few weeks ago and seemed to be doing well, told me some cute stories about the kids at the commune school and seemed to be happy. Katherine always asks about you, and she said that she understood why you hadn't spoken to her since she joined the commune. She also said that she missed you and that if you ever seemed interested in talking to her to just let her know. Since it's such a sore subject, I didn't bring it up."

Gino slammed his fist on the table and yelled, "What the hell is this world coming to?"

CHAPTER 26

January 8, 1969

As Katie climbed out from under her lavender bedspread and put on her robe and slippers, her heart ached for her dad. He had just sat in his chair the day before, staring into space. He didn't want to eat; he didn't shave or shower all day, which was so unusual for him. As she padded out quietly into the kitchen, she noticed him sitting at the kitchen table. He was still in the clothes he had on the day before, hadn't shaved or cleaned up, and was staring blankly at the front page of the *San Francisco Examiner*. On the front page was a picture of her Aunt Katherine taken a couple of years before, in her traditional nun's habit. Next to it was what looked like her mug shot from the day before. The headline read, "Nun Arrested in Drug Raid at Hippie Commune."

"Dad, I'm so concerned about you—did you sleep at all last night?"

"A little, on and off."

"Let me make you some breakfast for a change, and some coffee?"

He answered flatly, "No thanks, I'm not hungry."

"Well, we better start getting ready for church. Mass starts in a little over an hour."

"You go ahead and go; I'm not going."

Katie was taken aback because her father always went to Sunday Mass. She had never seen her Dad so depressed, even when Maggie died, as grief-stricken as he was; he had continued to take care of himself and stayed with his routine.

Katie ate a bowl of Wheaties cereal and had a cup of hot Lipton tea, and then took her shower and got dressed. She was brushing her teeth when the phone rang. On the third ring, she picked it up. It was her cousin Laura. She and her parents had just seen the paper and were in shock. What did Katie know about it, she wanted to know? Katie said she didn't know any more about it than what was in the newspaper and that her dad was taking it really hard. She said that she really needed to get off the phone and hung up. Katie sighed and thought, "It is probably going to be ringing off the hook today." It rang again. She answered the phone with her usual, "Pulli residence."

There was a pause, a deep breath and then the voice choked out, "Hi, Katie, this is Katherine, and I just wanted to let you and your dad know that I have been released from jail on my own recognizance, pending a court hearing. We think there was an informant who was posing as a commune guest and that this raid had been planned for a while."

Katie, at a loss for words, stammered, "I'm, uh, glad you called, Aunt Katherine. I have been so worried about you. What are you going to do now?"

"Somehow Mother Superior from my convent found out. She was so kind; she called the jail, and asked if I needed to be bailed out, and I told her no, that it must be so embarrassing for her and all of the other sisters. I said I was so sorry that I have put everyone through this. She asked me to come and see her as soon as possible, so a friend gave me a ride to the convent when I was released. We met privately; I told her how sorry I was and that I would not be returning to the convent, which I don't think was any surprise to her. She explained the process that I would need to go through to be released from my vows, which includes asking for permission from the Vatican. I'm staying with my friend overnight tonight and then she is going to give me a ride back to the commune tomorrow. I have been so concerned about how your dad is taking all of this."

"He is taking it hard, Katherine. He'll be relieved that you are out of jail, but he isn't going to be happy about you going back to the commune. Can't you go somewhere else? Maybe you could even stay here."

"I need to go back, Katie. That's my home and we need to get things back to normal and be with the children. This has been terrifying for them, especially those who had parents arrested. I need to go now. I am so sorry that I have caused you all this worry, Katie. I love you and your dad so much; please always remember that."

"I love you, too, please keep in touch and take care of yourself." Katie wiped away tears as she hung up the phone.

CHAPTER 27

February 2, 1969

Katie loved the weekend mornings and not having to rush off to school. She yawned and stretched and, realizing it was almost 9:00 am, thought, "I better get up and get ready for church. I wonder what Dad is up to?" She padded out to the cheery yellow kitchen. She realized that there was no activity, no smell of coffee or bacon cooking. She noticed a note from her dad scrawled on the back of an envelope on the white Formica counter. "Had to go. Back ASAP."

Where would he go? The grocery stores weren't even open yet. He certainly wouldn't have gone to church without her. She knew that he had been under a lot of stress and working lots of overtime because of the riots at San Francisco State. She winced every time he went on a tirade about the awful students being on strike and arresting some of the unruly ones. She knew that Eric was a regular demonstrator there, and he had told her that once her dad was one of the arresting officers when Eric and a bunch of his friends were taken to jail. Eric said her dad hadn't seemed to recognize him, which he attributed to having only seen him once at the game at Candlestick. Since then he had grown a full beard, his hair was much longer, and he wore John Lennon glasses. She swooned when she thought of Eric, and wished so much that she could see him openly. At least with her dad's busy schedule, she had been able to talk to him more often over the phone.

Katie decided to make breakfast and just as she was putting the Corning Ware coffee percolator on the stove, her father walked through the front door. "What's the matter, Daddy?" She said when she saw how drained an exhausted he looked.

He set down his hat, collapsed on to the couch, and croaked, "The Commune burnt to the ground this morning."

"Oh my God, is Katherine all right?"

"Yes, she spent the night last night in Berkeley so she wasn't there. Miraculously, no one was killed or seriously injured. Some of their pets died, but, thank God, all the kids got out all right. I worry so much about those young kids out there and whether the parents keep a good eye on them. Ron has a radio scanner, and he called me early this morning and said that the place was on fire, so I jumped in the car and went there and when I got there—there were flames ravaging the buildings. All the people were standing outside, so I frantically searched the crowd for Katherine and she was nowhere to be seen. I panicked and I started screaming, 'Where is Katherine Pulli? Is she still in the building?' I ran up to the firemen and was begging them to let me try to go in and find her, when a young woman with a baby on her hip yelled to me, 'Katherine isn't here. She went away for the weekend. She's in Berkeley.' I was so relieved, and all I could think was that she could have died this morning and—"

Katie sat down beside him and put her arms around her father whom she loved so much and their tears of strain and relief mingled.

CHAPTER 28

March 1, 1969

The house was filled with the delicious aromas of butter, cinnamon, and brown sugar. "Good morning, Dad, that smells delicious!" Katie said brightly as she sat down at the breakfast table. "After I finish the laundry and the vacuuming, I'd like to go to the Rafael Theater for the 2:00 matinee to see *Romeo and Juliet.*"

"What is that movie rated by the Legion of Decency?"

"Its Romeo and Juliet—the Shakespeare play—I'm sure it's considered appropriate for anyone to see," Katie hedged.

"I've never cared for Shakespeare myself, but I know you and your mom always liked that stuff."

"Who are you going with?" Gino asked as he pulled a cinnamon coffee cake out of the oven.

"Carol wants to go," Katie lied. "I would go over to her house and then we would head over to the bus stop and take the 1:00 bus to the theater. The movie is a long one, so we'd take the 5:00 bus home."

"I was hoping you'd go grocery shopping with me today. I'm going to Cala Market; they have some great deals on meat this week, but it would be nice for you to get to the movies, especially something that is educational. Okay, go ahead." Gino said as he cut the coffee cake into neat squares.

"Thanks, Dad," Katie answered as she poured a cold glass of milk and sat down to eat her steaming piece of coffee cake.

"I'm so proud that you got into University of San Francisco's nursing program. I know they don't just take anyone."

"Thanks, Dad. I sure appreciate all of the saving you did through the years to help me with my college education. You know I plan to work in the summers to help pay as much as I can."

"I'm glad I can do it for you, Katie. I would have loved to go to USF myself, but that was out of the question financially for me, and I always wanted you to have the opportunity to go to a top-notch college. You have been such a good girl and deserve only the best."

Katie squirmed as she took a drink of her milk and changed the subject. "This coffee cake is amazing. I love the crumb topping."

While her dad was outside doing the yard work, Katie used the old gray Hoover Upright to vacuum every room carefully. "Such a good girl—if my Dad only knew how much I lied to him so I can see Eric. I wish he weren't so overprotective and then I wouldn't have to," Katie rationalized.

At about 12:30, Katie took one last look in the mirror, brushed her long, shiny, brown hair, grabbed her purse and her jacket and said, "Dad, I'm leaving now."

He replied, "Here, I packed up some coffee cake for you to give to Carol and her mother. Are you sure you don't want me to give you a ride? You have to walk at least five blocks from the bus to the movie."

"Uh, no thanks, we'll be fine. We could use the exercise. And besides you are heading the opposite direction to go to the market. See you about 5:30," she said as she gave him a kiss on the cheek and hurried out the front door.

She walked around the corner to Carol's house and knocked on the door. Carol was dressed in navy bell bottoms and a plum-colored, tight, ribbed sweater and wore huge pink hair rollers designed to straighten her curly hair. As she opened the door she took a drag off of the Lucky Strike cigarette that she was holding. "Hey, Carol, I need you to cover for me again. I told my Dad that I was going to take the bus and go to the movies with you."

"Eric?" Carol smiled. "No problem, what are we watching this afternoon?"

"*Romeo and Juliet*—and I am taking the 1:00 bus there and the 5:00 bus home. Oh, and here is some coffee cake that my Dad wanted to give you. I can't thank you enough." Carol and Katie talked on the front porch until they could see the bus a few blocks away, and then Katie walked quickly over to the bus stop, her heart pounding in anticipation of seeing Eric

When she got to the theater, she bought a loge ticket from the old-fashioned stand-alone ticket counter and proceeded into the theater. There he was sitting in the back row of the loges with a big box of popcorn, a huge coke, and a gigantic grin, winking at her. She longed to run up and hug him, but instead she smiled at him, and sat down a few seats from his seat. She watched as people entered the theater and was relieved not to see anyone who knew her (or more precisely, knew her Dad). After the lights lowered, she scooted over next to Eric and he grabbed her hand and gave her a quick yet passionate kiss.

Eric had seen this version of *Romeo and Juliet* before, and he was very excited about sharing it with Katie. He loved having her head resting on his shoulder and his arm wrapped around her slender shoulder. This Franco Zeffirelli movie was being acclaimed as the best film production of a Shakespeare story ever. The young actors, Leonard Whiting and Olivia Hussey, were about the same age as Eric and Katie. Starting with the prologue narrated by Laurence Olivier and the amazing musical score, it was the most romantic movie that Eric had ever seen. He was so in love with Katie. He could relate to Romeo, but somehow he had to make sure his love story with Katie had a happy ending.

It had started to rain hard as Gino drove home from the grocery store, and he thought about Katie having to walk those five blocks from the movies in the rain. She hadn't taken an umbrella or a rain coat. He would call the theater and see when the movie was ending and pick her and Carol up. After he unloaded the groceries and put them away, he called the theater and found out the movie would be over at about 4:30. It was a long movie! Well, that gave him over an hour before he needed to head out. He sat down at the kitchen table with his big porcelain cup of coffee and decided to read the *Monitor*, the Catholic newspaper that had arrived with the mail a few days previously. As he flipped through the *Monitor*, he noticed the Legion of Decency column, which rated the current movies. He scanned the review to see what they had rated *Romeo and Juliet*. What? "Objectionable due to nudity." Gino was stunned as he thought with a scowl, "Did Katie know that? That sure isn't appropriate for her and Carol to see. I will need to have a talk with that young lady." At about 4:10, Gino picked up his keys from the hook by the door and headed out the door.

As the movie was ending and Katie was dabbing her eyes with a Kleenex, Eric reached for her face and lifting her chin toward him gave her the most passionate kiss of the afternoon. Katie's heart was pounding when he said, "I love you, Katie, and I want to see you every day! I hate never knowing when we can get together and then sneaking around. Katie, I totally want you to go to the Winterland Ballroom with me. I'd love to take you for a show. Jimi Hendrix and Jefferson Airplane will be playing, and it is going to be so—"

"I know, Eric, but things will be better next year when I'm at USF, and we are both in the city. My Dad sent in the dorm deposit yesterday. We just need to be patient."

As they walked into the lobby and saw through the window that it was pouring rain, Eric sighed. He tucked his shoulder length blonde hair behind his ears and said, "Well, at least let me drive you to your neighborhood. I could drop you off at Carol's and you could walk from there."

Katie looked around and, not seeing anyone she knew, hesitated and then replied, "Okay." As they walked out of the theater, Eric took her hand. Then he caught sight of Gino standing at the curb next to his Oldsmobile.. Katie dropped his hand when she saw the look of fury on her dad's scarlet face.

Gino grabbed Katie roughly by the arm and screamed, "So is this that Bill Smith's hippie kid? What have you been up to all this time—lying to me, sneaking around with this loser after telling me you wouldn't see him anymore? Get your butt in the car."

Eric tried to intervene. "Mr. Pulli, let me explain."

"Shut up, punk, let me explain to you—if I ever catch you around my daughter again you will be so sorry. You are damn lucky I don't knock your block off right here." A group of moviegoers froze and gawked at the spectacle. Gino glared at Eric as he pushed Katie into the front seat of his car and she tried to choke back her tears.

Gino drove the four miles home through the ravaging wind and rain in icy silence. When they drove into their hedge-lined driveway, Gino got out, slammed the car door, and opened the creaky garage door. Katie scurried into the house, went directly to her room, closed the door, and flopped on the bed. She wept about the two men that she loved and knew she could not have both. She thought, "Shouldn't I be able to be with the man I love? I can't bear thinking about life without Eric. I am almost eighteen, and I have already tried to stay away from him for almost two years. It is so unfair of my dad! Doesn't he remember what it was like to be young and in love?"

October 17, 1989

5:04 p.m.

Eric was driving his van south on Highway 101 on his way to Gino's house. He was glad that his sons had this opportunity to see the World Series game with their grandfathers, and he hoped that things were going well.

He had decided to get an early start so he could see the game in San Rafael at Gino's, and was now passing through Santa Rosa. It was about 5:00, so he turned his radio to the sports channel KNBR to catch the pre-game banter. He also wanted to make sure to hear Stevie Wonder sing the Star-Spangled Banner. Stevie was one of his all-time favorite singers and Eric was sure that he would give a great performance.

All of a sudden, Eric's van started veering to the side. "What the hell is going on? Did I get a blow out or something?" He headed to the shoulder to check on his car, and he noticed a number of other people were doing the same. The commentator on the radio at Candlestick saying that there was an earthquake and that the stadium was swaying. "And my kids are there—crap!" The radio went dead, and Eric was stunned. What should he do? He decided to get back on the highway—maybe he should head toward Candlestick to get them?

After a few minutes, the radio broadcast resumed and the announcer reported that it appeared that although badly shaken, the crowd seemed to have survived the earthquake and that no casualties or major injuries were being reported. Eric breathed a sigh of relief. The announcer continued to say that no one should head into the city. Unless people needed medical treatment, they should stay at home and keep roads open for emergency vehicles. There were reports that the Bay Bridge had collapsed and that hundreds may have been killed. Eric panicked. "Oh, no, Katie was going across the Bay Bridge to meet Rosemary just about that time. Oh, God, please don't let Katie be one of those people," Eric prayed.

He realized it would be best for him to go to Gino's and be there to answer the phone in case anyone called. He arrived at Gino's house about twenty minutes later, retrieved the hidden key under a clay pot on the porch, and quickly opened the front door. He headed to the old wall phone, and he found the well-worn address book on the small table next to the phone. He looked up Katherine's number and her cousin Laura's number, but when he tried to call all the circuits were busy. What about Rosemary's sister? He had no clue what her married name was.

He turned on the TV so he could get any updates, and thankfully they had resumed service. Even though there wasn't any electricity, they were able to use a news van generator to transmit. He sat in Candlestick on the couch, feeling helpless, waiting and worrying about the safety of his family.

CHAPTER 29

May 1, 1969

The peeling, putrid green living room walls were covered with psychedelic posters of the Fillmore and Winterland Ballroom from the last two years, featuring the Grateful Dead, Jimi Hendrix, Big Brother and the Holding Company and a poster that read "What If There Was A War and Nobody Came?" John, Eric's roommate, had opened all of the old windows that weren't painted closed to try to get rid of the lingering smell of incense, cheap marijuana, and roach spray. Eric was standing at the chipped red linoleum counter warming himself some soup on a hot plate when John came out of the bedroom that he and Eric shared, carrying a large bag of trash. It was hard to believe there had been that much trash in there, since their room was very small, containing only their twin beds, boxes that held their clothes, and some shelves made from cinder blocks and warped boards.

"Tonight's show at Winterland is going to be so out of sight—can't wait! My two favorite bands—Jefferson Airplane and the Dead will be on the same stage. You going, Eric?" John asked.

"No, not tonight, I'm going to hear this guy named Jim Jones talk about his vision for the People's Temple. You know he has this commune thing going on up out of Ukiah and they are starting a group here in SF and I want to check it out. He has a vision of truly having a rainbow family and he walks the talk. He and his wife have adopted a bunch of kids, including three from Korea."

"Are you still thinking about joining a commune, Eric? I can't imagine, all that commune stuff seems so—"

"I'm not talking about joining the Moonies or Hare Krishna group or anything. This guy is totally different. I mean he grew up poor in Southern Indiana, fought segregation, and he was the director of the Human Rights Commission of Indianapolis. He is a friend of Mayor Moscone and Cecil Williams. He really reaches out to minorities and the marginalized. Anyway, that's what I'm doing."

"You need to get out and have some fun, buddy. This whole year you have been doing such serious stuff. You have done nothing but go to school, study, picket at SF State, and pine over that girl Katie all year. What's that saying? 'All work and no play make a dull boy,'" John joked.

Eric retorted, "That's not true, last week I saw Jefferson Airplane at Fillmore West, and it was a hell of a show, too. "

"Yeah, but you went by yourself and didn't even get high. Ended up taking care of those kids who were out there with bad acid trips—you need to enjoy yourself, my man; don't you see all those girls ogling you? If I had your looks, I sure would take advantage of it."

"I'm just not interested in anyone else. I'm hoping maybe things can still work out with Katie and me. "

"Eric, you are damn crazy. You are lucky that her Italian cop Dad didn't kill you either when he arrested you at the riots or when he caught you with his daughter after the movies. Good thing he didn't have his service revolver with him then or we probably wouldn't be having this conversation. Wise up, Eric, this Catholic school girl is out of your reach and always will be. Why do you think the old man changed their phone number? He probably has her under lock and key with every cop in the Bay Area on alert."

"Well, she is not always going to be under his authority. You know she is going to turn eighteen soon, and I hope she will get in touch with me then. I can't imagine feeling about anyone else the way I do about her, and I believe she feels the same about me."

"You're nuts. Anyway, I need to get going. I told Michelle I'd pick her up at her dorm about 7:00, and I'm hoping that she'll come back here to spend the night, and so I was wondering—"

Eric smiled. "Now I know why you cleaned up the bedroom! Okay, I'll take the couch."

John answered gratefully, "Thanks, buddy, have fun at your seminar or whatever it is. God, I wish we lived some place better than this dump."

"What else are we gonna get for $100 a month? Working at $1.65 minimum wage doesn't go far!" Eric replied.

"Yeah, well, the price is pretty good. I sure look forward to when I'm out of school and can get a decent place," John yelled as he flew down the four flights of steps with the garbage bags in hand and thought, "I better not get too messed up if I want to get back up these stairs tonight."

CHAPTER 30

July 20, 1969

Gino and his former SFPD partner, Ron, fought through the crowd to get to their seats. Gino heaved a sigh of relief when he discovered that the Smith seats were empty, and he prayed they stayed that way. He couldn't bear to see that smug Bill Smith, and if he ever brought that hippie son of his, he would have a hard time restraining himself from taking a swing at him. He hoped someday he could bring his daughter to the game and not worry about running into them. Maybe he should consider changing seats, but they were so prime, and the other guys who shared the seats with him would want to know why, and he certainly didn't want to go there.

"Gino, it has been ages since we went to a game together. My son loves that I have been able to take him to so many games, but it's great to go with an adult for a change," Ron said as he settled into his bright orange seat and situated his black and orange Giants ball cap on his head.

"Yeah, weekends have been busy with Easter, Katie's graduation, a family wedding, and last week Katie's eighteenth birthday," Gino replied. He left out that ever since he had caught Eric and Katie together he had felt that he needed to keep a good eye on her. He made her come with him everywhere on the weekends and of course, he didn't want to bring her here. It had been four months since the incident, and she had promised not to see him again, so he had to start trusting her sometime. In less than two months, she would be going to University of San Francisco and he wouldn't be able to watch her every minute, but he sure wished he could. She was in a dorm with strict rules and curfews and had agreed to come home every weekend, so he would give her a chance. However, if there was any problem, home she would come; he would see to that.

Ron reminisced, "Wow, she's eighteen already. I remember when we became patrol partners, she was only about eight. I was newly married and now my boys are five and nine. Where does the time go? You must be extremely proud, Gino, that she did so well in high school and getting a scholarship to USF; she is such a smart girl."

Gino thought, "I wish she was smarter about the kind of guy she is attracted to." Instead he said, "Yeah, she takes after her mom. Maggie always did well in school. I'm sure she'd be proud that she is following in her footsteps and becoming a nurse."

They stood as the Star-Spangled Banner started, and both of them took their hats off and reverently placed their hands over their hearts and sang with the conviction that only war veterans could share. At the end of the anthem the announcer blurted out, "News just in. Neil Armstrong has just set foot on the moon. Can you believe this: President Nixon actually talked to him on the phone. The news service is reporting that when Armstrong set foot on the moon he said, and I quote, 'That's one small step for man, one giant leap for mankind.'" The crowd went absolutely wild, whooping, hollering, whistling, and slapping each other on the back and chanting, "U-S-A." Gino laughed and yelled to Ron above the roar of the crowd, "Go figure, when Kennedy said that by the end of the decade we'd be putting a man on the moon, I scoffed at the idea, thinking it was impossible. But by God, we did it, and we beat those Russian commies while we were at it!"

The L.A. Dodgers were up to bat and the umpire yelled, "Play ball!" In the first inning, the Dodgers scored three runs. Things looked very dismal for pitcher Gaylord Perry, especially since the first two innings were scoreless for the Giants. In the third inning, Perry was up to bat and the crowd braced themselves. The Giants were behind 3–0 and, like most pitchers, Perry was not considered a strong hitter. Although no one expected him to be the hitter that his teammates Willie Mays, Willie McCovey, and Bobby Bonds were, his fans hoped he would walk or possibly get a single. . . This was just too painful to watch! Claude Osteen pitched the ball, Perry took a strong swing, and it flew high in the air and yes, over the outfield fence. Gino looked up as Perry started his victory lap through the bases. "Unbelievable!" This was Perry's first home run with the Giants, and the team was absolutely ecstatic, and the fans were wild with excitement. The announcer came on and could hardly talk. "Perry's old manager Alvin Dark was said to have joked, 'They'll put a man on the moon before he hits a home run,' and he was right, but just barely. Congratulations to Gaylord on his first major league home run!" Everyone laughed, clapped, and cheered.

The Dodgers didn't score again and the Giants won the game 7–3 with Barton, McCovey, Lanier, Mays, Hunt, and Bonds all scoring. Gino and Ron couldn't stop smiling and shaking their heads as they walked back to Ron's new white El Camino pick up. They didn't even mind crawling through the traffic from Candlestick Park and over the Golden Gate Bridge. They listened to KGO radio to get the details about the Apollo 11 mission. What a day!

CHAPTER 31

August 5, 1969

John said, "Eric, You are damn lucky to go to that music thing in New York. That is going to be so out of sight. I hear Hendrix, Jefferson Airplane, and Creedence Clearwater Revival are all going to be there and that it will probably be the biggest rock festival ever."

"Yeah, Janis Joplin, Grateful Dead, Country Joe and the Fish, and a lot of others, too." Then he noticed John's envious expression. "Sure wish you could come along, John. You know I could ask the other guys if we could squeeze you in."

"Hey, thanks, man, but you already got four guys and two dogs in an old VW bus going across the country with no air conditioning. Phew, I can just smell it now! Unfortunately, I need to stick around and finish this construction job with my uncle. I finally got something that pays decent money—you know."

"Well, it won't be the same without you. We have shared so many great music shows together like the Beatles at Candlestick. I had no idea that would be their last live concert. They say they won't do another—would rather spend their time becoming self-actualized and recording their stuff."

"Yeah even though we couldn't hear the Beatles over all the screaming, it was electrifying to be there and see them at Candlestick.

Fantasy Fair and Monterey Pop Festival were amazing, too. And the shows we've seen at Winterland and Fillmore. You know, to be in the heart of the Summer of Love and the entire music scene the last few years has been totally amazing! Hey, exactly where is this place—Woodstock, New York?"

"Actually, it's not going to be in that town anymore because the locals were against it and they couldn't get permits. Now it is going to be at some guy's farm in Bethel, New York, which is about forty miles from there. They are still calling it Woodstock, though."

"When are you guys heading out?"

"We are taking off on Thursday; we figure it will take us about five days to get there. We'll probably drive a lot during the night, especially across the desert. We'll try to find some shady spot to sleep during the day; we may spring for a cheap motel once or twice. Anyway the concert starts on the sixteenth and we're trying to get there early to make sure we get a spot. We heard that lots of people are just going to head over there even if they don't have tickets, so it could be super crazy."

"So how'd you meet these guys?"

"You know I've been volunteering at the Haight Ashbury Free Clinic for a while now. Well, I know two of the guys from there and the third guy is their friend. A fourth guy was supposed to go, but then his girlfriend gave him a bad time about it and he decided not to go, and so they offered me the spot."

"No way! He let some girl talk him out of it? What a waste!"

Eric thought about Katie and how he would so much rather go to Woodstock with her than with the guys and dogs. She hadn't been far from his mind these five months and he had tried everything to try to contact her. He had even contacted her cousin Laura. She wouldn't give him her new phone number, but he convinced Laura to give Katie a message. When he called her back the response was, "I gave Katie the message and she doesn't want you to contact her again. She has promised her dad to never see you again, and she is going to keep that promise. And Eric, please don't call me either because it puts me in a really bad spot, knowing how her dad feels."

"But, can you at least tell me, Laura. Is she okay? Is she still going to USF in the fall?"

"Yeah, she's fine. But she's not going to USF, she's decided to go to school up in Washington," Laura lied, knowing that Katie would want her to throw him off the track.

"Would you please tell her one other thing? That I still love her and if she ever changes her—"

Laura had hung up before he finished.

CHAPTER 32

August 6, 1969

Katie awoke to the smell of coffee percolating and bacon sizzling on the stove. She glanced at the clock, and thought, "It's 10:00 already, wow, I really slept in." She had spent the summer getting up on weekdays at 6:30 a.m. to leave with her dad and be dropped off at her babysitting job. The mother she worked for commuted into the city and needed to leave by 7:30. She had sure earned her money that summer with three children all under five and very high maintenance. She missed the job she had the previous summer that included a chauffeur. That family had moved away. She had less than a month to go and she would be starting at University of San Francisco in the nursing program.

She missed Eric so much, but she tried hard not to think of him. After the movie fiasco, her father had grounded her for three months, changed their phone number, and watched her like a hawk. She wouldn't be surprised if her dad didn't have the entire Marin and SF Police Departments watching her. That's how she spent her eighteenth birthday, being grounded. Of course, there was a big family birthday dinner for her, and she saw her cousins, but it was such a letdown. She had declined invitations to go to two different proms, and she was relieved to give the excuse that she was grounded.

Although she felt that her dad was unfair in forbidding her to see Eric, she had to admit that he had a point. She had fantasized about spending her life with him, but what kind of future did he have? He already had a police record and she knew he would go to any lengths to avoid the draft. Did she really want to spend her life like that? Well, no, so why did she miss him so much?

CHAPTER 33

August 10, 1969

Katie padded into the kitchen, tying the sash on her blue taffeta bathrobe with her pink hair rollers lose and bobbing as she walked. "Morning, Dad."

Her dad stared at the *San Francisco Chronicle* and slammed down his fist. "That crazy killer has murdered someone else and sent that article to all the papers yesterday calling himself the 'Zodiac' and taking credit for the atrocious murder of the young couple in Benicia and then in Vallejo. You know that is only about twenty-five miles from here. Now he's playing a cat and mouse game with the press and the police with his 408-symbol cryptogram. Some couple down in Salinas seems to have cracked the code, and it's supposed to say something about how he's collecting slaves for his afterlife. What the hell is that supposed to mean?

"And look at this; they have more details on yesterday's murder of Sharon Tate and her friends down in Southern California. For God's sake, the woman was eight months pregnant—what kind of beast does something like that? Whoever did it must have been all hopped up on some kind of drugs. Now they think the same group was responsible for some other murders down there, too, but so far no leads."

Katie's eyes got wide and her stomach lurched as she put her hand on her dad's shoulder and answered, "That is so awful, I just can't believe that anyone could do such a terrible thing. She was so beautiful and I loved her in the movie *Valley of the Dolls*. You know that her dad was in the army and that when they were stationed in Germany, she used to babysit for my friend Lori and her brothers because they lived near each other on the base. Lori said she was very nice and down to earth, and they were so excited to have known someone who had become a movie star."

"Katie, the world has become a dangerous place. I have spent my whole adult life trying to keep people safe, most importantly you. I want you to stay home and not go to USF. I can't stand thinking of worrying about you and not having any idea if you are all right."

"Dad, I know you are worried and I can see why, but none of these bad things you are talking about happened in the city. It's not like I'm going to be in the Tenderloin District or any other bad area. I'll be on the campus of a Catholic University, in a girl's dorm that has strict rules. And I have already agreed to come home every weekend, at least for now. I'll call you every night, if you'd like. But I need to live my life, Dad. They have the best nursing school around and if I do two years at Marin J.C. there is no guarantee that they will take me at that point."

"I see your point, Katie, and I don't want to get in the way of such an opportunity for you. I just worry so much about you. You know my father always instilled in me that a man's most important job was to protect his family, especially the girls. I always felt such a responsibility to be the protective big brother to Katherine and look how that turned out. And as much as I tried, I couldn't save your mom and it's so overwhelming to take a chance that something could happen to you. It scares me to death."

"Dad, you did everything in the world you could for Mom. There was no way you could have done anything that would have kept her from dying of MS. And as for Katherine, she is on her own path, and it has nothing to do with you. Since she left the commune last month, she is building a new life up in Mendocino County and seems happy. She is finding herself, making new friends, having time to write her poetry without interruption. She may be a published poet someday."

Gino looked up at Katie and groaned.

Gino wanted her to forego attending USF her first two years of college, stay home, and go to Marin Junior College. She knew why. He was afraid she would get together with Eric if she was living away from home and in San Francisco where he was pretty sure Eric was living. Katie had tried to convince her dad that she had promised not to see him and that she would keep that promise. Besides, she had won a partial scholarship to go there and wouldn't it be a shame to waste it? She had put away money from her summer jobs that would help, but USF tuition was very expensive and there was the expense of her room and board, so she needed to depend on her dad for a lot of her expenses.

Finally, Gino conceded. "Okay, I will let you go to USF and live in the dorm with the following conditions: You keep up your grades, you come home on the weekends, and you don't see any boys unless I approve of them. Needless to say, you better keep your promise to never see that Smith kid ever again. If you don't keep these rules, I will not continue paying any of your expenses and you will need to move back home immediately."

Although Katie thought these restrictions were unreasonable, she agreed. Eighteen was not even considered legally an adult. Technically speaking her father still had jurisdiction over her unless she was married or turned twenty-one. Did that make any sense? She sure hoped that eighteen would become the legal age of adulthood. It drove her crazy that so many young men were considered old enough to fight in a war but not to vote. Girls could even get married at eighteen, without a parent's signature, but the guys had to be twenty-one to sign for themselves. Anyway, she had agreed to the conditions, hoping that he would become more lenient as time went by. She knew that a lot of it was about rebuilding her trust with her dad, and she was slowly doing that. There were times that she greatly regretted promising her dad that she wouldn't see Eric again, but a promise was a promise. She had worried about being at USF and Eric pursuing her there. She was glad that her cousin Laura had been quick to think of throwing him off by telling him that she was going to college somewhere else. She knew there was no hope for her and Eric, so why did she think of him every single day?

CHAPTER 34

August 26, 1969

Returning from work, John perked up when he saw Eric's bright orange Volkswagen van painted with flowers and peace signs parked at the cracked curb. He flew up the stairs, taking two at a time, and when he barged through the door, Eric was sprawled on the couch. "You look like hell, brother. When did you get home?"

"A few hours ago, and thanks a lot for waking me up. You have no idea how exhausted I am."

"No complaining, Eric, you have just been at the party of the century with all the best bands in the world, so don't be crying to me about how tired you are. Woodstock has been all over the news since you left. I can't wait to hear a firsthand account of what happened. Is it true that they had like over 400,000 people there and it was just one big orgy?"

"The orgy part is totally exaggerated, but yeah, there were about that many people and you know that they had a permit for only like 50,000 people. And there was lots of rain and naked people—that part is true. They knew more than 50,000 would show up, but they had no idea how many people would bust through. The doctor who was put in charge for emergency services had planned for the original number. I mean he had done the crowd services for big civil rights demonstrations, but come on, this was a whole different story. He had like a thirty-bed medical tent with two doctors and four nurses working shifts throughout the event, which wasn't nearly enough. They put out an appeal that they were desperate for help from anyone who had experience. The other guys I went with and I spent a lot of time volunteering at the first aid stations."

"The Woodstock promoters hired about eighty guys from the Hog Farm Commune to run 'trip tents' because they knew there would be a lot of LSD and other drug situations. So they took care of the people having bad trips. They didn't give them more drugs like Thorazine to help them come down though. Instead they worked with them one on one to help them calm down and talk them through it. Of course, the serious cases were handed over to the medical personnel. The roads were so blocked that they couldn't get the ambulances through, so they airlifted about 250 people out for medical services. There were a lot of physicians, med students, and nurses who had come to hear the festival, who just jumped in to help, so that part was cool. Some physicians even flew in from other areas to help out. It was such a feeling of camaraderie and non-judgment."

"I heard some people died," noted John.

"Yeah, a teenage girl who was sleeping in a field and got run over by a tractor, and one guy died of a heroin overdose. Ironically, I heard the guy was a Marine who was on leave, which is not what you'd think of. As sad as that is, it's miraculous that more people didn't get seriously injured or die. The most common injury was foot lacerations and in fact, they treated over 900 people with foot injuries. Most from people dancing barefooted. There was so much garbage and glass around that it was easy to get your feet cut up. I know it doesn't seem very glamorous, but I was on the 'foot team' and that's what I did. I helped clean up people's cut feet—the ones that didn't need stitches. We put on antibiotic ointment and bandages and covered their feet with plastic bags to protect them from contamination—you know it was a working farm—so lots of potential to get tetanus or something. We told them to spread the word for people to wear their shoes, at least while dancing. Lots of people didn't have any shoes with them and it was so crowded they couldn't see where they were stepping. It was pretty interesting, though, talking to all of those people while bandaging their feet. People were from all over and they all had a story to—"

John interrupted impatiently, "Enough about feet, Eric. I want to hear about the music."

"Yeah, well it was good that we got there more than a day early, because even then there was hardly any parking. With all the rain they had been having, the parking area was like a swamp. But once we got into the festival there was such a cool vibe. I mean even though it rained most of the time and was so muddy you were slipping around—everyone helped each other out, and I felt like there was a unity that is hard to describe. The first night was pretty mellow. Richie Havens did the first set, followed by Swami Satchidananda who did an opening speech and invocation. Ravi Shankar played through the rain, and then Arlo Guthrie and Joan Baez played next. Baez is six months pregnant and was kidding about being out in the rain singing at 2 a.m.."

"On Saturday afternoon, Country Joe McDonald, Santana, and some other bands played. I was busy helping in the med tents most of the day, but got back to see the Grateful Dead that night. Their set got cut short because the stage amps overloaded during, 'Turn on Your Love Light.' By that time, Creedence Clearwater got on about 2:30 a.m. and half of the crowd was asleep or under any kind of tarp to get out of the rain. You know how much I like them, so I was so glad to hear them, especially after working in the infirmary all day. I flicked my old lighter to make sure they knew someone was listening and yelled at Fogerty, 'Don't worry about it John, we're with ya!' He laughed and they put on a great show and I felt like he was playing especially for me. They were followed by Janis Joplin and the Who. Jefferson Airplane didn't play until 8 am Sunday morning because of all the rain delays."

"On Sunday, Joe Cocker and the Grease Band played, and then

there was a huge thunderstorm that shut down the events for several hours. Of course, there was so little shelter for people, and some people started to leave only to find their cars blocked and sometimes stuck in the mud, so they came back. Johnny Winter, Blood, Sweat & Tears, and Crosby, Stills & Nash finally were able to perform late Sunday night and into the morning. By the time Jimi Hendrix got on as the headliner, it was Monday morning at 9:00 and half of the crowd had left. He didn't seem to care though. He got onstage wearing a blue-beaded white leather jacket with fringe, a red headscarf, and blue jeans. He sure rocked 'Star-Spangled Banner' on his electric guitar. It was pretty amazing just to be there."

"Yeah, I saw that on the TV news, and the footage of people dancing in the rain and mud; looked incredibly wild." Just then John looked at the clock and jumped up. "Oh crap, sorry I didn't notice what time it is, I'm supposed to pick up Michelle in fifteen minutes, and I gotta clean up first. We are going to Ocean Beach, and you are welcome to come, too."

"Thanks, John, but I'm just gonna crash here and catch up on my sleep." Eric was standing at the counter near the phone where they left messages on an old notebook paper. He looked through the messages that had been left for him, which included a message from his brother Stephen. He had been back from Vietnam for almost a month and they still hadn't seen each other. There was an assortment of other messages, but none from the person who he always hoped would call. He hadn't seen Katie for five months and still thought about her every day. He had met a lot of cute girls on his Woodstock trip, and he had spent time with a couple of them, but he still yearned to be with her. It was a hopeless situation and she had said that she didn't want him to ever contact her. He wondered where she had ended up in college. Laura had said a school in "Washington," but that could be a lot of places. How he had hoped she would be at USF so he could see her. It was obvious that she had moved on and wasn't interested in keeping in contact. She probably had a new boyfriend. So why couldn't he just get her out of his mind?

CHAPTER 35

December 1, 1969

Katie walked quickly back to her dorm, dodging rain drops and trying to avoid the puddles that had settled into the cracks in the sidewalk. She had been at University of San Francisco for almost three months and had been acclimating to life in the city. Her classes were going well, and she was getting good grades. Although the university had only been totally coeducational for the last four years, there was a good blend of guys and girls in her general education classes; it was a welcome change to be in a big university rather than an all girls' school. Although it was considered a Catholic college and was run by Jesuit priests, there were many non-Catholics, including students from all over the world, so it made for interesting conversation. No one forced religion on anyone or checked to see if people went to church or anything like that. Most of the professors were non-religious, and the ones who were often wore regular clothes, and you wouldn't even recognize them as priests.

As she had promised her dad, she went home every weekend; he would pick her up on his way home from work on Friday and then bring her back either Sunday night or Monday morning. So far, it was working out because she had so much studying to do that she didn't have time for a social life. She was striving to get all A's, and so far, it looked like she might meet her goal.

As she collapsed her blue umbrella and shook it off, she opened the heavy oak door and walked into her dormitory. It was an old, charming Victorian-style building that dated back to the early part of the century. She ran up two flights of stairs, gliding her hand along the smooth oak banister and burst into her room. Her roommate Rosemary was not there, so she must already be down at dinner. She dropped her leather book satchel, hung up her yellow rain jacket and umbrella, changed into some dry socks and shoes, and headed down to the dining room. She thought of how fortunate she was to have a roommate like Rosemary and how well they got along. She had always wanted a sister, and this was the closest experience she had to that. Their room was small and could barely fit the twin beds and dressers that also doubled as their desks. They had fixed up their cozy space with posters, cute paisley bed spreads, and stuffed animals. Rosemary came from a Polish family in Chicago and had been very homesick. It was too expensive for her to fly home for Thanksgiving, so she had come home with Katie and experienced a big crazy Italian family's celebration that included pasta and other Italian foods in conjunction with the traditional Thanksgiving turkey dinner. She said she understood because her family had to incorporate Polish sausage into all their celebrations. Rosemary had also come home with Katie on several other weekends and had greatly appreciated Gino's hospitality, and Gino loved having Rosemary stay with them.

Katie flew down the stairs and into the dining room and stood in the cafeteria line for her dinner of meatloaf, mashed potatoes, salad, green beans, and pecan pie for dessert. Although the food was not as good as the home-cooked meals she was used to, she had to admit that it was pretty tasty most of the time. She saw that Rosemary had saved a place for her at one of the long tables, and she slid her tray next to her saying, "Hey, sorry, I'm later than I thought I'd be, I was doing some research at the library and lost track of time."

Rosemary answered, "That's okay, but I was starting to get

worried about you with it getting dark so early. I came down a little early because I wanted to make sure that we were finished in time for the draft lottery. Mary and Susie are already in the dorm TV lounge and they are going to try to save us seats. It will probably be packed. Everyone has someone they care about who is going to be affected by the lottery. I'm praying that my brothers get decent numbers. They are just a little over a year apart and both have December birthdays: December 6, 1948 and December 29, 1949. They say that probably the first 200 pulled will get drafted for sure—and maybe more."

"Yeah, this whole thing is extremely nerve-racking. I know they are trying to come up with a more fair way to do the draft since a disproportionate number of the guys drafted are minorities or poor, who don't have the opportunities to go to college, and so they don't have exemptions. I can understand that, but it really is going to mess up a lot of guys who are in the middle of college and will need to go anyway," Katie said as she picked at her dinner. She didn't have much of an appetite after all. She was thinking of Eric and his June 17 birthday and she sure hoped he got a good number. "I've eaten enough. Let's go."

They walked into the packed lounge of probably 300 girls, and they saw that the couches and chairs were full, girls were sitting on the floor in the front, and Susie and Mary were motioning for them to come and sit on the carpet next to them. Everyone in the room had a fiancé, boyfriend, brother, or other relative who would be affected by this raffle. They all had their eyes fixed on the big console TV, which was tuned into CBS Channel 5. The TV announcer said, "Mayberry RFD will not be broadcasted tonight because of our coverage of the draft lottery. We are now joining Roger Mudd in Washington, DC at the Selective Service Office."

On the television, several gray-haired officials stood at the front of a fairly small room, and they held a black container that looked like a huge shoe box, which they shook around and dumped into a deep glass container. That fishbowl contained 366 sky blue capsules that contained the calendar days of the year, including February 29, and the fate of many baby boomers that were born between the years of 1944 to 1950. Alexander Pirnie, a New York Congressman, was asked to choose the first number. Rosemary braced herself for hearing any December dates, and of course Katie didn't want to hear the sound of June. He dipped his hand into the glass container, pulled out a capsule, opened it and announced, "September 14."

One of the girls on one of the worn leather couches in the back of the room gasped. "That's Ray's birthday. We were supposed to get married next summer." She burst into tears and started to run out the door as a friend followed her. Katie and Rosemary looked at each other solemnly. Talk about bad luck! One of the girls had made a chart like they had on the TV on a huge piece of butcher paper taped on the wall, so she could record the birthdays as they were called out next to the order that they would be drafted. The next number was called: April 24. Then Number 3—December 30. Thankfully no one seemed to be affected by those two dates. Number 10: December—Rosemary took a deep breath—6. Her eyes filled up with tears and she whispered to Katie, "That's Stan's number."

Katie put her arm around Rosemary and said, "I know. Let's pray that Chet gets a good number."

The numbers continued to be called out, punctuated by gasps, sighs, and tears from the girls in the lounge. Number 16: December 29. Rosemary yelled, "Not Chet too, that can't be." She headed toward the door and Katie followed her. She said between sobs, "I need to call my mom and dad, they must be just shocked." There were three pay phones on each floor and they searched for a phone where Rosemary could call. All of the phones were being used, and people were in line for the same purpose. They were trying to call loved ones whose numbers had all been called early in the raffle that no one wanted to win. Rosemary chose a line to stand in and encouraged Katie to go back to the lounge. Katie shook her head. She would know soon enough what Eric's number was, and there wasn't anything she could do. She waited with her friend and put her hand on her shoulder as she called home. From her end of the conversation she could tell that Rosemary's parents were reassuring her that things were going to be all right. They didn't think that they could draft two sons at the same time, especially when they were both successful college students and would soon get their degrees. At the end of the conversation, Rosemary said, "I know I'm going to be coming home for Christmas in two weeks, but I don't think I can wait, I am so homesick. Okay, I'll try to keep my chin up. Yeah, okay, I'll call you tomorrow."

They made the trek upstairs, and while Rosemary got into her pink, flowered pajamas and fuzzy slippers, Katie heated water in her old electric coffee pot and made some chamomile tea with two sugar cubes for Rosemary. She encouraged her to snuggle up under her cheerfully colored patchwork quilt and read something soothing while drinking her tea. Katie said, "I'm going back downstairs if that's okay with you. I'll be back in a little while."

Katie headed down to the lounge and took a deep breath as she looked up at the chart—was June 17 on there yet? She let out a sigh of relief when she saw that it wasn't posted and they were now on Number 70. There was now room on one of the couches since some of the girls had left. At the announcement of each number someone recognized their loved one's birthday. Some left the room, others sat stunned with their friends surrounding them. Number 71 was called. Then Number 72. And Number 73—June 17—there it was. He was sure to be drafted and she knew how strongly he felt about not participating in the war. What would he do? Head to Canada? Apply to be a conscientious objector? She wanted so badly to call him right now. Why had she made that stupid promise to her Dad? And why was she still so stuck on him anyway? He probably had a girlfriend and wasn't even thinking of her.

CHAPTER 36

December 2, 1969

Eric awoke to the sound of the buzzing of his electric alarm clock and pushed the button, grumbling. "Crap, how could it already be morning?" He rubbed his temples, yawning, and then it dawned on him why he was so hung over. He and John had been at the neighborhood tavern the night before and watched the TV there as the numbers were pulled for the draft lottery. He had gotten Number 73, which was a pretty bad number, but not as bad as his roommate John whose birthday was the twelfth number drawn. Now there was some rotten luck.

Eric stumbled out of the bedroom, stopped at the bathroom, and then headed to the kitchen where John was drinking strong black coffee out of a big white chipped mug, muttering to himself as he read the *San Francisco Chronicle*. He looked up at Eric and blurted out, "Look, I was right about the days not being evenly distributed. According to this, there were more than twice as many December numbers drawn early than would be expected in a random distribution. There is speculation that the capsules with the birthdates didn't get mixed up sufficiently in that big shoe box thing before they dumped it in the jar. Isn't it bad enough that December is such a crappy month to have a birthday? All the times I have gotten a present for my birthday and Christmas—"

"Yeah, John, I see what you mean, but maybe it's good news. Maybe they will have to do a new drawing so they can say it's random. Both of us could use a better number—cause from what I hear if we have a number less than 200, then we are probably gonna get drafted."

"I doubt if they will redo it because they'd probably have just as many people think that wasn't fair to do it over. I'm thinking that maybe I'll just bite the bullet and enlist. At least then, I could pick what branch of the service and maybe have more of a say what I'd do," John replied.

Eric was stunned. He said, "But John, you don't even think we should be in Vietnam. Have you thought of being a conscientious objector?"

"I could never do that. My family would be so disappointed in me, and I'm sure that my dad would disown me. All of my uncles and cousins have served and I know that everyone would think I was a coward, and even though I disagree with this war, I can't help but think that it's my duty and that it's not right for me not to go and someone else to go in my place. What do you think you'll do?"

"Well, I'm not as self-sacrificing as you, my friend. There is no way that I am going to serve in a war that I don't believe in. I have thought about going to Canada, but the thought that I could never come back to this country really bothers me, so I don't think I could do that. I'm going to apply for conscientious objector status, and if they don't approve it, I'll do the prison time. I hear that most guys get a two-year sentence, and I'd rather do that. As far as my family goes, my mom will totally support me on this, and I don't have any respect for what my dad thinks anyway. Last time I talked to my brother Stephen, I told him that I might be a conscientious objector. I thought he might have a big problem with it, being in the military himself, and serving in Vietnam, but he just patted me on the shoulder and said, 'Brother, there are lots of different ways you can serve your country, I trust you will find your own way.' It was such a relief and I was so grateful for his acceptance of my position. I know that being a conscientious objector can affect my future, and it could get in the way of employment, loans, background checks, but I will just need to take that chance. From what I understand, the first step is that I have to write an essay on my position and then I need to meet with the local draft board."

"I hope you can write a hell of an essay."

"I hope that you can stay out of harm's way, John, and that we can remain good friends even though we are handling our situations so differently." They looked at each other solemnly and shook hands and then gave each other a hug.

CHAPTER 37

March 13, 1970

Rosemary and Katie were in their dorm room getting ready for their walk over to the museum, when Janet, a friend from across the hall, knocked on the door. They all had the same professor for English 1A and this week's assignment was to write a descriptive essay about a piece of art. It was really handy that the de Young Museum was about a half mile from their dorm and in the middle of Golden Gate Park, so they had made this plan to go together. They grabbed their things and headed out the dorm front doors onto Fulton Avenue.

The sky was a dazzling bright blue with a few puffy clouds and was unseasonably warm for March. Rosemary was giddy. "I talked to my mom this morning, and it is only five degrees in Chicago today and snowing like crazy. She was so envious when I told her what a beautiful day it is here. I'm so glad I'm here and not there for that dreary, cold winter. When I was looking for a college, all I cared about was getting somewhere it never snowed. My parents said I could go to any Catholic university that I could get into, but they weren't too happy when I chose San Francisco. They worried I might come home a hippie, but they gave in. They definitely would have preferred that I went to Marquette or somewhere else in the Midwest."

Janet laughed. "I know what you mean, when my parents realized that USF was only a few blocks from Haight-Ashbury, they made me promise not to hang out on 'Hippie Hill' or do drugs. Since I live in Sacramento, I go home fairly frequently, and you can tell that they are always making sure that I haven't gotten too radical. Katie, I thought your dad made you come home every weekend."

"He's been kind of loosening up and letting me stay on the weekends if there is a specific reason. This weekend I told him about this assignment and that I needed to go to the museum and he was okay with that. Last night, he came over on his way home from work and took Rosemary and me for pizza. He loves Rosemary and thinks that she is a good influence, so I think that's one reason that he lets me stay. Believe me, it isn't roses having an overprotective cop for a dad, but I know he means well, and it was either this or stay home and go to the local junior college, so I go along with his rules."

Rosemary chimed in. "He is pretty strict, but he has been great to me, inviting me to come home with you all the time. I'm looking forward to going home with you for spring break. I'm trying to get all of my assignments out of the way so I can relax and enjoy the break."

As they crossed the street and started walking through Golden Gate Park, they noticed a group of about eight young people sitting on the grass, one of the guys playing "Alice's Restaurant" on his acoustic guitar and two of the girls singing with him. As they walked by, one of the guys yelled out, "Hey, want to join us?"

Janet called, "Thanks for asking, but we can't today"

As the girls walked on, a very good-looking guy with blonde hair and a beard glanced up. He jumped to his feet and headed toward them, and tentatively called, "Katie?" Katie immediately recognized his voice and froze. Janet and Rosemary turned around to see who was calling their friend. He ran up alongside her and looked into her eyes. "It is you!" He so wanted to give her a huge hug, but he restrained himself.

Her friends looked at her questioningly, and she took a deep breath and said, "Rosemary and Janet, this is Eric." Rosemary nodded knowingly, since she had heard most of the story about Eric and Katie. She also knew that running into Eric was something that Katie had said that she dreaded, though Rosemary thought that a part of Katie also had hoped for it. Janet was clueless, and only noticed how absolutely gorgeous this hippie guy was.

"Katie, I thought you were going to school up in Washington somewhere."

"Um, well. . ."

"Can I talk to you, please, Katie?"

Katie looked at her friends, "If it's okay with you, I will just meet up with you in the museum in a little while."

"Sure, we'll probably start out in the Renaissance section," Rosemary answered as they walked away.

"Shall we sit over there?" Eric pointed to a worn park bench under a budding flowering plum tree. "So, Katie, it's obvious that you don't want to have anything to do with me, but can you at least explain to me what's going on?"

"I am going to USF and those are friends of mine from the dorm. I know Laura told you that I was going to college in Washington, but don't be mad at her. She said that because I told her to throw you off the track, if you ever tried to reach me through her. I was afraid that if you knew I was here in the city that you would try to find me and—"

Eric's voice tightened. "And you didn't want to see me—"

Katie's eyes welled with tears, and she sputtered, "No, it was because I really wanted to see you and I just didn't know if I could be strong if you actually came looking for me. I promised my dad I wouldn't see you again, and I need to keep that promise. I told myself that it would get better with time, but in the last year, there hasn't been a day that I haven't missed you."

Eric put his arm around Katie and held her close. "I have missed you too, so much, and this whole time I imagined that you didn't care about me."

"Nothing is further from the truth, Eric, but I just didn't see any future for us and I—"

"Katie, I love you and you have never been out of my mind these twelve months. I know you don't want to go against your dad, but we deserve happiness, too, and I want to be with you. Would you please at least think about it?"

Katie took a deep breath and said, "I don't know, Eric, right now I need to go and catch up with my friends."

He touched her hand and said, "I know, but can we meet tomorrow morning? How about right here at this bench around eleven?" She thought for a minute and then looked up at him and nodded. They said goodbye, and she walked briskly through the gardens toward the museum and when she was about to turn the corner, she looked back and saw that he was still standing watching her. He gave her a big smile and a wave and she waved back. He couldn't wait to see her again, and he had new hope because she had looked back, hadn't she?

CHAPTER 38

March 14, 1970

As the USF bells tolled 11:00, Eric sat under the mimosa tree on the old weather-worn, green park bench and wondered if Katie would really show up. It was a blustery, cloudy day and a young dad was helping his little girl fly a beautiful turquoise kite shaped like a bird. Seagulls were squawking and swooping down to eat some yellow popcorn that had been spilled near the walkway. In the distance he saw a girl in a purple jacket walking toward him and his heart skipped a beat. He couldn't see her face yet, but he could tell by the bounce of her gait and her beautiful brown hair blowing in the wind that it had to be her. He started walking toward her, smiling his gorgeous smile, tucking his blonde locks behind his ear, and said, "I'm so glad you came. I wasn't sure you would."

She smiled and said, "I said I would."

He reached for her hand and said, "Do you want to go to the Japanese Tea Garden? It isn't far from here and we would be shielded from this wind."

"Yeah, that would be good. Even though my Dad doesn't work this area anymore, he has a lot of friends who do and it would be better not to be out in the open."

"You mean you don't think the cops hang out in the Japanese Tea

Garden?" Eric quipped.

"I think the coffee shop on the corner is more their cup of tea, especially since they get free coffee there," Katie joked.

They walked along the path, winding through the budding trees and the newly blooming yellow and white daffodils garnished with the fragrant smell of narcissus bordering the flower beds. The entrance to the tea garden was framed with ornamental cherry trees, which were bursting with pink blossoms. A young Japanese woman in a beautifully embroidered green kimono seated them in the corner that overlooked a beautiful fountain. Eric ordered tea for them and they sat quietly across the table from each other and looked into each other's blue eyes. For the last year, Katie had been trying to convince herself that she had exaggerated how handsome Eric was and how attracted she was to him, physically and emotionally, but she could see that the chemistry they had was something she could not deny.

The waitress placed a plate of Japanese rice snacks and two small white cups on the table, filled their cups with tea from a beautiful ceramic teapot that was painted with red poppies, and placed the tea pot on the table. She bowed and then said in heavily accented English, "Please, let me know if need anything else."

Eric thanked her graciously and then turned to Katie, squeezing her hand, and said, "Well, we have a lot of catching up to do. I want to hear all about how you like living in the city and going to USF."

"I love everything about it. I absolutely love my classes, and philosophy is my favorite one. My professors are all really great teachers and the students are motivated and want to be challenged. It is so much more challenging and interesting than high school. Right now I am taking anatomy, chemistry, English 1A, a philosophy class, and PE. Living in the dorm has been such a blast for me. You know, I always wanted to have sisters and now I have a bunch of them! My roommate's name is Rosemary, and you met her yesterday, the girl with the blonde hair. She is Polish and is from Chicago and we have become so close, and there are all the girls on my floor who are a lot of fun. The rules are strict. No male visitors except certain evening hours and then we need to entertain them in the dorm lounge area, with our head resident lurking nearby to make sure there is no inappropriate behavior. Most of us are in the nursing program, so we have that in common. We never have to worry about any guys being around so in the evenings, we get in our pajamas and hair rollers and visit each other's rooms, eating popcorn, drinking hot chocolate, and catching up on the latest gossip. Part of my agreement with my dad was that I have been going home every weekend. He picks me up after his shift on Friday, and brings me back to the dorm on Monday morning on his way into his precinct. It has taken me this whole time to rebuild my trust with him, Eric, and he is finally letting me stay in the city for the weekend if there is an educational purpose, and this weekend I needed to go to the de Young. I have such mixed feelings about being here with you. I did promise him that I wouldn't see you and—"

"Katie, I am sorry that you had to go through so much when your dad found out that we were seeing each other—I can only imagine."

"I was grounded for three months, and my dad watched me like a hawk and took me with him everywhere. It wasn't really that bad because I really wasn't interested in going out because I—" Katie stopped herself as he looked at her intently and then continued. "I guess I didn't want to go out with anyone who asked me."

He squeezed her hand and then changed the subject. "Hey, I have wondered what happened with your Aunt Katherine and the commune drug charges."

"The DA dropped the charges, which was a relief for everyone. Katherine has formally left the order of sisters that she belonged to, and then she left the commune after the big fire. Did you hear about the tragedy out there a few months after the fire, when two of the little girls drowned after driving a tricycle into the swimming pool?" Katie asked solemnly.

Eric sighed, "Yeah, that was so terrible. You know I believe that the founders of the commune had good intentions, but everything seemed to fall apart. I heard that people went their own way and no one is out there anymore."

She changed the subject, saying, "Tell me about you. One thing that has really been on my mind—is what you plan to do about the draft? We watched the lottery in the dorm and I saw that you pulled 73 and I have been so worried about you."

"Yeah, I have never claimed to be lucky, but my roommate John got Number 12, he has a December birthday. We had hoped that they might do the lottery again because of the belief that the capsules were not adequately mixed up, but that's not going to happen. John enlisted in the Air Force and should be leaving for boot camp at the end of the semester. I have been doing a lot of soul searching in the last few months. At first, I thought I might apply for a non-combatant status, but I decided if I oppose the war—any way I am involved is against my convictions, so I applied for conscientious objector status."

She rubbed her hand on his and quietly asked, "What's involved in that?"

"Well, the first thing I had to do is to write an essay to plead my position, which is tricky because currently draft boards accept pacifism cases based on specific religious beliefs only. I really can't claim religious beliefs, I consider myself an agnostic. So I presented the case that I was philosophically opposed to the war and that I had deep beliefs in the great writers such as Camus and Thoreau. I told them that I didn't think any wars could be justified now that we had nuclear weapons because we risk destroying the planet and all of humanity and I just can't be part of it. The conscientious objector counselor I have been seeing says that it sure would make it easier if I could come up with a religious belief defense like being Quaker or Mennonite, but even if I could get away with that, I wouldn't lie about it."

"Eric, my philosophy professor is a Jesuit priest and he said that this past October the United Catholic Bishops came out with a statement that if a Catholic is totally convinced in conscience that a war is unjust that he has the right and obligation to refuse to participate.

He also quoted John Kennedy saying something like: 'War will exist until the day when the conscientious objector is treated with the same respect as the warrior.'"

"Oh, I get it, you want me to become a Catholic, huh," Eric kidded.

Katie shook her head, laughed, and then asked him, "Well, what's next?"

He replied, "Since I am a student, I go to my hometown draft board so I'm waiting for the Woodside draft board to contact me and set a date for my appeal which should be in the next month or two. If they approve it, I will do some sort of alternative community service for two years. Somehow my dad got wind of it and called me to try to talk me out of it. He says I'm shaming the family and ruining the family name as well as giving up any chance of having a decent career. The good thing is that I told my brother and he is cool with it. I care more about his opinion anyway."

"Is Stephen still in the military?" asked Katie as she poured more tea for them.

He answered, "Yeah, he just has another six months and then he will be out. He plans to go back to college on the GI bill and get a master's degree in business, which should make my dad happy. Anyway, if they approve my request, I will be required to do some type of alternative service which benefits society and it needs to be at least one hundred miles from my home. I don't mind doing that, a couple of guys that my CO counselor knows worked up in Mendocino County at a school for emotionally disturbed boys and they always seem to need help, so that may be an option. If they deny my request I will either go to jail for two years in somewhere like Leavenworth or I take off and go to Canada. I had considered Canada, but that would mean I could never come back and I don't know if I'm prepared to leave this country for good. Although this war is something I don't believe in, I do love this country. Katie, how do you feel about all of this?"

"I respect you for being true to your beliefs, Eric, but I'm not sure what else to say. It's so complicated."

"Katie, I love you and I don't want to let you go, but I will understand if all of this is too much for you."

"Let me think about it, Eric. Next week is spring break and I'll be going home Friday for a week."

"Can I please see you during the week, Katie?"

"No, Eric, I need some time to think about all of this."

"Can I have your phone number and call you at the dorm?"

"Okay, but wait until I get back from break," Katie said as she wrote her phone number on a scrap of paper she had in her pocket.

Eric sighed impatiently. "When will that be?"

"I'll be coming home sometime the night of Easter. I have classes the next day."

"Okay, I guess I've waited this long—I should be able to wait a couple of weeks. Let me at least walk you back to the dorm."

As they walked back to the dorm, he put his arm around her and she didn't resist. When they got to the foot of the stairs, he looked into her eyes and leaned down to give her a hug. She walked through the door and turned around to see him still standing there. She blushed and waved.

CHAPTER 39

March 29, 1970

Easter morning

Katie was dreaming of walking across the Golden Gate Bridge in the dense fog with Eric when the buzzing of her old white electric alarm clock startled her awake. At first, she felt disoriented and then she remembered that it was Easter morning and she was in her canopy bed at her house, and her roommate Rosemary was stretching her arms and yawning next to her. It was 8:00 and time to get up so they could make it to the 9:30 Mass at St. Isabella's church. The house was filled with delicious smells from her father's cooking, including the cinnamon coffee cake that was sitting on the counter next to the white and blue Corning Ware electric percolator that emanated the smell of fresh dark-roast coffee. The marinara sauce, which infused the kitchen with the aromas of garlic, rosemary, oregano, thyme, and garlic and would smother delicious homemade ravioli later in the day, was softly bubbling on the stove.

Katie and Rosemary nodded and grunted at each other as they both crawled out of bed and headed to the bathrooms. As Katie exited the bathroom, her father came through the front door. He beamed and came over and gave her a big hug saying, "Happy Easter, honey! I decided to go to the 7:00 a.m. Mass so I'd have more time to get ready for our company. You can go ahead and use the car to go to the 9:30. Then when you girls get home, you can help me hide the Easter eggs in the backyard. Looks like we are going to have about eighteen for dinner and that includes six kids." He pointed to the huge basket of brightly colored Easter eggs, which Katie and Rosemary had helped dye the day before. Gino was in his element; he loved having Katie home and having the extended family all here for Easter and cooking a big traditional meal, which included antipasto, ravioli, lamb, and many side dishes.

Rosemary had just entered the kitchen and said, "Thanks, Mr. Pulli. It has been so nice to spend this whole week with you and seeing all the Northern California sites. You know I had never even seen the ocean until I came out in September and for you to take your vacation this week to take us all the way up the California coast and then down through the redwoods is just so nice. They are so stupendous; my photos just don't do them justice. Anyway, now I'm looking forward to meeting all of your family."

"We are glad you can be here with us, Rosemary, and it was so nice for your mom to send that big box of Easter goodies, especially that beautiful lamb cake that she made and sent." He looked over at the beautiful lamb cake that had the place of honor at the center of his table. Gino had not told Rosemary that the cake had needed some "First Aid" and that he had spent some time patching the rear of the lamb with white frosting before she had seen it.

"Yeah, I'm so glad that it made the trip okay. It's a Polish tradition and I always help her with it. She had a lump in her throat as she said, "Only two more months and I'll be back home. I didn't realize that I would get so homesick. I feel bad that my brother Stan is at Camp Lejeune and will be finished with his training in about two weeks. It's looking like he will have a short leave and will be going back to Chicago, but I won't be back by then, so looks like I'll miss him. I am so relieved that Chet has the medical deferment. I just couldn't handle if both of them had been drafted."

Katie changed the subject, saying, "Hey, let's have some of that scrumptious coffee cake my dad made. I'll get out the orange juice and milk. We need to leave in about a half an hour. It's sure good that we can eat up until an hour before having communion instead of the three-hour rule that it was when we were younger."

Gino replied, "Hey, that's nothing girls, when I was a kid we couldn't eat or drink anything after midnight the night before if we wanted to go to Communion. "

The girls finished getting ready and then climbed into Gino's 1964 long green 98 Oldsmobile for the 10 minute drive to church. Katie said, "I'm glad that my dad isn't going to church with us because he'd probably wonder why I'm not going to Communion."

"Because of Eric?" Rosemary asked.

"Yeah, I mean I have been lying to my dad, I disobeyed him, and if that isn't bad enough, I think French kissing is a mortal sin," Katie confided.

Rosemary's eyes widened, and she answered, "I don't know what to say about that." And after a pause she asked, "Have you decided what to do about Eric?"

"No, I am still in turmoil about the whole situation. I thought it would help to have this week off to make a decision, but I still don't know what to do. Okay, well let's go in. I really like this Mass because it's the Folk Mass and I know one of the girls who plays guitar. The music is really cool. Would you ever have believed when we were little kids that church would be so different?" Katie remarked.

Rosemary replied, "I know when we were kids we had to wear a hat or veil, the Mass was in Latin, and the songs were always accompanied with serious organ music. Things have changed in a short time, and it makes me wonder what the world will be like in another ten years. I'll pray for you and your decision about Eric. Would you pray for Stan's safety? "

Katie nodded solemnly. "Of course I will."

8:00 p.m.

As the foggy wind blew behind them, Gino carried Rosemary's turquoise blue Samsonite suitcase and Katie's red plaid suitcase into the lobby of the dorm. Katie gave him a hug and kiss, saying, "Thanks, Dad, for driving us back and everything. You must be exhausted after all the cooking and company, and you have to get up so early in the morning to get to work."

Rosemary piped in. "Yes, thanks so much Mr. Pulli for the wonderful week at your house. I had such a great time and the food was fabulous. You are such a great cook. Thanks for showing me all around Northern California and it was great to meet all of your relatives; I felt so at home."

"It was my pleasure to have you, Rosemary, and I'm really glad I was able to take a week of vacation and revisit some of the places I haven't seen for a long time with you girls. I hope you can come home with Katie again soon."

"Thanks, I'd like that," Rosemary said as she gave Gino a hug.

The girls waved at Gino as he placed his brown tweed cap on his head and he headed out of the dark oak doors and down the stone steps and glanced back. Then they walked over to the front desk and asked the girl who was behind the desk to check their mailboxes for mail and messages. She came back and handed Rosemary two envelopes and a postcard and Katie an envelope and two handwritten notes. Katie's mail was all from Eric. He had come by the afternoon she had left, saying that he had hoped that he could see her before she left on vacation. The other was a message saying that he had called about an hour ago and wanted her to call him when she got in. She could tell that the envelope was a card; she'd wait until she got to her room to open it.

Rosemary sighed and said, "The postcard is from my brother, Stan. He will be shipping out to Vietnam probably sometime in May." As they walked down the hallway, Rosemary tore open the envelope and pulled out a card decorated with a cross and Easter lilies from her parents. She choked back her tears as she said, "Sure wish I could go home and see Stan before he gets shipped out. I also wish he didn't choose to join the Marines. I have heard that is the most dangerous branch of the service, especially for young officers like him. I am sure glad that my brother Chet didn't get drafted after all, because of his asthma. It's hard enough having one brother face Vietnam." Katie gave her a sympathetic nod as she unlocked their door and walked into the cramped room.

They plunked their suitcases on the floor and Katie opened her envelope as her heart pounded. It was an Easter card from Eric. It had a picture of Snoopy on the front trying to impersonate the Easter bunny and then on the inside he had written, "I hope you have a nice Easter. Can't wait to see you. Always, Eric." There were also two different pink "while you were out" notes that said he had called and wanted her to call him back.

Rosemary asked, "Those are from Eric, huh—what did you decide to do?"

"I am still so torn—I want to see him so badly, but I know I shouldn't. I feel in such a bind since I promised my dad. I had hoped that my Aunt Katherine would be at our Easter gathering and that she and I could have some time alone and that she would help me sort things out. She has met Eric and likes him. She knows that we have really liked each other for three years, and she also knows how difficult my dad can be. Anyway, she couldn't come because of some demonstration that she is involved in to save the redwood forests in Mendocino County—my dad doesn't know that part; he thinks it's just because she is working. I got a letter from her about a week ago telling me about that. I wrote to her about the whole Eric thing and this other letter is from her," she said as she tore open the tan envelope made from recycled paper containing a piece of binder paper with beautiful cursive handwriting.

"It says, 'Follow your heart, Katie. I know you don't want to disappoint your dad, but you also deserve to have happiness. You and

Eric have cared about each other for a long time and maybe it's time to see if you are meant to be together.

"'I have never told you this, but just before I entered the convent, I met a guy named Harvey and had such a crush on him, but felt I had committed to being a nun and would disappoint my family. I guess I also was worried that he might not feel the same way about me, so I decided to take the safe route. I've always wondered about him and whether we could have had a life together. Remember, Katie, this is the first day of the rest of your life—live it! I wish I had a telephone at my place, so I could give you a call.

"'By the way, the demonstration to save the old-growth redwoods will start on Friday, so I could be in jail by the time you receive this letter. It's bound to be in the paper, and I hope I'm not featured, because I really don't want to deal with any more of your dad's disapproval. Guess I need to practice what I preach, huh? Your dad is a strong man and has always taken good care of the women in his life and I appreciate it, but we are strong women and need to live our own lives. Let's support each other in doing that. Love you always, Katherine.'"

Rosemary smiled and said, "You are so lucky to have an aunt like that; she sounds so cool. I could never talk to my little Polish aunties about anything personal. I mean they are all very sweet and every time I am at their house they feed me Polish pastries and talk about the news from our parish, St. Stanislaus in Northwest Chicago, and who won bingo that week. Wow, to have a hippie aunt, who used to be a nun! I sure hope I get to meet her someday."

Katie smiled and said, "Want to take a Greyhound bus to Mendocino County Jail tomorrow?"

"I'd like to, but I think we better show up for our midterms this week," Rosemary bantered. "I'm going to study for a while and then try to get to bed early. Your Italian family wore me out. Are you going to call Eric?"

"The thought of going out in the hall to use the pay phone to call Eric and deal with the traffic of all the girls on the floor walking by is more than I can bear. And what would I say anyway? I'll try to get my courage up and call him tomorrow after class."

CHAPTER 40

March 31, 1970

Dodging the raindrops as she ran back to the dorm, Katie thought about how exhausted she was. She had tossed and turned all night thinking about her dilemma regarding Eric, and then all of her classes had been especially taxing, not to mention that she had mid-terms and a major paper all due this week. When she got to the dorm door, Candy, who lived down the hall from her, was coming out and squealed, "Some really cute guy is waiting for you in the visitor lounge and all the girls are ogling him; he's been here for at least an hour." Katie's heart skipped a beat because she knew it was Eric, and he would want his answer.

She took a deep breath, walked through the door, and there was Eric sitting on an uncomfortable brown imitation leather chair. "Hi, Katie," he said as he awkwardly stood up and walked toward her.

"Hi, Eric, sorry I didn't get back to you—um, it was pretty late by the time I got back last night and—" She noticed three girls at the front desk and two sitting across the room, and she knew everyone was pretending not to listen.

"We need to talk, Katie."

"Okay, well let me put my books and stuff away. I wish I could invite you to my room, but we can only have boys visit on Sundays from 1:00 till 4:00 in our rooms and of course we need to keep the doors open. Maybe we could go to the coffee shop down the street." She certainly didn't want to have their conversation where all these snoopy girls could hear.

"Okay, I'll wait for you here."

Katie burst into her room, dropped her books on her bed, quickly changed from her wet sweater to a dry one, and grabbed her blue raincoat. She looked in the mirror at her long, wet, wavy hair, ran a comb through it, and headed down to the lobby.

As they walked out the front door of the dorm, Katie flipped her hood over her head and looked at Eric and felt the butterflies she had always experienced with him. They walked quietly to the little coffee shop and sat at a little table in the back corner. She ordered tea with lemon, and he ordered coffee with extra cream.

Then he started. "Katie, the last two weeks have been the longest in my life. I need to know—do we have a future or not?"

Katie gulped, "I thought having a couple of weeks to think about it would help me decide, but to tell you the truth, I feel even more conflicted than before. I really missed you and I like you so much, Eric, but I just spent the week with my dad and he loves me so much and was so good to Rosemary and the thought of sneaking around—"

"I love you, too, Katie; your dad and I have that in common. It was wrong for us to sneak around to see each other before. What I would like to do is go see your dad and talk to him—man to man—and tell him I'm sorry about the past and tell him that I am going to date you and that I want to be up front about it."

Katie responded, "Eric, I really appreciate that and being direct and honest is the right thing to do. But I know my dad, and he has taken a stand on this issue and he is really bull-headed, I know he won't back down. If anything, I should be the one to talk to him, because I was the one who made the promise not to see you, but I'm just afraid to do it."

They sat silently for a while and then Eric said, "I don't know why you have such a hold on me, Katie, but ever since that day in Candlestick Park, I can't get you out of my mind. You are a beautiful girl with an amazing personality, but there is something more. I told my friend Hal about it and he said maybe we knew each other in former lives—I don't buy that reincarnation stuff but sometimes I wonder. I mean I've gone out with plenty of other girls, but no one has ever got under my skin like you."

Katie replied, "Well, I have only gone out with a couple of guys and nothing serious, but I feel the same way about you. Sometimes I wonder if the reason that we are so attracted to each other is because of the forbidden aspect of it. Maybe if we really spent a lot of time together, we'd get sick of each other and want to move on, and telling my dad would not be an issue."

"I can't imagine ever getting sick of you, but you may have a point about really getting to know each other. How about if we just take it slowly, goes out some, and see where it leads us?"

"Yeah, I still feel badly about my dad, but no use upsetting him if I can help it. You know, last time we talked about this you said that we deserve happiness. I received a letter from my Aunt Katherine last night and she said the same thing. She really likes you, Eric and encouraged me to follow my heart."

Eric reached out for Katie's hand, "Do you know how lucky we are to be young and living in San Francisco in this time? The music scene is so incredible. Have you ever been to any of the Winterland shows? I have tickets to the April 25 Joe Cocker-Van Morrison show. It's a Friday night, wanna go? It should be pretty mellow."

Katie smiled, "I'll try. I would really like to experience more, but I really don't want to get into the drug scene at all."

Eric said, "I'm with you. I mean I smoke a little pot here and there, but I'm definitely not interested in any of the hard stuff. Did you know that I have been doing volunteer work for the Haight Ashbury Free Clinic, and it is so sad how strung out and permanently damaged some of the young people are. Actually, that is how I got the tickets to the Winterland show. Bill Graham, owner and promoter of Winterland, gives some tickets to volunteers at the clinic—it is a show of his support for what we do and also provides more unofficial help during the concerts to help with those who overdo it."

"I will be done with my EMT courses at City College in June, so it has been good experience working at the clinic. I haven't heard whether my draft board will allow me to do alternative service but I'm hoping to hear in the next six weeks. I visited the school for emotionally disturbed boys in the Boonville area; they seemed interested in having me start in September there if I'm approved. I would supervise about ten boys—probably night shift. They really liked that I have first aid and basic medical skills because that could come in handy. "

"That sounds good, Eric. I really hope that comes through instead of you going to jail. I can totally see you working with those kids. Do they provide a place to live?"

"Yeah, they have a little cabin that needs a lot of work and doesn't have indoor plumbing, but I could make it work. Whether jail or Alternative Service, I have at least the next six weeks to enjoy life and I hope you can enjoy it with me."

CHAPTER 41

April 25, 1970

Eric stretched over to pull Katie close to him, nuzzled her neck, and whispered in her ear, "I love you, Katie, and I am so glad that you decided to spend the night with me. It was amazing for me, was it good for you?"

Katie wasn't sure how to answer that question; she didn't have anything to compare it to since it was her first time. However, she felt a glow that she had never felt before, and being safe in his arms was exquisite. She sighed and answered, "It was pretty good, but I like this cuddling part even better. I think I love you, too, Eric, it's all so new to me and I guess I feel a little guilty, because I, uh, always thought I'd wait until I got married before I, you know,"

"We can jump in my little VW van now and head to Reno because I'm that sure about us."

Katie smiled and asked, "Is that a proposal? I don't think I'm quite ready for that—besides, I don't want to get married in Reno! Hey, this conversation is getting too serious, what time is it anyway?"

"It's about 9:30. What did you think of the show last night?" Eric asked.

"I had a blast! It was interesting to see how they convert Winterland from a skating rink into a music venue," Katie replied. My dad took me ice skating a few times there; it was quite the hangout when he was growing up. Van Morrison really put on a great show, but I really was hoping he would sing 'Brown Eyed Girl.' I guess he wanted to promote more of his newer stuff from his new *Moondance* album; it seemed to have a rhythm and blues edge to it."

"Yeah, and how about the pipes on Joe Cocker? No one sings 'A Little Help from my Friends' like him. It was a mellow crowd last night, not like when the Grateful Dead or Jefferson Airplane play—way different crowd. That's why I wanted to take you for your first time," Eric said as he caught Katie's eye and they both laughed at the double meaning of "first time" as it pertained to the previous night.

Eric changed the subject. "How about if I put on some coffee and then maybe we can take a shower and have some breakfast? I asked John to couch surf last night and leave us alone until 11:00, so maybe we can leave about then?"

Katie appreciated that Eric's roommate had left for the night to give them some privacy, but she felt awkward and really wanted to be out of there before he came home. "How about if we leave by 10:30 so I can get back to the dorm. I don't want to hold up Rosemary in case she wants to go anywhere. I signed out of the dorm saying I was going home, and she was going to cover if the front desk or my dad was looking for. . ."

Eric stopped her mid sentence with a kiss and pulled her close to him. "In that case, maybe we should just skip breakfast and…" No more words were necessary.

CHAPTER 42

May 23, 1970

Gino put the key in the ignition of his long green Oldsmobile and headed out of the Travis Air Force Base parking lot. It had been grueling for Rosemary to say goodbye to her brother Stan as he was deployed to Vietnam. He had to report for duty early that day and had joined a group that was transported by bus to the Air Force base. However, she was able to sit in a waiting room and wave goodbye to him as he boarded his plane and she appreciated that.

Rosemary was choking back tears as she said, "Thank you, Mr. Pulli, for bringing me here to see my brother off and having him stay at your house for his leave before heading out. I'm so glad that I got a chance to spend a lot of time this past week with him. Thanks for taking us all over; he loved seeing San Francisco."

"It was my pleasure, Rosemary. He and all the guys who are going over there to do their duty are heroes in my book. I was glad I could put him up and show him around Northern California instead of him staying at the barracks or something. I'm glad he was able to use the last week of his leave here and spend time with you."

As they were exiting the gates of the base, Gino spotted some protesters on the outside of the gates with signs saying, "Hell, no—just don't go!" and "Make love not war." The signs were aimed at an incoming bus of soldiers who were probably being deployed to Vietnam from Travis. Stan had mentioned these protesters when they had seen him off.

Gino barked, "I can't believe those punks, and I'd roll over in my grave if you were with one of these creeps." Katie squirmed and Rosemary's eyes widened. She had always thought that Katie's depiction of her dad's inability to tolerate Eric might be an exaggeration, but she saw the rage in Gino's face and heard it in his voice and knew why Katie had been afraid to be straightforward with her dad. Katie could see Gino's face get beet red as he rolled down the window and screamed, "You cowards, grow a pair, or at least get a job and a haircut instead of harassing these guys who are doing their duty."

A guy with long brown hair and a beard limped toward Gino's Oldsmobile, pointed to his prosthetic leg and his other arm, where there was a hook instead of a hand, and said, "You have no idea, sir. I did one-and-a-half tours in Vietnam and I'm just trying to save these other guys." Gino did not respond, but closed his window and continued on.

Katie had just learned the previous week that Eric's appeal for conscientious objector status had been approved by his draft board. This had been a relief because it meant that Eric would not spend the next two years in jail. Instead he had been accepted by the Boonville Residential School for Emotionally Disturbed Boys and would be beginning work in September. Eric still wanted them to tell Gino about their relationship; he seemed to think that he could win him over, but Katie knew her father better than that. She had agreed that she would tell him after school was out.

Changing the subject, Katie said, "I'm sure looking forward to having dinner with all of the cousins this afternoon in North Beach."

Rosemary chimed in, "Yeah, how cool it is to have a family that has a top notch restaurant. I got chicken parmesan last time; do you have anything to recommend, Mr. Pulli?" The diversion worked and Gino started listing all of the delicacies and his favorite dishes made from his mother and auntie's recipes, and reliving stories from the days when he worked in the family restaurant.

As they drove over the Bay Bridge and into San Francisco, the girls encouraged Gino to continue to regale them with anecdotes about his childhood growing up in the North Beach neighborhood during the Depression. He obliged, and ended by saying, "The thing I loved to do the most was ice skate at the Winterland. Too bad it's ended up being a hangout for all those hippies who are all hopped up on drugs and all those loud bands. Glad I'm not on nights or have to do patrol work there anymore." Katie gulped and glanced at Rosemary as they climbed out of the car and headed toward the restaurant. Gino put his arms around each of the girls. "I know I promised to get you back to the dorm early since you have finals this week, and I sure want my girl to get all As again," he said proudly.

CHAPTER 43

May 25, 1970

Katie glided toward the dorm, relieved that her chemistry final was over and that she thought she did pretty well on it. Well, three finals down and two to go, and it was such a gorgeous, sunny spring day. The tulips were blooming as well as the rose bushes that garnished the area around her dorm, and she was going to see Eric tonight. He was going to take her to have dinner at a little Japanese restaurant that he had told her about, and she couldn't wait.

As she walked through the dorm door and saw the expression on the front desk receptionist's face, she knew something was wrong. Just then, Miss Moore, head resident of the dorm, came out of her office and approached Katie and said, "Please come to my office." Uh-oh, had she found out that she had been sneaking out to see Eric?

As they sat in the leather chairs in her office, she somberly said, "Your roommate Rosemary got very bad news today. Her brother was killed in Vietnam."

Katie was stunned. "There must be some mistake, we just saw him off at Travis two days ago and. . ."

"Yes, I know it is quite a shock, I'm sure. From what I understand, he was disembarking the airplane that had transported him there, and he was shot by a sniper. It seems that the Viet Cong targeted Stan because they could tell he was an officer by the rank on his uniform."

"Where is Rosemary now?" Katie asked as tears streamed down her crumpled face.

"She is with Father O'Rafferty in the chapel. Her parents called and asked that a priest come and break the news to her. He came about an hour ago, and she was able to talk to her parents in Chicago. We are working on letting her professors know that she will be unable to complete her finals now."

"Can I go be with her?"

"Yes, Katie, I think that would be a good idea. I know how close you girls are and I think it would be a big comfort to her. She wants to take the next airplane out tonight, which I certainly understand. She may need help packing her essential things; we can send the rest of her things on later."

Katie walked down the dorm hall, to the little chapel nestled in a corner overlooking the courtyard. She took a deep breath and then knocked at the mahogany door and the old, slim priest opened it. There was Rosemary, sitting on a small wooden bench in front of a stained glass window, sobbing into a man's handkerchief. Katie wrapped her arms around her friend, hugging her tightly and saying gently, "I'm so, so sorry, Rosemary, this is so awful, but you are going to get through it—I promise."

CHAPTER 44

June 16, 1970

The fog was rolling in over the Golden Gate Bridge as Gino and Katie approached the toll plaza and Gino pulled out the change for the bridge attendant. "Remember when you loved to pay the man the quarter when we drove over the bridge? You would be standing behind my shoulder in the back seat and lean through the window to give the man the money. It actually was quite the bargain during that time period. When the bridge opened in '37 it cost fifty cents and if you had more than five passengers you had to pay an extra nickel for each person." He laughed and continued. "I can remember hiding in the trunk of my cousin's Desoto so we could save a nickel when we were heading to Russian River. Times were sure tough during the Depression and good pay was about twenty-five cents an hour, so we pinched every penny."

"Yeah, those must have been some really tough times, Dad," Katie responded. He told her stories so often, and she knew that it was his way to keep the past alive.

"I hear they are taking the turnstiles out that make pedestrians pay a dime. Starting in December it will be free to go across the bridge," Gino said.

"Really?" Katie responded, but her mind was focused on Eric.

Tomorrow was Eric's birthday and she planned to meet him at Muir Woods. Once again, she was going to sneak around hoping she didn't run into anyone who knew her dad.

"It should be quite the game today against the Chicago Cubs. Sure hoping we can get to the World Series this year. It's hard to believe that with the great players that we have, we haven't made it since '62. You remember that last game of the World Series, Katie, and what a heartbreaker it was," Gino reminisced.

"Yeah, I sure do, Dad, and I can remember how grown up I felt and how exciting it all was. Well, hopefully they will make it to the World Series this year. Glad we can go to this game together and get dinner after to celebrate Father's Day. I wish that we could have gone on Father's Day; too bad they were playing out of town then."

"Yeah, it's good to get the day off and go to a weeknight game, less crowded, less traffic." He was really thinking that there was less of a chance for Bill Smith to be at a weekday game. In fact, he couldn't even remember seeing him there except on weekends and not even then in some time. Most of the time, strangers were sitting in the seats, who he assumed were Smith's clients or friends. Sometimes his seats even went empty. He could only hope that Smith would sell the tickets again so he never had to lay eyes on the stuck-up drunk or his hippie son.

Gino parked his big Oldsmobile, and they pulled out their warm parkas and red plaid picnic bag bulging with a thermos bottle of hot chocolate and lots of goodies. The salty wind was blowing hard and he hoped it would die down. As they made their way through the bustling crowd, Gino put a protective hand on Katie's shoulder, guiding her through the throng of people. What a beauty she was, looking so much like her mother except for her beautiful dark hair that she got from Gino's mother. It was hard to believe that Maggie had already been gone three years; how he missed her. How proud she would have been of Katie getting straight As in all of her classes two semesters in a row at a place like University of San Francisco.

The smell of hot dogs and popcorn filled the air along with the kid yelling, "GET YOUR PROGRAMS!" After going through the ticket turnstile, they made their way to their seats just in time to hear the Star-Spangled Banner. Gino was relieved to see that the Smith seats were occupied by a middle-aged couple. The woman was flaunting a mink coat. Unbelievable! They must be some wealthy clients of Smith's.

Gaylord Perry was at the pitching mound as the Chicago Cubs went up to bat. Popovich, Callison, and Williams all had a chance for the Cubs, but none of them scored. The sun was going down and it was getting even chillier as Katie tied her blue parka hood, reached into her pocket for her gloves and covered herself with the old red plaid stadium blanket.

The Giants were up to bat against the Cubs pitcher Bill Hands. "What a funny last name for a pitcher," she thought. Bobby Bonds, Al Gallagher, and Willie Mays all got a chance at the ball and they were all called out.

Gino pulled the thermos out of the matching bag and unscrewed the cap and the delicious bittersweet aroma of Ghirardelli chocolate wafted toward Katie. Gino poured the hot cocoa into the red plastic cup and handed it to Katie. "Here, honey, hope this will warm you up. It's hard to believe that when we left home it was about eighty-five degrees and here less than thirty miles away it's barely fifty degrees, and the wind is so piercing."

"I'll be okay, Dad." McCovey was up; Hands walked him, which was not unusual since he was known as such a heavy hitter. Ken Henderson hit a single, and then Dick Dietz was up. He hit a fastball over the outfield fence. The crowd whooped and hollered, waving their Giants banners as the players rounded the bases. Three more Giants players were up and out and it was the end of the inning.

"You know, Dad, I've always meant to ask you why we have so much red plaid stuff. Mom's suitcase, which is mine now—all this stadium stuff. "

Gino laughed. "Most of the stuff was gifts that your mom received from my family. I think that they thought that all Irish people liked plaid and of course, they liked red so that's what they chose. Your mom thought it was sweet."

The next four innings were scoreless as Gino and Katie ate the dinner that he had packed. The sourdough rolls stuffed with turkey, ham, salami, and provolone cheese and garnished with fresh lettuce, pesto, and peppers were delicious. For dessert, he brought homemade biscotti.

At the top of the seventh inning, Chicago had two outs and one man on base when Ed Santo stepped up to the plate. Gaylord Perry had been pitching a great game, but he slipped and gave Santo a pitch that he belted over the fence, bringing in his teammate and changing the score to 3–2. The Giants needed to hold on to the lead.

The Giants did not score the bottom of the seventh, and neither did the Cubs in the top of the eighth. Regan relieved Hands in the eighth inning to pitch and again no score. After a scoreless top of the ninth, the Giants walked off with a 3–2 win.

As they gathered their stuff and started to walk up the stairs toward the exit, Gino was excited. "I think this is going to be the year, Katie! You know the last five years we have come in second in the National League West and haven't gotten to the series, but I think this is going to be the year, Katie, my girl, it is time!" Behind them the hungry sea gulls swept through the thick fog to scavenge the bits of food that had been left behind by the happy fans.

CHAPTER 45

July 3, 1970

Eric had wanted to tell Katie's dad about their relationship ever since they started seeing each other again. She had been putting it off: first until school got out, then she decided to wait until after Father's Day, and most recently until after the big Pulli Family Fourth of July celebration at Russian River. This had been a tradition for many years, reminiscent of the times in the past when the mothers and kids stayed at the cabins all summer and the dads came on the weekends, making the long trek by streetcar, ferry, and train to join their families. In recent years, since the older generation had passed on and everyone was so busy, families took turns going to the rustic cabins, but when the Fourth of July rolled around, it was expected that everyone would show up. Supplementing the cabins, the younger generation brought campers and tents, and some slept under the stars in sleeping bags.

On the way there, Gino once again told Katie the story about meeting her mom and pointed out Monte Rio where they had first danced under the stars. He also elaborated that, throughout the years, the area had become run down and was no longer the vacation spot it had been in earlier times.

The food was absolutely wonderful, which could only be expected from a family that had run one of the finest Italian restaurants in

San Francisco for many years. Ice chests filled with antipasti, meats, cheeses, rolls, along with delicious marinated meats to barbecue and delicious salads and ample wine and beer provided quite a spread for their gourmet campout.

Katie really enjoyed spending time with her cousins, especially Laura. Laura had been attending Sacramento State, and so the girls had not seen each other much during the school year. Katie had told Laura earlier in the summer that she was seeing Eric again and her cousin was not surprised.

The two cousins declared that they were going for a walk, and then Laura said, "Fill me in on what is going on with you and Eric. I always thought it would be just a matter of time before you guys found each other and got back together."

"Eric insists on telling my dad that we are seeing each other. He says that he will not sneak around anymore, and that he doesn't want a relationship built on sneaking around and lies. He says that he'll probably be mad at first, but since I am the apple of my dad's eye that he will come around, and that being honest is the best way to go. I am so scared of what his reaction will be, but I've decided to tell him on Monday."

Laura sighed and put her arm around Katie. "Yeah, I see Eric's point, but I also know your dad and his temper and can see why you'd be nervous. I think someone should be there with you."

"Eric wants to be there when I tell my dad, but I know that would just make matters worse. We have worked out a plan where I am going to tell my dad around 10:00 in the morning. Eric is going to park across the street from my house and wait for me to open the door, and then he will come and join us."

"If your dad kicks you out, you could come to our house."

"Thanks, Laura. I don't think it will come to that, and I don't want to get you guys involved. I think that would make matters worse."

"Does Katherine know what's going on?"

"She doesn't have a phone. I sent her a letter about a week ago and it usually takes a while for her to pick up her mail at the post office and then to call me or write me back."

Laura said, "We better head back to camp, it's almost time for dinner."

Katie answered, "I'm so nervous, I can't eat, but I will get a plate and do my best."

Laura squeezed Katie's hand and said, "I'm here for you, cousin, let me know if you need me."

"Same here, Laura, thanks for being like a sister to me."

CHAPTER 46

July 5, 1970

Katie awoke with a start. Her stomach was in a knot because she was going to tell her Dad about Eric today. She lingered in her room rehearsing what she would say, and then around 8:30 she padded out to the kitchen where her father was sitting at the table sipping his coffee from his old white mug. He looked up at her over his reading glasses and put aside the newspaper. "Good morning, honey, what sounds good for breakfast?"

"Thanks, Dad, but you don't need to wait on me."

"I like to make my girl breakfast," he said and gave her a kiss on her forehead.

"Okay, well then how about something like hot cereal," Katie replied, though not at all hungry.

"You got it, how about some oatmeal with some bananas and strawberries."

"Thanks, Dad. Maybe I'll go take a shower while that's cooking." Gino nodded and Katie headed to the bathroom. She showered, got dressed in shorts and an embroidered peasant top, and came out to the kitchen.

She said, "Smells good, Dad—oh, and thanks for making me tea, you know I love Earl Grey tea." She remembered that was Mick

Jagger's favorite tea, but didn't think her dad would be impressed with that piece of trivia.

"I've been meaning to ask you if you've heard from Rosemary recently," Gino said. "How are she and her family doing?"

"Rosemary is still having a really tough time. You know that her family sent a nice thank you note for the flowers that we sent along with a holy card from Stan's funeral. I talked to her a couple of days ago and she has made the decision not to come back to USF; she feels her mom and dad need her to be close by, so she'll enroll somewhere in the Chicago area."

Gino replied, "My heart goes out to them, nothing harder than losing a child." Then changing the subject, he said, "I need to catch up on some yard work today, wash the car, and pick up my uniforms from the cleaners. So what do you have going on today, sweetheart?"

"Actually, I'm planning on going to Bodega Bay today. A friend is going to pick me up in about half an hour."

Gino was surprised that Katie hadn't mentioned this before. He realized that she was almost nineteen and probably didn't need to ask permission every time she went somewhere, but this was unlike her.

"So is this a guy friend?"

Katie nodded and stirred her oatmeal, taking small bites, but could barely swallow them. Then she picked up her tea cup and her hand was trembling. Her dad noticed and said, "Katie, are you okay?" She glanced at the clock and saw that it was only 9:45. She shouldn't tell her dad yet.

"Yeah, I'm okay, Dad; I just have a lot on my mind."

"Well, tell me about this guy."

"We have known each other for a while and he is a really nice guy, and we really enjoy each other's company."

"Does he go to USF; is that how you met him?"

"Uh, no, but I did meet him in the city."

"Why didn't you tell me about him before? I thought we had an agreement that I would approve of anyone you dated. Why haven't you brought him around?"

"Well, Dad, it's complicated. I have liked this guy for a really long time, but because you didn't like him, I really tried to deny my feelings and not see him, but I really can't do that anymore. It's Eric, Dad," she explained quickly.

Gino's face started getting red and he slammed down his mug, "What? I hope you are not referring to that long-haired Smith kid? You promised me you would stay away from that hippie, Katie. I trusted you!" he screamed.

"I have tried, Dad, but we love each other. I didn't see him for a whole year after that time you caught us at the movies, but we ran into each other in March and we really feel we belong together. We could have continued seeing each other secretly, but Eric insisted that we be honest with you. In fact, he wanted to be here when I told you, but I thought it was better if you and I talked first."

"Big deal, so you broke your promise and you've been sneaking around for the last few months and now I should be happy that you are being honest with me? What kind of future can that loser provide you? I can't believe he has any kind of decent job. He's probably a draft dodger on top of everything else."

"He has a job up in Boonville starting in September at a school for emotionally disturbed boys. He is doing it as alternative service to the draft."

"Oh, for God's sake, is that supposed to make me feel better?" As he was pacing and throwing his hands in the air, he said, "I suppose you have been sleeping with this guy?"

Katie's eyes dropped to the floor and Gino bellowed, "You don't need to even answer, I can tell by your reaction. I am so disappointed in you, Katie. My dream was to walk you down the aisle in a beautiful white dress and give you away to a man that I could respect and would take good care of you."

"Dad, he does love me and he wants to marry me. I just thought we should wait until. . ."

"Let me make myself perfectly clear. I will not support you, help you with school, or even have you in my home if you choose to continue to see him."

"Dad, please don't put me in this position. I love both of you and want both of you in my life. You have told me before that Mom's family didn't want the two of you to get married, but you did and—"

Gino yelled, "Don't you dare make that comparison! Your mother's family just didn't like the idea that I was Italian, but I was nothing like your marijuana-smoking boyfriend. I served my country, had a career, and always took good care of her."

"Yeah, I know Dad. I'm just saying that I need you to give Eric a chance. I know you got a bad impression of him, but I think if you gave him a chance, you might grow to—"

"Not a snowball's chance in hell, Katie. I know his type and you are just setting yourself up for heartbreak. He has a police record. I even arrested him once. I don't think he thought I recognized him. I also saw him lazing around Candlestick Park with his loser friends more than once."

Since Katie could see that this was getting nowhere, she went to the front door and opened it. Eric was already there and as he stood at the threshold he said, "Mr. Pulli, I'd really like to talk to you, I know this is hard for you, but I want you to know that I love your daughter and—"

Gino stormed from the living room to the front door and appeared to be ready to punch Eric. Katie stood between the two men as her father roared, "Don't you dare step foot into my house, you bastard. You have stolen my girl's heart and taken her virtue and I'd like to get my service revolver and let you have it. If you know what is good for you, you'll get your ass off my property and never come back, and don't you dare see my daughter again!" Gino hollered angrily.

Katie took a deep breath, dried her tears and looked at Eric and then back at her dad and said, "We are going to the beach, and I will be home around 4:00."

Gino replied angrily, "I forbid you to go out that door with him, and if you do, don't come back."

Katie had worried this would be the way her dad would react, but she hoped that with some time he would cool off. She picked up her purse and her beach bag, turned to her father and said, "I love you, Dad, but I need to follow my heart." She went to give him a hug, but for the first time in her life, he pushed her away. She walked out the door and started to follow Eric to his beat-up Volkswagen, and then Katie turned around and her heart sank as she watched her dad, with his head slumped, turn around and go back into the house. He suddenly looked so old to her. She looked at Eric and then back at the door and sensed that she was making the biggest decision of her life.

Eric took her hand as they walked across the street, and she started to sob. Eric opened up her car door as she fished around in her purse for a tissue to wipe her runny nose. Eric said softly, "I love you Katie; I think things are going to be all right. Let's go pick up some sandwiches and head out to the beach. We'll give him some time to cool off and then come back and maybe we can sit down and talk with him."

Katie nodded and blew her nose; Eric started up his van and turned on the radio to KFRC, and "White Rabbit" was playing. He reached over and took her hand and really hoped that Gino would have a change of heart.

They drove through the town of Novato along the rolling hills and windy roads of West Marin, which were peppered by many Hereford cows grazing on the hillsides. They stopped at the French Cheese Factory in Nicasio to pick up sandwiches and a couple of cokes and headed to Salmon Creek Beach at Bodega Bay. It was still overcast but the sun was starting to peek through the clouds. They climbed the sand dunes and found a secluded spot. He reached over and hugged her and gave her a tender kiss. Although her eyes were red from crying and her cheeks stained with tears, she had never looked more beautiful to him. He dabbed her tears away with a paper napkin and then snuggled up to her and gently rubbed her back, reassuring her that things were going to be okay. After a while, Eric reached into the brown paper bag to pull out the sandwiches. Katie declined, she couldn't even imagine eating. She did drink part of her coke, which was not cold anymore. They climbed down the dune and to the shoreline, and the small freezing cold waves teased their bare feet as they walked with their arms entwined. The wind was softly blowing their hair and the sun was bright and warm in their faces.

Around 2:30, they headed back to their car for the return trip to Katie's house. This time they took an alternate route on Sir Francis Drake Boulevard past Samuel P. Taylor Park, which was the home of many majestic redwood trees. They stopped and walked through one of the campgrounds, and Eric marveled, "There is nowhere that I feel nature's beauty as keenly as when I am in the midst of these giants—and to think that some of them are over 1,000 years old, it just blows my mind. I admire your Aunt Katherine for wanting to protect them; it's hard to believe that people would want to cut down old growth like these."

Katie answered, "Yeah, they are amazing. We used to come here a lot when I was a kid for picnics and sometimes even camp overnight." She grew silent again and Eric knew that she was thinking about her dad. They headed back to the car, and Katie looked at her watch. "If we leave now, we should get to my house around 4:00."

When they arrived at the Pulli house, Gino's car was gone and on the front door was a note inside an envelope. Katie ripped it open and it read, "I have gone for a drive. You have two choices: break it off with him for real, or make it on your own without me or my support. You are not welcome in my home as long as you associate with him." Katie showed Eric the note.

Eric took a deep breath and said, "Katie, I'm so sorry, you know I really love you, but I will understand if you decide not to go against your dad."

Katie squared her shoulders and said, "I love you and we have tried to stay apart, but I believe we were meant to be together. I am going inside to pack some things."

Eric said, "Considering how your dad feels about me, I will wait for you in the car. I think it would be disrespectful for me to go in."

Katie unlocked the front door and headed toward her bedroom. She got her old red plaid suitcase out of the closet and packed essential clothes and her photo album, then she went into the bathroom and got her toiletries. She zipped up her suitcase, carried it to the kitchen, grabbed a pad of paper and a pen, and wrote, "Dear Dad, I am sorry that it has come to this. I love you and I always will, but I also love Eric. I want both of you in my life. I will call you tomorrow and I hope we can work this out. Here is my house key. Love, Katie."

As Katie left the house and started down the driveway, Eric saw her and came running to help her with her suitcase. He hugged her and said, "Katie, I would love for you to come and stay at my apartment, or I can take you somewhere else if you'd rather."

"What about your roommate?"

"He'll be gone for most of the summer and we can figure the rest out later."

"Okay, yeah, I want to stay with you."

With that, the young couple in the VW van headed toward Highway 101, across the Golden Gate Bridge, into San Francisco and toward their future together.

CHAPTER 47

July 6, 1970

Gino sat at the kitchen table looking into his coffee cup, tortured by the memory of the previous day. After his drive through Napa Valley, he had come home around sunset, and he saw that the envelope had been taken from the front door. He had thought once she knew that he had really meant business that she would tell the loser to get lost. He wasn't prepared for her note and key declaring that she was choosing Eric over her family, her education, her reputation. She had always been such a good girl, doing the right thing, respecting her parents, but all this had changed. Now she was an ungrateful brat running off with this draft dodger and throwing her life away. Damn it, this world was going to hell in a hand basket and it had corrupted his sweet daughter.

Well, he was a man who did not back down once he said he would do something. If they thought by staying out all night and getting him all worried that he would back down, they had another thing coming. He had considered reporting her as a missing person, but what good would that do? She was eighteen, he couldn't force her to come home, and he would just drag the family's name through the mud if he called the police.

The phone rang and he jumped up—that must be her now. He answered it, "Pulli speaking."

"Hi, Gino, this is Katherine, is Katie there? I—"

He screamed into the receiver, "No, she's not, and it's your fault, you and all your hippie ways—you have been a goddamned bad influence on her. I don't ever want to speak to you again." He slammed the phone, sat down at the table, and cried the tears that he had been holding back for so long.

Stunned by her interaction with her brother, Katherine hung up the pay phone receiver. She had just picked up her mail and received Katie's letter informing her that she was planning to tell Gino about Eric, and obviously she had already and it had not gone well. She assumed that Katie was with Eric. She wished she knew Eric's phone number or address so she could reach her, but she would need to wait until Katie wrote again. She closed the door of the phone booth, walked out to the highway, and stuck out her thumb to get a lift.

October 17, 1989

5:04 p.m.

Katie had tuned her radio to the World Series, and was listening to the pre-game banter as she got to the end of the Bay Bridge. She was thinking of how much she was looking forward to seeing her old friend Rosemary and her sister Helen. Just as she got past the Cypress Viaduct her car started veering—what was going on? She looked in the rearview mirror and saw the Cypress structure collapsing and heard the horrendous crash. Oh, my God, what was happening? On the radio she heard the announcer say something about an earthquake, then the radio went dead. She panicked, thinking of the boys at Candlestick. What should she do? She couldn't turn around and go to Candlestick, the bridge had collapsed. She decided that it would be best to go ahead to Helen's house. It was only a couple more miles, and she could try to use her phone and figure out what to do next. Her hands were trembling and her lips quivering as she proceeded to her destination.

When Katie drove her yellow Datsun up the driveway, Rosemary came running out the door and yelled, "Oh, my God, Katie, I was so worried about you. I knew you were probably coming over the Bay Bridge when the earthquake hit, and it's reported that hundreds of people were probably killed there and at the Cypress Viaduct, and I was so afraid that you had—" Rosemary cried and hugged Katie tightly as she got out of her car.

Katie sobbed and sputtered, "I had just gotten on the other side of the bridge when the earthquake hit. I looked in the rearview mirror and—and saw it collapse. If I had been one minute later. . . Now I'm really frantic about my boys and my dad. They are at Candlestick and I hope they are okay and can get home."

"The good news is that the announcer is saying that it doesn't appear that there are any casualties or serious injuries. Your dad will take good care of your boys—they will have their own personal cop to keep them safe," consoled Rosemary.

"Can I use your phone, Helen?" she asked as they made their way through Helen's front door. Helen and her two daughters were picking up things that had fallen off the walls and out of the china cabinet. Helen embraced her as she said, "Of course, Katie, I'm so glad you are okay." She pointed to the phone on the blue-tiled kitchen counter.

First, Katie tried to call Eric because he might still be at home. She got a recording that said, "The circuits are busy," and then she tried to call her dad's in case Eric or someone else was there, but she got the same recording. Next she called her cousin Laura, and then her Aunt Katherine, and was unable to get through to them either. She thought about her options and then declared, "Going across any of the bridges right now seems impossible, so I am going to go around the Bay and go through Vallejo and around that way. I'm going to leave the numbers here, so that you can continue to try to call them. Please tell them that I am okay and that I will head toward my dad's place. I will trust that my dad will find a way to get them back there."

"Of course, we will keep trying to call, Katie. Please take something to eat and drink with you, who knows how long it will take you to get back home?"

Helen grabbed some water and a can of soda along with some fruit and crackers and stuffed them in a bag. "Are you sure you are okay to drive, Katie, you seem really shaken, maybe one of us should go with you?" In the background, the TV reporter was warning people to stay at home if at all possible, not to head into San Francisco, and to avoid bridges until they were judged to be safe.

"Thanks so much, but I'll be okay. If you came with me, we'd need to find a way to get you back here and I think it's going to be a real mess for a while. Sorry we didn't get to visit, Rosemary, I'll call you when I get to my dad's place

and the circuits are clear." Helen gave Katie a map of the area, marking the back roads to follow to get to Highway 80 which would lead her to Vallejo. She knew her way from there.

They all said their goodbyes, Rosemary gave Katie a big hug, and Katie headed out to brave the traffic. It was starting to get dark, the adrenaline had worn off, and she was starting to feel the stress that had been masked before.

She wove her way through the back streets to avoid the Bay Bridge area, and then merged onto Highway 80; it was bumper-to-bumper traffic and going at a snail's pace. She listened to the radio and found out that fires had erupted in the Marina district, that the Golden Gate Bridge was closed, and that it was nearly impossible to get out of the city. She was relieved that the reports about Candlestick were continuing to seem positive. She got off Highway 80 at Vallejo and started to drive west on Highway 37 toward Marin. As she inched along the highway at about five miles an hour, she prayed that her father and sons were safe and were finding a safe way out of San Francisco.

CHAPTER 48

August 2, 1970

As Katie ran up the flights of steps, she could hear her phone ringing in the apartment. She hastily unlocked the door and ran to pick it up. "Hello," she said breathlessly.

"Hi, Katie. This is Katherine. How are you?"

"I was hoping it was you. I am doing so well; Eric and I are so happy and so in love. I got a job at the pizza place where he works and we have both been working long hours, so we can save money."

Katherine replied, "Well, that explains why I have had such a hard time getting a hold of you. After I got your letter telling me your address and phone number, I wrote to you—you got that didn't you?"

"Yeah, that's how I knew you were going to try to call me. Sorry I've been so hard to reach."

"No problem. I'm just glad you are well and you are happy."

"I have some news for you, Aunt Katherine, are you sitting down?"

"Well, no, I'm in a phone booth at a gas station."

Katie laughed, "Oh, yeah. Well, Eric and I are going to get married."

Katherine exclaimed, "Really? Congratulations, I'm happy for you, but isn't this sudden?" Then she paused, "You are not, uh—"

"No, I'm not pregnant, we are really careful about that. I went to the Haight Asbury Clinic and got on the pill a while back. I know it's sudden, but we love each other and know we want to be together always. We probably would have just lived together for a while longer, but Eric has that job up in Boonville to do his alternative service, and he will have a little cottage to live in. If we are married, I can live there, too."

"I'm really excited for both of you, Katie, but does that means you are going to quit school?"

"Yeah, for now. I'll go back later, but I don't have any way to pay for school right now anyway. Besides, I don't want to be away from Eric. The director of the school where Eric will be working says that they need some part-time help in the office and also cleaning the dorm, and so I hope to do that and make a little money."

Katherine interjected, "Tell me more about the wedding."

"We have decided to get married in Muir Woods among the redwoods three weeks from today, on August 22, and it will be very small. Our neighbor is a Universalist minister, so we have asked him to officiate. Stephen, Eric's brother, will be the best man. And Aunt Katherine, would you please be my maid of honor?"

Katherine was touched. "It would be my honor," she said softly as she wiped tears from her eyes and fumbled in her pockets for money to feed the pay phone for three more minutes of time with her precious niece.

CHAPTER 49

August 22, 1970

Katie and Eric drove up to the little Mill Valley café and Eric climbed out of the old van and opened the door for Katie. Her figure was complimented by her white halter-style sundress and her beautiful shiny, wavy brown hair that cascaded over her shoulders. When she flashed her beautiful smile at him, Eric's heart melted. The tall groom was dressed in dark green pants and a white, gauzy long-sleeved shirt that had a Nehru collar, his blond hair pulled back in a pony tail, and his green eyes sparkled at his bride.

He took her hand and they walked into the café. His brother Stephen was already sitting there waiting for them, and he stood up and gave them each a hug, "Wow, you both look great! Ready for the big day?"

Katie had only met Stephen once before, and she had liked him immediately. Since he had been discharged from the military the previous year, he had been working on his master's degree in Business at Stanford University. There was a strong resemblance between the brothers, though Stephen was five years older, and, although he no longer had a crew cut, was still very clean-cut. She said, "Thank you for standing up for us today."

"I wouldn't miss it for the world! Since I got here a little early,

I thought I'd have breakfast. This omelet is out of this world. What do you guys want?" Just then the waitress came to take their order, and Eric ordered coffee and Katie asked for tea. They were both too nervous to eat.

"When is everyone else supposed to show up?" Stephen asked

"My Aunt Katherine is coming down from Mendocino County and should be here any minute. Our friend Mark, who is going to perform the marriage, should be along shortly, too. We decided to keep it really small." Katie had once dreamed of a big wedding, but because of her dad's position on their relationship, she had decided not to even invite her cousin Laura. She knew it would put her in the middle of things and she didn't plan on letting her dad know about the wedding until later. She knew it would be hard for him, but he had left her no choice. She had called him every week to try to talk to him and each time he got angrier with her. He had told her she was living in sin, and the last time he told her not to call any more until she had come to her senses.

Mark arrived, met Stephen, and ordered coffee, and the four of them chatted while Stephen finished his breakfast. About twenty minutes later, Katherine rushed through the door, apologizing for being behind schedule. She had borrowed her friend's old red Toyota pickup and had some difficulties getting it started initially. "If it's okay, I'll just leave it parked here for now, but I'm probably going to need a jump when we come back."

"No worries," said Eric as he hugged her and made introductions.

Katherine gave Katie a big hug and a kiss and marveled, "You look absolutely beautiful, and Eric, you look so dashing!" She gave him a hug and he smiled warmly at this woman who would soon be his aunt.

The little group headed out to the parking lot. Stephen offered to drive Mark and Katherine in his dark blue Dodge Swinger, so the two cars headed out of Mill Valley and up the steep windy road to Muir Woods.

When they arrived, Eric reached in the back of the van, pulled out two florist boxes and handed them to Katie. She opened the first box and exclaimed, "I love it." She put the beautiful wreath of fragrant blue flowers in her hair. When she opened the second box and discovered a small bouquet of roses, blue flowers, and baby's breath, she squealed, "It's perfect!"

Katherine helped her bobby-pin on her wreath and then said, "Okay, you have something old, new, borrowed, blue?"

"I did borrow a shawl from my neighbor in case it got cold. Oh, I don't think I have anything old."

Katherine smiled as she pulled a beautifully hand-embroidered handkerchief from her leather shoulder bag. "This was your grandmother's. I want you to have it." Katie's eyes welled with tears as she thanked her aunt and gave her a hug.

Eric put his arm around Katie and they all walked together to the grove of redwoods that Katie and Eric had sat in the first time that they had visited they park together. They had since declared it to be "their grove," so it was fitting to have the ceremony there. As they stood under the giant tree, Katherine thought that she had never seen a more beautiful couple or one that was more in love.

Mark said a few words about Katie and Eric and what a pleasure it was knowing them both. Katherine read a poem she had written for the occasion, and then Stephen read a passage that the couple had chosen from the book *The Prophet*. Katie and Eric then exchanged the vows that they had so carefully written for the occasion. Katie had cried intermittently throughout the ceremony and had made good use of her handkerchief. When Eric asked her if she was okay, she said, "I'm fine, just tears of joy," which was partially true. She also was sad that her mother and father weren't there and that her dad wouldn't accept Eric. She had vowed that she wouldn't let that ruin her wedding day though.

Stephen went back to the car and brought back a big picnic basket that he had put together for the occasion. The others helped him put a tablecloth on a rugged redwood picnic table and unpack the lunch that included champagne, crackers, cheese, salami, fruit, and a small wedding cake. The five of them ate heartily and enjoyed each other's company. The coastal fog started blowing in and the group said their goodbyes and headed back to their cars. When the young couple reached their VW van, they realized that Stephen had decorated their van with white shoe polish declaring "Just Married," and tied cans on the back bumper. They laughed, and Eric said, "Stephen must have done this when he said he was going to the bathroom." They climbed in and rode off as the others waved and cheered them on.

As they were heading north on Highway 101, Katie said, "Could you do me a favor and take the next exit. I need to do something." Eric was puzzled, but did as she said.

She directed him to the Catholic cemetery, and as they drove into the driveway, Eric understood. She took him by the hand and led him up the side of the hill. They stopped at her mother's grave marker and Katie said, "This is Eric, Mom. I really wish you could have been at our wedding today. I hope you are happy for us; please pray that Dad will come around. I love all of you so much." She wiped her nose with her handkerchief. She looked at Eric and said, "I'd like to leave my bouquet here, is that okay?"

Eric said, "I think that's a nice idea." He took the bouquet from Katie and set it on the grave and said softly, "I promise I will always love your girl and always take really good care of her, Mrs. Pulli."

After standing there for a few minutes, Katie nodded and they headed down the grassy knoll to the car.

Eric and Katie would head to an inexpensive hotel in the Bodega Bay area. They would return to San Francisco to pack up Eric's apartment the next day. They were due at the Boonville School in a week, and they were ecstatic about starting their married life.

CHAPTER 50

November 15, 1970

"Hey, how are you doing? Thanks so much for calling me back, Laura. We have so much to catch up on," Katie said into the old tan wall phone that had recently been installed in their home.

"Yeah, it's great to hear your voice, cousin, it's been too long. What's it like to be a married lady?" Laura asked.

"Eric and I are so happy and it's so beautiful here on the ranch. Eric works long hours with the boys here, but he really likes it. I have a job helping in the kitchen for a few hours a day and also fill in for the secretary during her lunch break or if she needs a day off. It is an old ranch that they have converted into a residential school, so there are a lot of outbuildings. The school director said we could have any of the unused structures and fix them up to be a house for us. Believe it or not, we chose an old chicken house that hadn't been used in years. We have been fixing it up with a fresh coat of paint, some floor coverings, and lots of plants; it really turned out well. Tell me how you are doing."

"I am having such a great year, Katie. I joined a sorority and we have a lot of dances and mixers with the fraternities. I met this guy, Tim, in my chemistry class and he is so cool—he just met my parents last week and they really like him. Did you know that I changed my major to chemistry; I have decided to be a pharmacist."

"How cool—the guy, and the pharmacist part." Katie was thinking about how envious of her cousin she was. No so much of the sorority, parties, and promising career, but of the fact that her parents liked her boyfriend. How much easier it would be if Gino accepted Eric. "Have you heard anything about my dad and how he is doing?"

"I saw him at church last week when I was home and he looked okay," Laura fibbed. He had looked haggard and depressed, but telling Katie that would make her feel bad. "The family is planning to get together for Thanksgiving at our house this year. I wish you would come."

"I wish we could, but I think it would just cause a scene. My dad still won't talk to me, even though I have called multiple times and have sent a number of letters," Katie said, choking back tears. "I don't know if he ever will."

"I know it's tough, Katie, but I think that he will come around eventually. You know how hard-headed our Dads are, and the way the Italians tend to hold on to their vendettas, but I know how crazy your dad is about you and he is bound to come around."

"I hope so, but I do worry so much about his dangerous job. It scares me to think that something could happen to him while we are estranged. I do tell him that I love him in my letters, but I am not sure that he even reads them. If you do talk to him, you might leave the chicken house and cleaning job out of the conversation. I am not thinking he would be impressed."

Laura laughed, "Sure thing. What is most important, Katie, is that you are happy. Oh, sorry, I need to go, Jim just showed up and we are going for a bike ride."

"Okay, thanks for calling, and tell Jim that I look forward to meeting him," Katie said before she hung up the receiver.

She looked out the window and saw Eric driving his VW van up the dirt driveway, causing billows of gray dust to permeate the air. She went out to the porch and although he had only been gone a few hours, he ran up to her, swept her off her feet and gave her a romantic kiss. "I sure love you, Katie."

"I love you, too, honey. Did you get all of the stuff for our bookcase?"

"Yep, cinder blocks and boards. It will be great to get our books out of boxes and onto shelves. While I was in Ukiah at the hardware store, I ran into this guy named Tim that I knew from when I went to some of the People's Temple meetings. They have their home base in Redwood Valley, which is only about ten miles from here. They of course expanded to SF and other places, but quite a few of them still live there. Anyway, he invited us to come to a meeting next week. He's excited because Jim Jones is setting up a new place in Guyana, you know in South America. He said that if we were interested, we might be able to get in on the ground floor. Wouldn't that be exciting to live in South America for a while after we are done here? Anyway, let's check it out."

CHAPTER 51

October 3, 1971

Gino and his former SFPD partner Ron drove across the Golden Gate Bridge on the way to Candlestick Park. "Gino, this is the big year when the Giants will go to the World Series; I feel it in my bones. It's been almost ten years since we even got a crack at it, which I have never been able to understand, with players like Mays, McCovey, Marichal, Perry. We have a great record with ninety wins this year, and now all they need to do is beat Pittsburgh two more games and we'll have the National League pennant and be on our way to the Series," said Ron.

Gino answered, "Yeah, they won the game yesterday in eight-and-a-half innings and with two home runs. They just need to do it again. With all the rotten things that seem to be happening in the world, it would give us something to be happy about."

"Yeah, I know what you mean; I thank God every night that I have gotten home safely to my family, especially after stuff like at Atticus Prison last month. Imagine 1200 inmates gaining control of the facility and taking fifty officers and civilians hostage for four days—and ten of them ultimately dying. My wife wants me to transfer from the jail because she's worried that could happen to me," said Ron solemnly.

"Yeah, I know, but I don't know if being a street cop is any safer. You know, I really used to like my job, but it has gotten damn stressful dealing with everything from hippie kid protesters to the Zodiac killer and what that wacko might be up to next," said Gino. "I had thought on and off through the years about applying for the San Rafael Police Department even though they pay a lot less, because it would be safer. After that shootout at the Marin County Civic Center last year, which was only a few miles from my house, I realized no community is immune to violence."

"Yeah, Marin County is one of the most affluent places in the country, and that didn't keep those guys from shooting up the courthouse, taking the judge, prosecutor, and those poor women jurors hostage. Horrific, huh, for Judge Haley and three other people to be killed? They have proof that the SF State professor, Angela Davis, bought the guns, and they don't think she can get a fair trial in Marin, so they are moving the trial down to San Jose."

Ron continued, "And you know what else has really been bugging me? That the Supreme Court overturned Cassius Clay's conviction of draft evasion."

Gino answered sarcastically, "Don't you mean Muhammad Ali? What the hell is that Black Muslim stuff about anyway? Wasn't that what Malcolm X was?"

"Yeah, I think so. Anyway, now Clay can box again and get back his titles. What does that say to all the other yellow draft-dodgers?" Ron hesitated when he remembered that Gino's son-in-law was a conscientious objector. "Sorry, Gino, I didn't mean—"

"No need to apologize, I feel the same way about him and all the rest."

"Have you seen Katie?"

"No, I told her as long as she was with him, I didn't want to see her. She writes to me and sends me cards and sometimes phones, but she burned her bridges when she married that loser."

"I know all that broke your heart, Gino, but you are being bull-headed. I know you really miss her and life is unpredictable. Maybe you could come up with some type of compromise."

As they approached the parking lot, Gino snapped, "Drop it. I'm here to see a game. With any luck they will take care of business today and then just have one game in Pittsburgh to have the three out of five they need to take the National League pennant."

As they got out of the El Camino pickup, Ron slapped his friend on the back and said, "Sorry I brought it up." Gino nodded and pulled his red plaid blanket and picnic bag out of the back seat and they walked toward the stadium and the familiar smells of hot dogs, popcorn, and stale beer. The sky was blue with some wispy clouds thrown in, and it was warmer than usual. Maybe Gino wouldn't need that blanket after all.

After buying a couple of beers, they made their way down to their seats, squeezing past the bustling crowd. Smith's seats were vacant, so that was good news. Gino sat down and took a gulp of his cold, frothy beer. He was not much of a drinker, but he did like the taste of a cold beer on a warm day.

Gino was pleased when the Giants showed their stuff, with Willie Mays hitting a home run in the first inning. In the second, both teams scored one run, followed by a scoreless inning. At the bottom of the third inning, with the Giants ahead by one run, he looked over and saw that Bill Smith was making his way down the row of seats. A middle-aged platinum blonde in bright pink hot pants and black stiletto heels was hanging onto his arm as he squeezed through heading to his seat.

Luckily, Ron was sitting in the seat next to Bill rather than Gino. Ron whispered to Gino, "Ignore him. Let's just concentrate on the game." The Pirates were up to bat and their first baseman Bob Stephenson was at the plate. Unexpectedly, he cracked the ball over the fence, resulting in a tie game, followed by another Pirate run that put them in the lead. Gino was doing his best to keep his eyes on the game. He did notice that Smith had ordered several beers and Gino was sure that he had been nipping from his flask as well.

During the fifth inning, Pittsburgh got another run, and things weren't looking very hopeful for the Giants. The Pirates didn't score during the sixth inning. At the bottom of the sixth with two outs and two men on base, Willie Mays was up. The fans hooted and hollered, "Home run, Willie!" He would get them out of this fix. As the fast ball came over the base, Willie cracked the ball high and long into the gap in right field—it was sure to be at least a double! The runners were advancing when Roberto Clemente leaped into the air and snagged the fly. Now Pittsburgh was up and soon they had two on base, and—oh no, that Stephenson kid was up again. He hit a homer and brought in two others in the top of the seventh, resulting in a score of Pirates 8 to Giants 2.

Gino threw down his hat in frustration. "What the hell happened to the Giants who played such a good game yesterday?" he grumbled to his friend. What a letdown after having so much hope for the game. As the organist started playing, "Take Me Out to the Ballgame," signaling time for the seventh inning stretch, Bill Smith squeezed past Gino, stepping hard on his foot without apology, and headed toward the exit. Gino's face turned beet red with anger but he contained himself as he asked himself whether Smith had done that on purpose. Bill's date stayed in her seat looking bored as she filed her long, painted finger nails and used her compact mirror to put on matching hot pink lipstick.

The eighth inning was scoreless, and just as the Pirates were getting up for the top of the inning, Bill came staggering down the stairs with two beers in his hand, once again squeezing through the row past Gino. Just before he passed Gino, he tripped and spilled the large cup of beer down Gino's lap. Gino jumped up, grabbed him by the collar, pushed him into the aisle, and screamed, "You drunken son of a bitch, what the hell are you doing? Isn't it enough that you and that damn kid of yours have ruined my life and my kid's life? Now you have to step all over my feet and pour a beer down the front of me!"

Bill stood up. He was nearly a head taller than Gino, but did not have the strength or training that Gino had. He slurred, "You little wop cop, you think you are so tough. Bring it on." As he lifted his fists,

Ron intervened and pulled Gino away.

Just then Bob Stephenson was up to bat and made another home run for the Pirates. Three homers in a playoff game was a record. The Giants fans were disheartened. The fans near Gino and Bill were enthralled with these two middle-aged men about to fight. One fan said, "I'm getting Security."

Ron grabbed their stuff and pulled Gino toward the steps. "We gotta leave. Don't need bad publicity for the department."

As they were heading up the steps, Smith yelled after them, "Go to hell. You think you are so high and mighty. Your daughter is—" The next words were drowned out by the cheering of the crowd because the Giants pitcher had struck out the next Pittsburgh player.

Ron and Gino silently walked to Ron's small red Datsun pick-up, and then they turned on the radio. The final score was Pirates 9 to Giants 4; the Giants had scored two more runs in the ninth inning. They listened to the post-game banter on the radio as they made their way up Highway 101 to Gino's. As they climbed out of the car, Gino grabbed his plaid picnic bag and blanket and said goodbye to Ron. Ron grabbed his hand and shook it. "You know, I'm always here, partner, if you ever want to unload."

Gino nodded and said, "I know, thanks, Ron." As Ron drove away, Gino walked up his wooden porch steps, unlocked his door, and went into his empty house.

CHAPTER 52

October 9, 1971

Katie was drinking her tea and reading the newspaper when the phone rang and she answered it with a bright, "Good morning!"

"Hi, Katie, you sure sound chipper today!"

"Oh, hi, thanks for calling me back, Aunt Katherine. I wanted to wish you a happy birthday—how was it?"

Katherine replied, "I got together with some friends and we had a great time; my friend even made me a delicious chocolate cake. You know, I'm forty and I'm feeling kind of old, especially with such young people dying. It's still hard to believe that Jimi Hendrix, Janis Joplin, and Jim Morrison all died this past year and within nine months of each other. It is so eerie that they were all twenty-seven years old. They were all amazing musicians and it is such a loss to so many."

"Yeah, I know. Eric was really affected by their deaths. Because of his volunteer work with the Haight Clinic at Winterland he had actually met Jimi and Janis. I mean, not that they would probably have even remembered him, but they made an impression on him, and for them to all die of apparent drug overdoses is such a waste."

Katherine asked, "Is Eric still helping out at concerts?"

"Yeah, the founder of the Haight Ashbury Free Clinic has formed a group called Rock Medicine, and Eric goes to help out. They provide basic medical care for people at events like concerts and deal with things they can, and when necessary they call 9-1-1. Of course, he needs to work around his schedule here at the school but he enjoys it and gets to see free concerts. I go with him sometimes, but to tell you the truth, the scene is usually really wild, and most of the time I'd rather stay home," Katie replied.

"What else have you been up to?"

"Last night Eric and I went to an information meeting at the People's Temple commune in Redwood Valley. This guy that Eric knew from the city has been calling us and inviting us to the meetings ever since we moved here, and we finally went last night. Jim Jones spoke about their plans to move the commune to Guyana and—"

Katherine cut in with a gasp. "You are not thinking of joining up with them are you? It is more than a commune—it's a dangerous cult and I have known people who have had really bad experiences."

Katie replied, "No, we saw that for ourselves last night. I think this Jim Jones guy is really unstable. I know he did some good things for people early on, but he really seems like an egomaniac now."

"That's an understatement, Katie, Jones is an evil lunatic and nothing but trouble. I'm glad you saw that for yourself. If you are interested in joining a commune, there are a lot around that I can recommend, but steer clear from him and any of his members."

"No, I don't think we are interested in joining a commune anymore. I think what we'd really like to do after leaving here is to have some land, build our own home, and raise our own food. Neither of us is interested in going back to the hustle and bustle of the Bay Area," Katie replied.

"You know, there is land outside of Willits that is beautiful and wooded and going for really low prices. If you want, I can look into it for you. The parcels tend to be around forty acres, but some people have land partnerships and share the land with another family."

"That sounds great, Aunt Katherine. I'll tell Eric about it. Are you still teaching for the community college?"

"Yes, I'm teaching a poetry class and a writing class, and I am really enjoying it. I still have time to write, and my little house in the redwoods is the perfect place to be creative. On another note, have you seen your dad?"

"No, although I write and call him, he is not budging. I had hoped with time he would come around, but it's been over a year and I don't know if he ever will," Katie said as she choked back her tears.

"My heart goes out to you, Katie. He has always been so stubborn, and when he was a kid my mother always called him 'testa dura,' which means 'hard head.' I think it is good that you continue to write and call him, and eventually I think he'll come around. My relationship with your dad is another story. I don't think he will ever forgive me for being a bad influence on you."

"You haven't been a bad influence. In fact, I really don't know what I would have done without you. Your support means so much to us."

"I hope we can spend the holidays together again this year."

"Absolutely. Let's talk again in a few weeks about Thanksgiving; by then Eric will know his schedule. Love you, Aunt Katherine."

"Love you more, Katie. Goodbye."

As Katie was hanging up the phone, Eric walked through the door. He was pale and obviously upset. "Are you okay, babe? Did something happen at school? You look like you've seen a ghost."

As Eric collapsed into the kitchen chair, he said, "Stephen just called me at the school and told me some very bad news about our mother. She—she. . . was killed in a car accident last night," he stammered.

Katie said, "Oh, my God, I am so sorry." She reached out to take his hand. "What happened?"

"She was driving home from Sedona after an Arts Council meeting and she went off the road and over an embankment. She was alone and they think that she may have fallen asleep at the wheel. I just can't believe it, Katie," Eric said as he started to cry. "Although

I rarely saw her, or even talked to her, I loved her so much. She was never really cut out to be a mother, but she did love us unconditionally and I will miss her so much."

Katie responded, "I really wish that I would have gotten to know her better. She was such a creative, interesting person. I'm glad that I met her last year when she was here for that Meditation Retreat and we spent some time with her." She was also thinking that now that she and Eric were both motherless, when they had children they wouldn't know either of their grandmothers.

"I told them at school that I needed to take the next week off. I want to go to Sedona and so does Stephen; do you want to go with us?"

"Of course I do," Katie replied as she dried his tears with a cloth napkin and gave him a big hug.

CHAPTER 53

June 18, 1972

As the sun rose, Katie and Eric sat on their little porch at their tiny round wooden table made from an old cable spool. Eric had to work early today since it was Father's Day; he was taking another guy's shift so he could visit his dad. As Eric drank his strong coffee laden with cream and a little honey, he looked over at Katie, and once again remembered what a lucky guy he was. He noticed that a tear was running down her cheek. He took her hand and said, "You are feeling sad because of Father's Day, huh?"

She nodded and asked, "Are you sad, too, Eric? I mean it's been so long since you've spoken to your dad. Do you miss him?"

Eric shrugged. "Not really. I miss what I wish we had together, but I have come to accept that he is who he is and I am better off not having contact with him. It's different for you, Katie. I know you really miss your dad and I feel bad for both of you and feel kind of guilty about it. Gino is a good dad, and although he is strong-willed and won't back down, I think he has always had your best interests in mind."

"You are so sweet, Eric; he has really treated you badly, and yet you say something nice about him," Katie said as she grabbed the napkin from the table to wipe her tears.

"I can't hide that I have been pretty mad at him for shunning us, mostly because it has hurt you so much, but Gino and I have one thing in common, Katie. We both adore you." He came over to Katie and started rubbing her shoulders. "You know what I think you should do, honey? I think you should jump in the car, head down to San Rafael, and just go to your house and knock on the door. I know that you have written letters and called without success, but I have the feeling that if he saw you in person, he would not be able to resist."

Katie sat straight up in her chair and said, "Do you really think so? I guess the worst thing he could do is tell me to go away, and of course I'd be hurt, but I think you are right that it is worth a try."

An hour later, Katie was backing up their old orange VW van and heading down the driveway. She reached over and put in an 8-track cassette of Crosby, Stills, and Nash and sang along to "Teach Your Children Well." She prayed that everything would go well with her dad.

Two hours later, she pulled into the driveway that she knew so well. It held so much sentiment for her; she had learned to skate, play hopscotch, and even ride her bike there. She looked in her rearview mirror, brushing her waist-long hair and applying some lip gloss. She even pinched her cheeks to give her color as her mother had advised her to do.

She slowly walked up to the door, knocked twice, took a deep breath, and when Gino answered the door cried, "Happy Father's Day, Daddy. I couldn't bear another holiday without you and I want you know that I love you and I'm sorry that I hurt you. Please forgive me."

Gino grabbed Katie into his arms and gave her a long bear hug and whispered in her ear. "I love you, too, baby and have missed you so much and I am glad you came home." He looked out to the street and asked, "Is he here, too?"

Katie answered, "No, he's working, but he was the one who encouraged me to come see you today. He knows how miserable I have been without you and says that even if you don't want to ever see him, he would like you and me to have a relationship."

Gino said, "Are you happy, Katie?"

"I have been really happy, except for missing you, and now I hope you and I can rebuild our relationship."

He looked at her waist-length hair, long flowered skirt, sandals, and gauze top and smiled, "You look like you just stepped out of the Bible." They both laughed, and he said, "How about some French toast, and I still have some of that Earl Grey tea that you always liked."

Katie replied, "Sounds great!" as she put her arm around her dad and they walked into the kitchen.

CHAPTER 54

July 4, 1973

The clear water shimmered at the swimming hole near the Pulli family cabins at Russian River. Katie and Laura had been swimming and were now soaking in the rays of the sun as they had always enjoyed. Two of their little male cousins were bobbing around on inner tubes splashing and laughing.

As Laura was slathering more baby oil on her legs she said, "It's sure good to have you back at the family gatherings, everyone missed you so much. I'm glad that you and your dad made up. How's it going?"

"It's going pretty well. I come down to see my dad about once a month and the two of us either go to the movies, to a ballgame, or out to eat. He is still not ready to have Eric around, but he seems to have come to terms with our marriage and his inability to change that."

"How does Eric feel about that?" Laura asked.

"It bugs him that my dad still hasn't accepted him, but he's a good sport about it. He knows how much I missed my dad and he's glad that we aren't estranged anymore. I try to go down and see my dad on the weekends that he needs to work. I pray that someday he can accept Eric, but until then it seems like the best compromise that we can come up with."

"Tell me about your land. You really bought twenty acres?"

"Yeah, it's about thirty minutes from Willits and it's gorgeous, with a few old growth redwood trees, a couple of natural springs, and lots of wildlife. I'd love for you to see it. We got the land for a really great price and we paid for it with the inheritance money that we received from Eric's mother. We even had some left for some building materials, and we are building the whole place ourselves. Eric designed it with the help of a friend and we have been working hard on preparing the building site."

"Wow, that's amazing! Where are you living now?" Laura asked.

"Actually we are living in a teepee on the property." Noticing the surprised look on her cousin's face, she continued, "It's actually not that bad because we really have everything that we need. It's kind of fun actually," Katie hedged. "It's taking a while because you know Eric is really busy between working at the school and volunteering for Rock Medicine." What Katie was really thinking about was how frustrated she was that they weren't making more progress. "We are going to have a work party two weeks from now, and our neighbors are going to come and help us for a couple days, you know, kind of like the old barn-raising parties. We are hoping to get the house closed in at least, so that we can live in there this winter."

Laura said, "We are probably getting burned; we should flip over to our stomachs." As they did, she couldn't help but notice that Katie had quit shaving her legs and underarms. Laura guessed that was part of her new way of life along with becoming a vegetarian. "I heard that you are a phlebotomist now?"

"Yeah, the local community college had a program and I got a certificate. Right now I have an on-call job at the Willits Hospital, but I am hoping I can get on full-time somewhere soon," Katie replied. "Enough about me, tell me about your life, college graduate."

"Next week, I am leaving for a four-week trip to Europe with some of my friends. We have a Eurail train pass and we are going to go to Italy, Spain, and France, and I am going to see our relatives in Tuscany. However, my big news is that a few weeks ago I received notification that I have been accepted to the Pharmacy College at University of Chicago, and I am so excited because they have an exemplary program! Tim has been accepted there, too! My parents are going to announce it tonight after dinner and have a cake and stuff for me, but I wanted to let you know first."

"Congratulations, Laura, I am so happy for you. That trip sounds great and you will make a great pharmacist." Katie couldn't help being envious, but she didn't want to show it. "Hey, do you remember Rosemary, my old roommate from USF? She lives in Chicago, and I know that she would love to show you around. She has a great family and they would be sure to take you under their wings."

"Oh, yeah, I remember Rosemary, wasn't she the one whose brother got killed in Vietnam? That was so sad. How are they doing?"

"It's been tough, but they have their faith and they are a tight-knit family, so that helps. Rosemary went back home after her brother died and transferred to DePaul University, which is actually the largest Catholic University in the United States. She graduated magna cum laude with a degree in Business and will continue there for her MBA. I know you guys would really hit it off."

Just then they heard feet running on the sand, the sound of giggling, and were doused with buckets of cold water. The girls squealed, jumping up and chasing Laura's little brothers down the wooded path that led back to the cabins. "You little brats just wait till we get our hands on you!" Laura screamed.

CHAPTER 55

August 29, 1974

It was the top of the fourth inning and the Giants were playing the Pittsburgh Pirates for the third night, having lost the other two games. "I'm glad you could make it to the game with me tonight, Katie," Gino said to her as he poured her a cup of hot chocolate from his old red plaid thermos.

Katie, shivering from the foggy, windy evening, took the cup and smiled. "Thanks, Dad, that Ghirardelli chocolate smells so delicious. I'm glad I could come, too. It's been a long time since we've been to a game."

"Yeah. Hey, look at that, we are up already and at least we are ahead, one to nothing. It's been a bad year, haven't won too many games; hopefully you will bring them luck. As you can see, lots of empty seats, lots of fickle fans, I guess. Okay, one out, and Kingman, our first baseman, is up."

Katie said, "I don't recognize any of the players on the program. What happened to Mays, McCovey, Marichal, Perry—aren't any of them on the team anymore?" Just then Kingman hit a home run and the crowd went wild as the ball flew over the fence and he ran the bases, smiling at the crowd, acknowledging their exuberance.

Gino answered, "Yeah, I always forget that you don't have a

television and probably don't read the sports page. We have lost a lot of guys. They traded Willie Mays to the New York Mets for Charlie Williams and $50,000 in 1972, and that same year they traded Gaylord Perry to Cleveland. Marichal got traded to the Boston Red Sox about a year ago, and then McCovey got traded to the Padres just about six months ago. I guess the managers thought getting rid of some of the older guys and getting some younger talent would turn things around, but obviously it didn't work that way. None of the new guys have been what they were cracked up to be, and we lost all those great players in the mean time," Gino grumbled.

The fifth inning was under way and Katie put her hood over her woolen cap, and with her gloved hands adjusted the trusty red plaid blanket on her lap. She had forgotten how cold these August nights in Candlestick Park could be. Gino put his arm around his daughter and asked, "Katie, are you too cold? Should we leave?"

"No, I'll be Ok," She certainly didn't want to cut the evening short. She knew her dad had been really looking forward to the game and didn't want to spoil it for him.

"We still have Bobby Bonds, though, but he hasn't played the last couple of nights. You know, he and Willie Mays are good friends. Willie is the godfather to Bobby's oldest boy, Barry. Sometimes I go up to the press seats where the families sit, and it's really fun to see the players' kids rooting for their dads. Bonds has three young boys and they go crazy yelling, 'Go, Daddy, go!' when he is running the bases."

Katie smiled knowingly because she knew her dad had always been crazy about kids, and she could see him slipping up there to the press seats just to enjoy seeing the children's reactions. She hoped that she and Eric would make him a grandpa someday, but they had been trying for about a year and no luck yet.

The fifth inning was scoreless. As the Pittsburgh Pirates got up for the top of the sixth, Gino asked, "Did you hear about your father in-law and I having a confrontation a couple of years ago when we were playing the Pirates for the championship?"

Katie said, "No, what happened?"

"Well, you know how I have always felt about him, and thank God he hardly ever comes to the games. His seats are often empty or he gives them to clients or friends, but he showed up at that game. Sometimes I think he just keeps those seats to spite me. Anyway, he was drunk, stepped all over my feet and then spilled beer in my lap."

Picturing the scene, Katie bit her lip to keep from laughing. "Then what happened?"

"Well, I grabbed him and threw him in the aisle, and he yelled, 'Bring it on!' And if Ron hadn't restrained me, I think we would have actually fought. He got me out of here before Security showed up, which was good, because the press could have had a field day with a fifty-year-old cop getting in a fight at the ball park, and more importantly, I could have lost my job over it, but I was so damn mad that I couldn't see straight."

"Bill wrote off Eric a long time ago, and he doesn't have anything to do with us, which is just as well. We do keep in contact with Stephen and he keeps us informed of how their dad is doing. You can see how severe his drinking has gotten, and he has had a string of floozy girlfriends. Stephen says he is drunk every night and all weekend, but somehow functions in his high-paying investment job. Stephen has done very well for himself; he is also an investment broker, lives in a very nice apartment in the city. He has been the perfect son for his father: scholar, officer, successful businessman."

"He seems like a heck of a nice guy. Is he married?"

"No, he's not, he keeps his love life private, so we've never met anyone he's dated. He comes up to visit us a few times a year, and it is always fun to have him. He's a great guy and we all get along really well. He and Eric have a great relationship and have a lot of mutual respect for each other in spite of their very different lifestyles. He is so good-looking and my friends always want me to introduce them to him when they see his picture, but Eric discourages me from doing any matchmaking. There have been a couple of disasters when I have tried to fix friends up."

No score for either team in the sixth inning or seventh inning, so the Giants continued to enjoy their 2–0 lead. Would this last? At the top of the eighth, Pittsburgh finally scored, making it 2–1.

When the Giants didn't score in the bottom of the eighth, Gino said, "They have to hold on to this lead and not let those Pirates score again." However, at the top of the ninth, with one out and Sosa pitching for the Giants, Stargell, the Pirates' first baseman, cracked a fast ball over the fence. The score was now tied, and if the Giants scored a run, the game would be over.

Gino looked at Katie and said, "Honey, if they go into extra innings, I think we should just leave. I think you are getting too cold, we could listen to the rest on the radio." Katie didn't argue; it had been over one hundred degrees all week at home, and though initially this cool weather was a relief, she was now aching with the cold. As the ninth inning ended and the Giants hadn't scored, she and Gino packed up their things and headed to the exit. By the time they got to the car, Gino turned on the heat and the radio. It was the top of the tenth inning and no one had scored.

As they were heading through the fog over the Golden Gate Bridge, at the bottom of the eleventh inning, Thomasson hit a double, followed by another double by Matthews that brought Thomasson home. Both Katie and Gino cheered and were glad that they had a happy ending to their outing.

Within a few minutes, Katie was starting to nod off to sleep. Gino was glad that she had agreed to spend the night. It was much too late for her to drive home, and it was actually the first time she had spent the night since she moved out.

He started thinking about what a crazy year it had been. Vice President Agnew resigned because of the allegations of taking bribes and evading taxes, the whole Watergate fiasco had happened, and just a few weeks ago President Nixon had resigned. It was unbelievable that neither the president nor vice president who had been elected were in office now. Gerald Ford, who had been a congressman from

Michigan, was now the president. There was a lot of controversy over whether pardoning Nixon had been the right thing for Ford to do, but maybe in the long run Ford had saved the country a lot of trouble. Gino had been a Democrat most of his life but had been voting for the Republican candidates for the last two elections, because he thought the Democrats had gotten too liberal. Now, he wasn't sure where he stood.

His mind also flashed back to the Patty Hearst kidnapping six months previously, and he couldn't help feeling sorry for her family. Imagine having your daughter kidnapped at gunpoint, not having any idea where she is or even if she's alive. Although the family paid a huge ransom to the kidnappers, they didn't release her. Then two months later she helped rob a bank in San Francisco and declared allegiance to that Symbionese Liberation Army and bad-mouthed her family. In addition to that, she reportedly used a machine gun to rescue one of her captors. When their hideout was surrounded and six of the SLA members were killed, the family didn't know if she was one of the dead until they made the identifications and found that she wasn't there. Now they had no idea where she was and whether she was brainwashed or what else may have happened to her. He longed for the seemingly more simple days of his time with the SFPD, when they dealt with plenty of bad guys, but not stuff like this. Zodiac Killer, gangs, revolutionaries, what next?

As he drove into his garage, he looked over at his beautiful sleeping daughter. Although she didn't have the life he had dreamed of, she was safe and seemed very healthy and happy. It still really smarted that he didn't even get to see his own daughter get married, but he could now see how stubborn he had been about the whole thing, and it was all water under the bridge now anyway.

He remembered Tevye, the father in the movie *Fiddler on the Roof,* who had disapproved of his daughter's marriage because she had married a man who wasn't Jewish, but had eventually come to terms with it. Of course that was a movie, and Gino wasn't sure that he could do that, but he missed her so much.

CHAPTER 56

August 26, 1976

Gino had been sitting in his old brown leather chair watching the Giants lose to the Pirates in Pittsburgh 2–3; the Giants were having another bad year. Just as the game was ending, Katie opened the door and her Dad jumped up to come and give her a big hug. "You look so radiant, Katie. There is just something about you."

Katie laughed as she sat down on the familiar well-worn sofa and patted the seat next to her. "Well, there is something I need to tell you." As he sat down she took his hand and said, "You are going to be a grandfather."

Initially Gino was speechless, and then he hugged her tightly and blurted out, "I am going to be a Nonno! When? Where? Tell me all about it!"

She answered, "My due date is February 24, so I am about twelve weeks along. We decided to wait until I was through my first trimester before we told anyone. And you are the first one to know, Daddy."

Gino gave Katie a big hug and felt his eyes well up with tears thinking about his baby having a bambino or bambina, and he was touched that Katie had called him "Daddy," which she hadn't done in a long time. "How have you been feeling?" he asked tenderly.

"I had a lot of trouble with morning sickness and fatigue, but I am starting to feel a lot better now. I am going to a wonderful midwife, and she says that I'm doing great; the baby's heartbeat sounds really strong."

"A midwife? Why aren't you going to a doctor?" Gino asked abruptly.

"Don't worry, Dad, she is really well qualified, and has delivered hundreds of babies. We are considering having a home birth so—"

"You are kidding, aren't you? Why wouldn't you have the baby in the hospital where they are set up if something goes wrong? Is it because of the money, because if it is—"

"No, it's not that, it's just that a home birth is so much more natural instead of the baby being brought into the world in a sterile hospital environment. Anyway, we aren't sure what we are going to do yet. We still have six months to figure that out. There is something else that I want to talk to you about that is really important to me."

"What's that?" Gino asked politely, although he was bristling about the home birth idea.

She took a deep breath and said, "I want us all to be a united family for this baby, and I want you to be a vital part of his or her life, so I need you to accept Eric and treat him like the son-in-law that he is."

Gino answered quickly, "All right, I will."

Katie was pleasantly surprised by his quick agreement; she had practiced a long speech trying to convince her dad to do so. Her dad had crossed paths with Eric several times in the last few years, and although he had been civil, he had been distant.

"Okay, great, Dad." She decided to leave it at that.

Her dad went on. "Are you all ready for the baby?"

"We are hoping to get our house finished before the baby is born." What Katie didn't tell her Dad was how frustrated she was that they had lived in their house for three years and it was still far from being finished. They had run out of money after getting the basic structure built, and Eric had seemed to lose his enthusiasm for working on the house. After his alternative service at the school in Boonville, he had been hired as an employee. He worked long hours, and he often did volunteer work with Rock Medicine on the weekends.

Gino seemed to be reading her mind. "You know I still have a savings account that was always meant for you, Katie. What would you think of me giving you some of that money so you can get the materials and maybe hire some help so you could finish up the house."

"Oh, Dad, really? That would be so wonderful. I need to talk to Eric about it, but I'm sure he would appreciate it, too," Katie said as she gave her dad a big hug.

"Nonno Gino, it has a good ring to it, huh?" He beamed.

"It sure does. You will be a fantastic grandpa, no doubt about it," Katie answered lovingly.

CHAPTER 57

February 26, 1977

The cold rain pelted the parking lot as Gino pulled into the 76 Union Gas station. Eric had called him early in the morning to tell him that his grandson had been born in Fort Bragg at 1:00 a.m. and weighed in at seven pounds, twelve ounces. Both mother and baby were doing well, and he was welcome to come to the hospital on the coast to see them. Gino was ecstatic!

He had a tiny black and orange Giants outfit that he had bought at Candlestick all wrapped up, as well as some crocheted baby blankets and booties that his mother had made for Katie and he had saved all these years. He also had stopped and picked up a beautiful arrangement of yellow roses with baby's breath in a teddy bear vase that said, "It's a Boy."

He drove up to the self-serve pump and started pumping his own gas and then washing his windshield and checking the car's fluids. He was still getting used to this change; there was a full-serve island he could use instead, but it cost more. He looked over and noticed an older woman in a long blue coat and a plastic rain bonnet pumping her gas. He went over to help her, mumbling under his breath, "I never thought I would see the day when a lady would need to pump her own gas, it's just wrong—and puts some people out of jobs, too." After he assisted the grateful woman, he headed into the store to pay and pick up a cup of coffee. On the newsstand, he spotted the latest *Rolling Stone,* which pictured the Golden Gate Bridge with Jerry Garcia and some other rock and roll musicians standing in the foreground and the headline, "What a Long, Strange Trip It's Been: A discordant history of the San Francisco sound as told by the musicians who created it." He took it off the shelf and set it down next to his strong coffee that steamed from the Styrofoam cup. As the cashier rang up the magazine, he looked up at Gino and smiled, but he didn't say anything. Gino thought about trying to explain, but decided it wasn't the kid's business anyway.

As Gino drove on the windy road to the coast in the fog and rain, he thought about how tough that ride had been for Katie about this time the day before. Gino had been relieved that she had gone the hospital route, but had worried about the hour-long curvy ride she needed to endure to get there. She had decided on having the baby at the Fort Bragg hospital because they had a very modern birthing center where she could have a natural delivery and a midwife but would be in a hospital center. Anyway, his prayers had been answered and everything had gone well, so he could relax now.

After he parked his car in the hospital parking lot, he headed toward the front door of the hospital with full arms, while he tried to avoid the huge puddles. When the volunteer at the front desk asked who he was there to see he stammered, "Katie Pulli—I mean Katie Smith." She directed him to the Obstetric Wing and Katie's room number and smiled at him and his armful of flowers and packages. As he walked quickly down the hallway, he yelled back at her, "I'm here to meet my grandson!"

When Gino walked into the room, Katie was holding little Samuel, and Eric was leaning over the bed and talking tenderly to them. Gino felt awkward. Was he intruding? When they saw him, Eric said, "Hi there, want to meet your grandson?" Gino set down the things he brought and went over to them.

Gino went over to Katie and gave her a kiss on the head and was relieved to see that even though she looked very tired, her color was good and she was beaming. Katie looked up at her dad, who had tears in his eyes, and said to the baby, "Samuel, this is your Nonno." Eric motioned for Gino to sit in the chair and then gently picked up the swaddled bundle and placed him in his grandpa's arms. Little Samuel with his brown curly hair, cute turned-up nose, and deep blue eyes, seemed to be making eye contact with Gino, who fell in love with him instantly. "He is absolutely beautiful, congratulations to both of you. Did everything go okay with the birth?"

Eric answered, "Katie did absolutely great. She used all the breathing techniques we learned in Lamaze and had the baby totally naturally without any drugs. I was so proud of her."

Katie beamed and said to her husband, "You were such a great coach, Eric; I couldn't have done it without you being there through it all."

"Things sure have changed since you were born. Back then, the dads had to just sit in the waiting room for hours with the other fathers; the cigarette smoke was so thick, you could hardly see. And when you finally got to see your baby, it was just for a few minutes and then they whisked her away to the nursery. I'm glad you get to keep Samuel right here with you. Mothers used to have to stay in the hospital a week to ten days. When will you go home?"

"Tomorrow morning, as long as everything goes okay."

Gino answered, "Things sure have changed. When you were born, you and your mom stayed in the hospital for about ten days." When the baby started to get fussy, Gino kissed him on the top of the head and handed him to Katie. He walked back to the entrance to the room where he had left the gifts. "The flowers are for you, Katie, and the wrapped packages are for little Samuel. And Eric, there is something for you in that bag that I thought you might like."

Eric opened up the bag and pulled out the *Rolling Stone* magazine and smiled. He knew it was Gino's awkward attempt at making peace with the past. "Thanks, Mr. Pulli, that was thoughtful. I also want to thank you for helping us with the money to finish up our house. I hope you can come visit us soon."

Gino smiled and said, "You're welcome, and you don't need to be so formal; you can call me Gino. "

Just then, Katherine walked through the door, also bearing flowers. When she saw her brother there, she started to turn around and leave. "Come here, Sis," Gino said and gave her a big hug. "Can we bury the past?" Katherine nodded and then hand in hand they went over to Katie and the baby. As they all stood there, marveling at the miracle of this tiny baby, Gino declared, "New beginnings and new life for this family—Samuel's family."

CHAPTER 58

September 23, 1976

Gino had invited Eric to the Giants vs. Dodgers game, and although he was glad to have the company, he also felt awkward about what they might talk about. Katie was usually around to be the buffer, but today she and little Sam had stayed at Gino's house watching the game on TV while the guys went to the game. The baby was seven months old and quite a little crawler, and wouldn't have been happy to sit on their laps for three hours. The weather was always so unpredictable, but it had turned out to be a pleasant evening with mild wind and no fog.

The early '70s had not been good years for the Giants, and the attendance had been really down. It was a combination of not having a winning team and it didn't help that Candlestick Point was cold and windy most evenings throughout the summer months. The fall was often better, as was tonight. In January, owner Horace Stoneham had almost sold the Giants to a brewery in Toronto. Luckily, Bob Lurie and some other investors had intervened and bought the Giants so they could stay. Many Bay Area fans had decided to root for the Oakland Athletics; they had won the World Series three times in a row in the previous five years. However, Gino was not a fickle fan, and stood by his team no matter what their standings were.

When Eric told his brother that he was planning on going to the game with Gino, Stephen made arrangements with his dad to get his own tickets. His dad had told him that any time he wanted to go just to let him know, so Stephen had. Bill Smith had told him that in recent years it was even hard to get his clients to take the seats because of the weather and the Giants' performance. Gino believed that Bill held on to the tickets just to spite him.

When they arrived at the game, Stephen was already in his seat, and he had brought along a friend. "I'd like you to meet my friend Tony," he said as he stood to shake Gino's and Eric's hands. Tony was a handsome young man with a slight build, dark brown hair, and expressive brown eyes.

The Dodgers got up to bat and scored two runs in the first inning. The Giants were up to bat and Eric, who was perusing the program, said, "Which guy did they trade Bobby Bonds for?"

Gino said, "Bobby Murcer, and he'll be batting fourth today. They originally traded him to the Yankees straight across for Bonds. They both were making $100,000 yearly salaries while most of the players make more like $15,000. Anyway, now they are paying him $175,000 which is the highest Giants salary ever. In 1972, Murcer led the league in runs and total bases, and yesterday he stole home for a 3–1 victory. Now we have two outs and no one on base, which would be a good time for him to hit a home run." However, when Murcer was up he hit a long fly that was caught, and that was the end of the inning.

As the Giants headed out to the field, John Montefusco headed to the pitcher's mound. Stephen leaned over to Gino and said, "What do you know about this pitcher?"

"Well, he's been with the Giants since 1974, when he a hit a home run at his first at-bat as a major league player, which is darn amazing for a pitcher, and that same year he was named National League Rookie of the Year. Last year, on the Fourth of July, he told everyone that they were going to beat the Dodgers, and he went on to pitch a shut out, which was impressive, but so far today he's given up two runs in the first inning." The Dodgers went on to score two more runs in the second inning, and the Giants scored none.

The Giants held the Dodgers from scoring in the third inning, and as they were going into the bottom of the third inning, things were looking very bleak. With two outs and no one on base, Jack Clark, center fielder, went up to bat, cracking the ball over the fence, and changed the score to 4–1.

Gino asked, "Do you two fellows work together, is that how you know each other?"

The two men looked at each other and then Stephen said, "No, we know each other because we live in the same building."

Tony chimed in, "I'm a waiter at Caesar's Restaurant." This provided a lot of common ground for discussion. Tony had eaten at the Pulli Ristorante and had been very impressed, and Gino had high regard for Caesar's as well.

The rest of the game was uneventful, with no more runs scored in the last six innings. As the four men were walking out of Candlestick, Eric asked Stephen, "How is Dad doing?"

"His drinking has really progressed. Miraculously, he has kept his job all these years, but I think that is coming to an end, too. His firm is encouraging him to retire and he has been fighting it, but it looks like he will be retiring at the end of the year. If his father had not been the one who founded that firm and our dad didn't have so much stock in it, they would have canned him years ago. After his last DUI, the firm has actually hired a driver for him who lives in the old pool house and drives Dad wherever he needs to go. I have talked to him a number of times about going to a rehab, but he just scoffs at me when I bring it up. But if he doesn't quit soon, I can't see him living much longer. "

Eric nodded sadly, "Even though Dad and I have been estranged for all this time, I do care about him. If there is ever something you think I could do, let me know. I would like him to meet Samuel, but I really don't want to deal with him if he's been drinking. It's so sad that we have already lost our Mom, and now for him to be drinking himself to death; it really gets to me. . ."

Stephen put his arm on Eric's shoulder and said, "We always have each other, little brother. Let's get together soon. I miss my little nephew."

"Yeah, let's do that. You are a great brother, Stephen, thanks for always being there for me."

CHAPTER 59

November 19, 1978

Katie sat near the crackling woodstove, enjoying the sound of the rain coming down and writing in the baby book. Sam was now almost two years old and delighted them with his curiosity and enthusiasm for life. He had brown curly hair and big blue eyes. He was starting to talk a lot and was always on the go. His nonno affectionately called him "Papagalo," which was Italian for parrot, because he repeated everything he heard. He had just gone down for a nap, so it was time for her to put her feet up and write some of the cute things that he had said recently.

Katie really enjoyed being a wife and mother and had never been happier. It had made a big difference to have their little house completed. She now had indoor plumbing, insulation, drywall, hardwood floors, and rugs, which made all the difference. They were able to buy the materials, and they had their neighbor Ted do the finish work, thanks to Gino's financial help. Although electricity still was not an option where they lived, they had wood heat, a propane refrigerator and stove, along with a generator and solar energy that supplied them with lights and hot water. She was really excited that shortly after Sam was born, telephone lines had been established nearby and they had been able to pay to be connected. She no longer needed to drive a half hour into town to use the pay phone every time she needed to call someone.

Of course, Gino was really happy about this because he had worried about her being isolated with a baby and not having a way to get help if there was an emergency. He was still baffled that they would choose to live so primitively; after all, his parents had electricity eighty years previously. However, he had learned to hold his tongue and let them live their lives. He had come to appreciate Eric and what a loving husband and father he was.

Gino was now retired, and they saw each other often; he and Sam had developed a strong bond already, and whenever Sam saw him he would squeal and run to his arms, calling out, "NO NO!" Gino loved seeing his little grandson in their big vegetable garden and helping gather the eggs from the assortment of hens that ranged free during the day.

Katie noticed that it was almost time for Eric to get home from work, so she lit the gas stove burner and placed the metal coffee percolator on to brew, and then she stirred the pot of vegetable soup that was softly bubbling on the back burner. Although their house was about 1,000 square feet, the open floor plan made it look larger. They had decorated in a country style in earth tones, and many of her furnishings were treasures that she had discovered at the local thrift stores.

Eric worked at the school in twelve hour shifts, three days a week, which worked well for them. It saved on commute time and gas. Eric, exhausted when he came home, would eat and then go to sleep for a while. He would be off for the next four days, and they were looking forward to going to the Bay Area to visit her dad. They were going to leave Sam with her dad one of the evenings and go into San Francisco to have dinner with Eric's brother Stephen.

She heard Eric's little pick-up truck drive into the dirt driveway. She went to the door to greet him, and as he climbed out of his vehicle, she noticed that he looked pale and shaken. "What's the matter, Eric?"

He gave her a hug and kiss and said, "Let's get out of the cold."

As they sat down on the couch together, Eric said, "Something really bad happened yesterday at Jonestown in Guyana. I just heard about it on the radio. You remember that we read in the papers that Congressman Ryan and a group were going to Jonestown to investigate allegations of abuse and holding people against their will?"

"Yeah, I remember that he was taking some of the family members there with him as well."

"Well, they did visit Jonestown, and they conducted interviews, and they took the members who said they wanted to leave. They then all traveled to the airstrip where they were scheduled to get on two small planes. Before they could get on the planes, some of Jim Jones's men ambushed them and killed Ryan and four others, including the NBC cameraman. Nine others were injured."

Katie gasped, "Oh, my God, that is terrible!"

"I haven't told you the worst part yet. Sometime later, when law enforcement officials arrived at Jonestown, they discovered that the members of the commune were dead. Katie, they think as many as 900 people died there, including Jones. Some of the members were able to escape and they are reporting that Jim Jones somehow got all those people to drink poisoned kool-aid."

Katie started to sob, "Even the children?" Eric nodded. This was personal to the two of them. They had attended those meetings in Redwood Valley and knew a number of the families. It was likely that some of them had perished.

"I know it's so horrendous, and to think that I considered joining them and—" Eric started to cry and reached over to take Katie in his arms and held her close as they wept for those who had died in this terrible tragedy.

CHAPTER 60

July 3, 1980

The cold fog was swirling from all directions at Candlestick Park, and Katie and her dad were bundled up watching the Cincinnati Reds head out to the field after a scoreless top of the first inning. Candlestick Park continued to have the reputation of being the coldest major league ball park, and visiting teams often dreaded the games there. When Gino and Katie had left San Rafael only twenty miles away, it had been over ninety degrees. The hotter the weather was inland, the more fog and wind was sucked into the areas close to the coast. Though the temperature was about the same as other places in San Francisco, the gusty wind often made conditions unbearable for the fans and the players. It had earned the nicknames "North Pole" and "Windlestick" through the years.

The Giants were up and Billy North, the center fielder, struck out. He was followed by third baseman Joe Strain who got to first, and then Jack Clark got a single. Willie McCovey was up, and the cheering from the crowd was deafening. Gino said, "He is such a favorite with the fans. You know he played for the Giants from '59 to '73 and then got traded to the Padres; we finally got him back in '77. The talk is that he will be retiring this season. You know he hit his 521st home run against the Montreal Expos just a couple months ago; he has made major league home runs in four different decades. The Reds better be careful, a couple of years ago, he made two home runs against them in the same inning."

Willie hit a hard line drive through the gap and hit the fence. He ran to first, then second, while his teammates both scored. Of course the crowd went wild, and Gino commented, "That guy is a legend!" Larry Herndon, center fielder, was then up and struck out and the inning was over.

"Thanks, Dad, for always remembering the blanket," she said as she shivered and tucked the old red plaid blanket around herself and pulled down her light blue knitted cap over her ears. Her hair was just as thick and wavy as ever, but now shoulder length rather than long as she had worn it in the past.

Eric was taking care of Sam so Katie could go to the game with her father, and Gino was thrilled to have this one-on-one time with her. Gino was impressed with what a good dad Eric was, and appreciated his patient, kind yet firm manner with him. He played a lot with him and did a good job including him in conversations, doing projects, and reading to him. Gino had really misjudged Eric, and had thought of trying to apologize to him, but maybe just leaving things alone was the best thing. "No use stirring stuff up," he thought.

Bill Smith arrived and started down their row, and when he passed Gino, the men gave each other a cool nod. Katie stood up and gave her father-in-law a hug, which he stiffly accepted. Katie said, "I'm so glad you came to the game, how are you doing?"

"I'm all right. Since I'm retired now, I go to more games, nothing much else to do. I thought Stephen was going to come, too, but some big client of his from Japan is coming in tonight, so he has to tend to that," he said proudly. Two years previously, Bill had been forced to retire from his firm because of his drinking. He drank even heavier for several months and had landed in the hospital where the doctor told him he had cirrhosis of the liver and that if he continued to drink it would kill him within a year. Reluctantly, he had gone to an expensive thirty day rehab in the Napa Valley, and as far as they knew, had not had a drink since. When he was in rehab, Eric visited him and went to some of the family meetings. He was relieved that his dad had quit drinking, but disappointed that his abstinence from alcohol had not changed his personality. He was still arrogant and distant; Eric had come to grips with the fact that he probably would never change. It was sad that Sam would never know his grandmothers, so Katie and Eric really wanted Sam to know Bill. They made a point to get together with him at least every six months, meeting for lunch. Although Gino and Bill were civil to each other, there was still an undertone of animosity, so Katie and Eric didn't push having them get together outside of the games.

Neither team scored in the second inning. "Want some hot chocolate, honey?" Gino asked Katie. She nodded and from his old red plaid thermos, he filled her cup with steaming hot chocolate that filled the cold air with the familiar delicious aroma of Ghirardelli chocolate. He then looked over to Bill and offered some to him. He declined, but Katie was very pleased that her dad had done so. He had come a long way, and she was proud of him.

In the third inning, both the Reds and Giants brought in a run which made the score 3–1. Bill leaned over to Katie and said, "How's Samuel?"

"He is doing great. He loves his preschool and all of his teachers there, and he is off for the summer. We have been doing a lot of swimming in the pond on our property and love to have his little buddies over. He especially loves to build with his blocks and play with his trucks in the sand."

Gino was trying to be a good sport, but he did feel possessive about his grandson. He had been the only grandfather in the picture for his first two years, and now he had to share Sam, even though infrequently, with another man—this guy he disliked so much. He would take the high road for Sam's sake though.

The fourth and fifth innings were scoreless and the wind was blowing as hard as before. Katie and Gino ate their sandwiches as it started to get dark in the stadium, and Bill flagged down the vendor and got a hot dog and cup of coffee. The Giants scored in the sixth, making the score 4–1. Some fans started to leave the stadium, and Gino asked Katie if she'd like to go. "I'm all right for now, Dad, but if it gets any colder, I might."

At the top of the seventh, Cincinnati scored two runs, and that changed the scoreboard to 4-3. They all stood for the seventh inning stretch, singing "Take Me Out to the Ballgame."

Bill said, "I'm going to take off and try to avoid some of the traffic. It's going to be a mess between Fourth of July Traffic and the ball game traffic."

Katie responded, "It was good to see you and we'll call you soon and try to make a time to get together. Sam would really like to go to the zoo."

Bill said, "Yeah, give me a call. I don't know if I'm up for the zoo, but maybe we could have lunch at the Cliff House afterward." He walked past her and shook her hand. He nodded to Gino, being careful not to step on his feet, and walked to the aisle and up the stairs.

The score stayed the same through the eighth inning, and when the Reds hadn't scored at the top of the ninth, the Giants walked off the field with the win. The fans were elated with the victory and delighted to go home early and get out of the cold. Though they had won thirty-six and lost forty-one, it was early enough in the season that they could still make it to the World Series.

They joined the bustling crowd, made their way through the stadium and to the parking lot. Gino unlocked Katie's door and opened it as he always did for women, and then quickly ran around to his side of the car, jumped in, and turned on the ignition and heater. The parking lot was gridlocked, so Gino just let the car idle until some of the traffic started moving.

Katie said, "I hope Sam fell asleep without too much trouble tonight for Eric. He has been so excited about going to the Pulli reunion tomorrow at Russian River and seeing all of his cousins. What time do you think we'll leave in the morning? I told Eric that I would let him know so he and Sam can get there about the same time."

Gino answered, "Oh, I think if we leave by 11:00 or so that should be fine. I'm glad you are spending the night and that we can all go together."

"Dad, Eric and I have some news for you. I was going to wait, but I just can't. We are going to have another baby."

Gino reached over and gave her a big hug and exclaimed, "Another grandbaby! How wonderful! When?"

"Beginning of February, so I am about two months along. Sam and the baby will be almost five years apart. I would have liked to have them closer together, but it didn't work out that way."

"Sam will be a good big brother; does he know?"

"Not yet, we are going to wait another month, when I have hit the end of the first trimester. We figure when Sam knows, the whole town will, so I want to make sure."

Gino asked, "How have you been feeling?"

"I'm still having a lot of trouble with morning sickness, but it usually passes by 10:00 or so."

"Nothing has made me happier than being Nonno, and now another bambino or bambina! Well, we better get you home and to bed, little Mama," Gino crowed as he squeezed her hand and put his car in gear to head toward home.

CHAPTER 61

February 4, 1981

Gino was delighted that he had been asked to come to Katie and Eric's home to take care of Sam during the labor and delivery. They had pre-arranged for him to be on call and to head out when Katie went into labor, and that a neighbor would take care of Sam until Gino arrived. He got the call around noon, and was at their neighbor's house by about 3:00. When he arrived Sam was outside playing in the snow with his little friends, making snowmen and sledding down the driveway. Gino was not really dressed for the snow, but couldn't resist throwing a few snowballs. It had snowed the night before and had been a novelty for all the little boys; it only snowed a few times a year and usually lasted only a couple of days.

Gino and Sam spent the evening eating pizza, playing with blocks, and reading a pile of storybooks, and then fell asleep together on Sam's bed. Periodically, Gino needed to remember to feed the wood-burning stove with firewood since it was their only source of heat. Around midnight, Eric called and reported cheerfully, "Nonno, we got another boy, and he weighs eight pounds, one ounce, and is twenty-one inches, and we named him Maxwell. He and Katie are doing great!"

"Congratulations, Eric; I am so glad all went well." It was such a relief that his precious daughter was all right, it was hard to think of her going through the ordeal of childbirth. And of course, it was always a blessing when a baby arrived safely. He said a little silent prayer of thanksgiving.

"Gino, would you be able to bring Sam over tomorrow afternoon? We really want him to meet little Maxwell. I mean, unless that is too much or it's snowing or something."

"I'd be happy to bring him over. The weather shouldn't be a problem; it seems to have cleared up," Gino answered.

Eric added, "Thanks so much. Give Sam a big hug for us and tell him we miss him and can't wait to see him."

"I'll do that. I can't wait to tell him about the baby. He is going to be so excited about having a little brother. Thanks for calling, Eric. See you tomorrow in the early afternoon.

"Okay, see you then, Gino."

CHAPTER 62

February 5, 1981

As Gino sat at the table having his third cup of coffee, Sam stumbled out of his room with sleepy eyes, and his Nonno announced, "You have a brother!" Sam squealed, twirled around, jumped up and down, and yelled, "It's a boy, boy, boy! Did they name him Max?" When Gino nodded, Sam continued, "I have a brother and his name is Max. I am so lucky!" Sam was so stoked that it was a boy, and that they had named him Max, short for Maxwell, as he had begged them to do. Sam's favorite book was *Where the Wild Things Are* and Max was the main character. When Katie and Eric were deciding on names, that was one of the possibilities, and Sam thought it would be the best name ever.

After they had eaten breakfast and dressed, Gino pulled out the present he had brought for Sam and let him open it. It was a Giants jacket and hat with a note that said, "Congratulations, Big Brother. I think you are big enough to go to ball games now." Sam hugged his Nonno and immediately put the jacket on, and then donned his Giants cap on his mass of brown curls. His big blue eyes sparkled with delight.

Gino had another package as well and gave it to Sam to give to his new brother. When Sam asked what it was he answered, "It's a smaller version of the jacket and cap I got you. You know he is going to want to be just like you!"

Sam grinned from ear to ear. His mom and dad had prepared him for the new baby, telling him that some things might be hard like the baby crying a lot or needing a lot of attention, but that all Sam's feelings were very important, and that he could tell them if he felt jealous.

Gino and Sam were packed up in the car to go to Fort Bragg and meet the new arrival. Gino scraped off the ice from his windshield, warming up the car and getting Sam settled. They headed down the windy road into Willits, and then the curvy road to Fort Bragg. Sam got sick on the way, and they stopped along the side of the road, near the old red school house. They took a walk around the beautiful redwood-studded park, getting some fresh air and exercise. They continued on their journey and arrived at the hospital around noon.

As they came into the room, Eric jumped out of his chair and quickly headed over to Sam, who jumped into his arms and gave him a big hug. "Buddy, are you ready to meet your little brother?"

Katie said gently, "Sam, come on over; I have missed you."

Eric carried him over to his mother who was holding a sleeping, swaddled baby with a little blond fuzz on his head. "Can I hug him?" Sam asked.

"Yes, come sit up here next to me and we will let you hug him. We know you can be very gentle." Sam kissed the baby on the top of his head and said, "Hi, little guy. I'm your brother Sam."

The parents of the two little boys relished the moment as did their grandfather. Gino stood at the doorway of the hospital room, not wanting to intrude on this little family's time together.

Eric said, "Nonno, what are you standing over there for? Come over here and meet your grandson."

Gino walked across the room and stood in awe of the beautiful new baby wrapped in a blue receiving blanket like a burrito. He gave Katie a big hug and kiss and shook Eric's hand.

"Would you like to hold him?" Katie asked.

Gino said, "I would love to." He sat down and Eric carried Max over to him.

As his grandfather received him into his arms, little Max awoke and looked right into his grandfather's eyes. Gino soaked in the miracle of new life as he looked into the baby's beautiful blue eyes. Sam came to snuggle in next to him. Gino was overcome with the emotion of having his two grandsons with him, and his voice cracked as he asked, "I forgot to ask you what Maxwell's middle name is."

Eric answered, "It's Gino." At that, tears streamed down the proud grandfather's face.

CHAPTER 63

June 30, 1983

"Dad, I really appreciate you taking care of the boys while I go to lunch with Rosemary. I have been really looking forward to it," Katie said, as she fixed sandwiches for Sam and Max.

"My pleasure, Katie; it's not every day that you get to see your old roommate, and I know it's hard to have an adult conversation with two active boys. I look forward to seeing her, too," he said, as he smiled at his two grandsons noisily playing in his living room with little Hot Wheel cars. "How long has it been since you've seen each other?"

"The last time we saw each other was about six years ago; she was here on business and we visited briefly. Her sister moved to Oakland a couple of years ago, and it looks like they are staying put, so I think we will see each other more often. She is now an executive with a major insurance company that insures huge building projects, so she travels a lot."

"Sounds exciting. Is she still single?"

"Yeah, she says she is married to her work, enjoys her freedom, and has a close relationship with all of her nieces and nephews. She seems very content." Their conversation was interrupted by the doorbell ringing. Sam ran to the door yelling, "I'll get it."

Rosemary looked stunning in a well-tailored navy blue designer suit and stiletto heels, her blonde hair swept into a sleek bun, and her makeup very artfully applied. She greeted the boys warmly and then spotted Katie and rushed over and gave her a heartfelt hug and kiss. Gino came out of the kitchen and greeted her with a big hug as well.

Katie was wearing jeans, a flowered blouse, and Birkenstock sandals, and said, "You sure look nice, Rosemary. I didn't bring anything dressy to wear; I thought we'd be just going somewhere casual."

"You look fine, Katie, it turned out that I had to go to a meeting on my way here today, and I didn't have time to change."

Rosemary noticed that the Giants game was playing on the old RCA console television, though the sound was turned all the way down. "I see you are still a Giants fan. In April, I saw them play the Cubs at Wrigley Field and I thought of you."

"Yeah, well it's been a long dry spell for us; I know you Cubs fans can understand that. This season was looking good, but we seem to have gone downhill. We are playing at Cincinnati today and it's the second inning, and the Reds are beating us 8–1. "

"Well, if it's any consolation, the Giants won the game I saw in Chicago. I bet you were excited about the 49ers winning the Super Bowl."

"Yeah, they did last year, so I am glad that Candlestick Park has brought them luck. I had hoped some of that would rub off on the Giants," Gino replied.

After playing with the boys for a while, the women got up to leave. Gino called after them, "Rosemary, I hope you can come back and stay for dinner. I am going to make spaghetti and meatballs, it's the boy's favorite."

"Thanks so much, I sure wish I could; I remember what a great cook you are, but my sister is expecting me for dinner. Can I take a rain check on that?"

"You bet," Gino answered as the boys hugged their mother and Rosemary goodbye, and they walked to the new black Lincoln

Continental that Rosemary's company had provided for her. As they drove away and Katie looked out the tinted windows, she was struck by how differently their lives had turned out.

Rosemary mused, "So many things have happened in the world since we saw each other last. My family is so excited about having a Polish pope, and our relatives in Poland are really hopeful regarding the Solidarity movement that Lech Walesa has inspired."

Katie said, "Yeah, that was really scary that Pope John Paul II was shot; it was miraculous that he survived those four gunshots. I heard that he even went to the prison and forgave the guy who did it."

"Yeah, that's true. And that was just a couple of months after Hinckley tried to assassinate President Reagan," Rosemary continued.

Katie added, "Yeah, it's been a crazy few years. We are still in shock that John Lennon was shot down the way he was, just going into his place."

"Yeah, remember when the Beatles were breaking up and we would play the two albums we had over and over?"

"Yeah, *Abbey Road* and *Hey, Jude*. And there was that rumor that Paul McCartney was dead and that there was some clue on *Sgt. Pepper's Lonely Hearts Club Band* if you played it backward, and some of the girls in the dorm were sobbing about it?" They had so many memories from the year they had lived in the dorm together.

They had reached the little French café where they were going to have lunch. They continued to reminisce as they sat on the ivy-draped patio, sipping white wine and eating their quiche and salad, when Rosemary said, "Katie, are you okay?"

"What do you mean?"

"There seems to be some deep sadness in you that I have never seen before. Are things okay with you and Eric?"

Katie hesitated and then said, "I can't keep anything from you, can I? You are right. I have been depressed lately. I know I have a lot to be grateful for, but I am really tired of living the way we do. It was exciting when we first moved there, and it was tolerable when we had one child, but now that we have two, it's a lot of work. Eric is gone so much of the time, working at the Boy's Ranch, and now he has also gone back to school to get his RN, and on top of it, he still volunteers for Rock Medicine at concerts. When he is home, he is tired, and though he is a good dad, he doesn't have the energy to finish projects around the house or for us to do anything as a couple. It's a lot of work with a woodstove and a generator. I had hoped that we might be able to hook into electricity by now, but the lines are still pretty far away, and it would cost a lot."

"Have you talked to Eric about it?" Rosemary asked.

"Yeah, I have told him that I want us to move into town. I spend so much time driving back and forth to take Sam to school and activities, and I'm just really tired of it. He says that he knows that it is a really hard time now because he is going to school, but that he will be done in less than two years. Then he will be home more, have a better paying job, and do the finish work on the house. He also says that he won't volunteer for Rock Medicine anymore, but he has said that before, and then someone calls saying that they are desperate for help and off he goes. He doesn't want to move to town, he feels like it would be giving up after all we have put into it. I have asked him to go to counseling with me, but he doesn't want to. He says that we are just going through a tough patch and things will get better once he's done with school," explained Katie.

Rosemary nodded sympathetically, and Katie started to cry. "To be really honest, I compare myself to you and feel like such a failure. We started out at the same place at eighteen, and I envy your success. You have a master's degree, an impressive career, and you get to travel all over the world. I have one year of college, no career, and don't even have electricity—how pathetic."

"Guess who I have been envying?" Rosemary said with a smile. "You, because you have those beautiful, bright little boys, a husband who adores you, get to live in one of the most beautiful places in the world, and have good weather. I know my life looks glamorous, but

I am seeing that I have forfeited a lot to pursue my career and I am starting to regret it. I used to think that I really didn't care if I got married or had children, but now I wish I did. You know, Katie, it isn't too late to pursue a career, if that is what you want."

"Yeah, I know, and I plan to. Eric and I have the agreement that once he finishes his degree, that I will go back to school. I would like to get a degree in social work."

"I can totally see you doing that, Katie; you have always been so good with people. I'm so glad we were able to be real with each other. None of us have it all, but like they say, the grass always looks greener on the other side of the fence," Rosemary added.

"That's right, and Rosemary, you are only 33, and it's not too late for you to get married and have children, if that's what you want, or even adopt a child on your own if you want to skip the marriage part."

Rosemary answered, "Yeah, that might happen, but right now I'm content with enjoying my nieces and nephews."

Katie glanced at her watch. "Oh, its past the time I said we'd be back, and those boys are probably really wearing their Nonno out! Thanks, Rosemary, for being such a good friend and such a safe person for me to talk to."

"Anytime, Katie," Rosemary said as she squeezed her hand. "I'll never forget how you were always there for me, especially when Stan died." She motioned the waitress for the bill and when Katie reached for her purse, Rosemary grabbed her arm and said firmly, "It's my treat today."

"Thanks so much, Rosemary," a relieved Katie responded. She hadn't realized how expensive this restaurant would be, and wasn't sure if she had enough money to cover her share. She was so grateful for having such generous people in her life, but it bothered her that she always had to worry about having enough money.

CHAPTER 64

November 12, 1984

Katie stood out in her front yard wielding an axe, chopping some kindling, and she was furious. Eric wouldn't be back until the following morning, and he hadn't made sure she had everything she needed to get a fire going, as he had agreed he would take care of before leaving. She was becoming more and more discontented with Eric being gone so much of the time, feeling isolated, wanting to do more with her life. She brushed her hair from her face and glanced over to check on Max, who was playing with his Tonka truck in the sandbox, and saw that Sam was still climbing a nearby tree. She loved her children immensely and had enjoyed being a wife and mother, but as she had gotten older she also craved a social life, a career, and an easier life.

She looked up to see Ted driving up her driveway in his big white Chevy truck. He lived a couple of parcels from them. He was a contractor and had been the one who had done a lot of the finish work on their house when Gino had given them money. They had developed a friendship then, and ever since he had stopped by periodically to say hello. He parked his truck, climbed out, and said, "You shouldn't be doing that, let me help. Why don't you and the kids go inside. The sun is going down and it's starting to get cold."

She answered, "Eric usually keeps the wood supply up, but I guess he didn't notice that we were getting low, and he's working tonight." She didn't say that she was really angry at Eric for leaving her once again without wood. He was so overextended with school and work and always so forgetful and tired when he was home. She did almost all of the other chores, including taking care of the boys, the chickens, the garden, and keeping the woodstove going, but splitting wood was really a push for her. She felt like a single parent most of the time, and resented that Eric still insisted on living this remote, alternative lifestyle even though he was rarely there. Sometimes she felt like she was living in the 1800s, and she was tired of it.

Ted took the axe from her hand, and as their hands brushed, she could feel electricity between them. He was medium height with a stocky build, had dark, curly hair, a beard, soulful brown eyes, and a New England accent that Katie found very attractive. He had moved onto his property with his partner Stella, but after an eight-year relationship she had left and gone back to Vermont. Katie had met her a couple of times at gatherings, but she always seemed very distant.

Katie took the children inside and made a big pot of minestrone soup, just the way her father had taught her. She told Sam to go out and invite Ted for dinner. He accepted, and the four of them chatted as they ate their minestrone soup and homemade bread. Katie sensed that he was attracted to her, too, and was flattered, but also felt guilty about it. He got down on the floor and wrestled with the boys as she cleaned up the kitchen. And she reassured herself that they were just friends and that she would not let it go any further than that.

CHAPTER 65

October 6, 1985

It was a beautiful fall day in Candlestick Park, sunny, with a breeze coming off the Bay. Gino was proud to have Sam sitting next to him at the last game of the season. He sure wished his team was doing better though. They had won sixty-two games and lost ninety-nine, which not only made them the lowest ranking team, but it was also the worst season in franchise history for the Giants. The stadium was less than half full; no fickle fans there today.

It was the bottom of the fifth inning and the Atlanta Braves were winning 6–0. The Giants won the last two games against the Braves, which wasn't saying much because the Braves were only one rung above them in the standings.

Bill Smith was in his seat next to his son Stephen, and Sam was sitting between Gino and his uncle. It was nice to see Sam interact with Stephen. He was a really nice guy, and Gino could tell how fond he was of his nephew. Gino noticed that Stephen had lost a lot of weight and was pale, and he wondered if he had been sick. He would ask Katie about it later.

"Want some ice cream, Sam?"

"Sure, thanks, Nonno," he answered, and his grandfather flagged down the ice cream vendor. Sam was now nine years old and tall for his age. He was a handsome boy with his mother's gorgeous blue eyes and brown curly hair. Sam's hair was longer than Gino would like to see, but he had learned to keep his opinions to himself. Sam was very bright and had a great sense of humor, which made him a delight to have around.

It was the bottom of the fifth, the Giants were up to bat, and they got three outs in quick succession. Gino loved to spend time with his grandsons and took Sam to weekend games whenever possible. Katie was at his house with four-year-old Max, and they would return home that evening. Next summer Max would be five, and Gino would start taking him to games, too.

It was time for the Braves to get up to bat. They also had a scoreless inning. At least they weren't getting any more runs. Stephen was reminiscing with Sam about when he and Eric were Sam's age and took turns going to the games with their dad. They had been in these very seats during the famous World Series against the Yankees. He and Eric had flipped a coin to see who would get to go to the last game of the series, and Eric had won.

"Nonno, were you at that game, too?"

"Yes, I was here and so was your mother. She wasn't much older than you are now."

At the bottom of the sixth, with the score 6–0, the stands had started clearing out and the fog was starting to come in when the Giants were up to bat. They miraculously scored four runs. With two men on base and two outs, Treviño stood at home plate, ready to swing. The discouraged crowd had become rejuvenated and stood cheering for this catcher who was known to be a strong hitter. Treviño came through, slugging the ball over the fence and bringing in three runs. The next batter struck out, but what an inning! They were now ahead 7–6.

Sam said with delight, "Those guys who already left are sure going to be sorry they missed this. We aren't fickle fans, right, Grandpa?"

Bill looked over at Sam and cracked a smile; he wanted to interact more with Sam, but he always felt awkward. His own dad had been stern and unavailable, and Bill felt sad that he had repeated the same pattern. He had never been the type to fuss over kids or be affectionate; it really wasn't him. He was glad that Stephen had suggested going to the game today. He hadn't seen him for a few weeks and was surprised at his weight loss. Bill had asked him if he was okay, and he said that he was having some lab work done. Bill was worried; he had never seen Stephen look this way.

During the top of the eighth, Atlanta came back, scoring two runs and changing the score to 8–7. The Giants fans, who had a temporary morale boost from the previous inning, became deflated. They reminded each other that their team still had two more chances to come up with a couple of runs. However, no more runs were scored, and the Giants lost the hundredth game of the season.

As they headed out of the stadium, Stephen joked with Sam and roughed up his hair. Sam looked up at his uncle adoringly and hoped that he would see him again soon. As they exited the park, Sam gave Stephen a hug and then hesitated as he wondered whether to give his Grandpa Bill a hug or shake his hand. He decided to give him a hug, and Bill was able to respond more warmly than he had in the past.

"Thanks for taking me to the game, Nonno. Too bad they didn't win more games, but win or lose; they are still our team, right?"

"Right, Sam, and one of these days we're going to get to the World Series again," Gino said as they headed to his car.

CHAPTER 66

December 15, 1986

Katie was driving back from town in her little yellow Datsun station wagon with the boys chatting about their day in the back seat. She had picked them up from school, gone grocery shopping, and now it was getting dark and snowing really hard. As she drove up the snowy incline of their road and was about to turn the corner to go up her driveway, she lost control of the car, and it slid into a ditch. Although no one was hurt, the boys were scared and crying, and Katie wasn't sure what to do. Eric was working and wouldn't even know they hadn't made it home. It was snowing hard. They were about a mile from home, and they weren't dressed for walking in the snow. It was getting dark, and the temperature was dropping fast. She wasn't even sure she could get the doors open. There were only a few neighbors who lived on the road past their driveway. She prayed one of them would come along and help.

A few minutes later, Ted pulled up from behind in his four-wheel-drive truck. He helped get the wedged back door open and get the boys out, and then said, "We won't worry about your car tonight. You and the boys hop in the truck and I'll take you home." He helped her unload her groceries into his truck, and Katie and the boys gratefully scrunched into the warm truck cab. For the previous two years, Ted had stopped by often to check on Katie and the boys. He frequently helped out with little odd jobs around the house or property, and would always spend time playing with the boys.

When they arrived back at the house, they shook the snow from their clothes, and headed into the living room. While Katie and the boys went to their rooms to change their clothes, he started the fire. When they came out, he insisted that Katie and the boys just relax and get warm because he could tell that they had been badly shaken by the mishap. He then went into the kitchen, put the kettle on the stove for tea, and yelled, "I am going to make supper tonight, but what I make best is breakfast; does that sound okay?"

Katie, Sam and Max chimed in that breakfast for supper sounded great. Ted went to work making pancakes and eggs, and found some rum and made hot buttered rum for Katie and himself and hot chocolate for the boys. They sat around the wood stove eating pancakes, and he told them stories of growing up in Vermont. Max fell asleep on the couch and Katie carried him to bed. Sam could hardly keep his eyes open and sleepily made his way to his bed as well.

They hadn't looked outside for a couple of hours, and didn't know how deep the snow had gotten. Ted and Katie poked their heads out of the door to see that it had snowed a lot, and the wind was blowing hard. Katie said, "You can't drive home—there's a blizzard out there."

Katie gathered blankets and a pillow for Ted to sleep on the couch. When she returned, he stood up, looked into her eyes and said, "Do you have any idea how crazy I have been about you for years?" He took her into his arms, and kissed her passionately. All of the pent-up passion that they had felt for each other through the years was expressed that night, and it was the beginning of their affair.

CHAPTER 67

October 2, 1987

Katie had been doing a lot of soul-searching and had decided to tell Eric that she wanted a separation. She had been saving money through the years that Gino had given her for Christmas and her birthday, and she had put a deposit down on an apartment in town the previous day.

She felt very guilty about her continued affair with Ted. There were times that she told him that it had to end, and then she would see him again, and she would weaken. She knew it was especially crass that she was doing this in the home she shared with Eric, with her sons in the next room, and yet she continued. What happened to the girl who was so moral and principled? She rationalized her actions by telling herself that Eric was always tired and inattentive, but she knew it was wrong and that she needed to come clean. Ted wanted her to leave Eric and move in with him, but she wasn't interested in doing that. She realized that Ted was much more serious about her than she was about him. What a mess she had created.

Eric had been sensing that something was wrong, but when he would ask her, she had been vague. Eric had this weekend off and she figured it would be a good time to talk to him. She arranged for the boys to go to some friends for an overnight stay.

She poured herself a glass of Chardonnay and offered Eric a bottle of beer. She told Eric that she wanted a separation and that she had put a deposit on a small apartment in town and planned to move there. He was dumbfounded and responded with a simple, "Why?"

"I have been unhappy for a long time and I need to try something different."

"Well, that is damn flippant," Eric answered angrily. "Are you saying you don't love me anymore?"

Katie answered, "I don't know anymore."

"Is there someone else?" he asked suspiciously. When she turned her head away, he said, "You don't even need to answer that, it's written all over you. Who is it?"

"It doesn't matter who it is. I have been unhappy for a long time, and I think it was a symptom of that unhappiness, not the reason I want to leave."

Eric grabbed Katie's arm and made her look at him, "What a crock of shit—did you read that in a book or something? Who is it?" Katie didn't answer, and Eric thought for a moment and then snapped, "It's Ted isn't it? The boys are always talking about how he comes around and fixes things for you—guess that's not the only thing he's doing, huh? That son of a bitch! How long has this been going on?"

Katie had known that Eric was going to take the news hard, but she was surprised by this display of a temper that she hadn't seen before. "Eric, it isn't Ted' fault; it just happened."

"Those things don't just happen. I asked you how long this has been going on."

"About ten months."

Eric exploded and jumped up from his chair. "Ten months! Where?" Eric looked at Katie and then yelled angrily, "Here, huh? Under my roof, with our sons here?"

"Yes, but we were always very careful for the boys not to witness anything."

Eric smacked the butcher block counter. "So that's supposed

to make me feel better? So you are just going to walk out on me and the boys."

"We can share custody—"

"You can walk out that door, Katie, but you are not taking the boys."

"What will you do when you are at work?"

"I don't know, but I'll figure it out."

She knew she had rights to shared custody. She would pursue that with him after he had cooled off.

"When should we tell them?" Katie asked hesitantly.

"It's your decision, you tell them," said Eric angrily as he started toward the door.

"You are not going to Ted's, are you?" Katie asked

"No, I'll leave that to you," he said sarcastically. "Tell me, do you love him?"

Katie sighed and said, "I don't know. I'm not leaving because of him, Eric. I know what I did was wrong and I am so sorry for all the pain it's causing you and will cause the boys. I need time to sort it all out. I am not going to go to him, that's not what this is about. I have rented a little apartment in town."

Eric yelled sharply, "Be gone when I come back."

"I'll pick up the boys in the morning, talk to them and they could stay with me or I could bring them here around noon," Katie said tentatively.

Eric glared at her. "This is their home. Bring them here." Then he went out the front door, slamming it behind him.

Katie had gathered some of her things, including a sleeping bag. She had the key to the apartment, so she drove there. The utilities were not hooked up yet. Using her flashlight, she scanned the apartment. Finding a place on the living room floor, she spread out her sleeping bag and pillow, lay down, and cried herself to sleep.

CHAPTER 68

October 3, 1987

Katie picked up some donuts and milk from the local bakery, then picked up Max and Sam at their friend's house and drove them to the local park, where they played on the playground equipment. She laid out a light blanket on the picnic table, setting the donuts and milk out. The boys were excited about the treat. She had been dreading telling them even more than telling Eric. After they had polished off their donuts, Katie gently said, "Max and Sam, I need to tell you something. You know that your dad and I love both of you very, very much, nothing could ever change that. And some moms and dads live together and some live in different places?"

Sam was stone silent, looking at his mom suspiciously. Max, with a milk moustache, looked at his mom and said, "Yeah, like Eli and Meadow?"

"Right, well, I have decided to get an apartment in town and live there for a while, and you boys will have two homes. You'll have your dad's house and my apartment in town. It will be an adjustment for everyone, but it is something I really need to do."

Sam scowled and demanded, "Why?"

"I am unhappy, Sam, and need to try something different. It has nothing to do with either of you; you haven't done anything wrong or anything, I want you to make sure and know that. We will both be your parents and will love and take care of you no matter what."

"So you don't want to be married to Dad anymore?" Sam asked angrily.

"I don't think so. He is very angry at me right now. I need time to think about all of this," Katie replied.

Max had started to cry and choked out, "Mama, I want you to live at our house."

"I know, honey," she said softly, giving him a hug.

When she tried to hug Sam, he pushed her away and, with his lip trembling, he said, "This sucks. I want to go home." He then ran over to the car, got in the back seat, and slammed the door.

Katie nodded, gathered her things, put her arm around Max, and walked to the car. They drove silently up the familiar road. When they got to the house, they jumped out of the car and ran to the front door. She watched as Eric opened their old wooden door, hugged each of them, ushered them into the house without making eye contact with her, and shut the door. Katie sat silently in the car for a few minutes, knowing that it was going to be a painful process for all of them. She prayed that she had made the right decision.

CHAPTER 69

October 16, 1987

Katie drove to Highway 101 and toward her hometown. Now it was time for her to tell Gino the news, and she felt almost as nervous as she had when she told Eric and the boys. On her radio, the Eagles song "Take It Easy" was playing. That sure was easier said than done, she thought. The week had been a tough one. Eric was still feeling very angry and betrayed, which she could understand. She had decided not to see Ted anymore, and he had been disappointed. He had assumed her leaving Eric was a sign that she wanted to commit to their relationship, but that had never been her intent. She needed to have time to herself and to really sort out what she wanted. So now the only two men she had ever been intimate with were angry with her.

Sam and Max were having a tough time, too. They still wanted things to be the way they were, but they never would be. She had told their teachers so they could be aware of the transition, and also had told Aunt Katherine, Laura, Rosemary, and some of her other friends. They were supportive, though they all liked Eric, and were sad to see them splitting up. Aunt Katherine suggested counseling, but Katie felt it was too late for that.

In the meantime, Gino was sitting in his recliner and was flipping through a *National Geographic*. Since he had retired, baseball had become even more important to him, and now that the season had ended he was feeling let down. It had been a terrific season, the Giants had won the National League West, and for the first time since 1971, they were in the National League playoff. They had been battling the St. Louis Cardinals for the last two weeks, and just the day before went into the seventh game in Busch Stadium with a tied record of 3–3. But they had lost the seventh game. He had so hoped that they would make it to the World Series. The good news was that they had gone in only two years from an all-time low to almost winning the pennant, and that was impressive. Will Clark, a young first baseman and a powerhouse hitter, had helped them make the turnaround.

Gino was thrilled that he had his two grandsons to take to ballgames now. At eleven, Sam was the perfect age for going to games, and even six-year-old Max went some of the time. Bill was often at the games now, but Gino was able to ignore him most of the time. If both boys wanted to go to the game, Bill often had one of his tickets available, so that was convenient.

A lot of construction was underway at Candlestick Park to make the stadium stronger in case of earthquakes. Some of the fans were annoyed with the inconvenience and the cost of the project. "Government regulations, we don't need all of that," some of them grumbled, because the price of tickets would be going up.

Gino was happy that Katie was coming by to visit today. She had called the previous day about coming, and she said that she would be alone. It was unusual for her to come without the boys. He had a pot of stew bubbling on the stove and was looking forward to having an early dinner with her.

Katie drove into the familiar driveway and parked her car; she took some deep breaths and opened her car door. Her father came out the front door and as he approached her, he could tell something was wrong. He gave her a big bear hug and kiss and said, "Honey, are you okay?"

Katie shrugged, holding back the tears, and said, "Let's go inside. There is something I need to tell you."

Gino froze, "Are the boys okay?"

"No one is sick or hurt. It isn't anything like that," Katie said as they headed into the house.

After they sat down on the couch, Katie said, "Eric and I are separating."

Gino was shocked. "What happened?"

Katie answered, "It's complicated. It was my decision."

"Is there another person involved?" he asked sternly.

Katie nodded and Gino flew off the handle, "That son of a bitch, how dare he do something like that to you!"

She interrupted him and said, "Dad, it wasn't him, it was me. I had an affair, and it was really wrong of me to do that, and I am not seeing him anymore, but I have been unhappy for a long time and I—"

Gino was stunned, "I—I just don't believe it. Katie, what about the boys? Have you thought about how hard this is on them?"

"Yes, and it has been tearing me up, but Dad, I just couldn't—" she said, as tears ran down her face.

"Katie, I think you are giving up too soon. Eric is a good man and good father and maybe you can go to counseling or something. You need to try to work this out."

Katie couldn't help but think how ironic it was that her dad was trying to talk her into getting back together with Eric after all of the years that he had tried to keep them apart. "Dad, one thing I have wanted to do is go back to school and pursue a career, and now that I will need to support myself it is even more important. I would like to go to Sonoma State and get my degree to be a social worker, and I am going to apply for financial aid, but I'm going to need some help."

"Yes, Katie, I will. I still have some of the money I had set aside for you."

He took a white handkerchief out of his pocket and started to dry the tears on her face.

"Thanks, Dad. I love you."

"Love you, too, Katie."

CHAPTER 70

September 18, 1988

A doorman greeted Bill at the front door of Stephen's apartment building. He called up to announce Bill's arrival, and then he escorted Bill to the elevator. Bill rode up to the top floor and exited the elevator and thought about how Stephen had really made it big to have a place like this. He knocked at the door, and Eric answered it. He had hoped that Eric would outgrow his need for a beard and long hair, but he hadn't, and he had added an earring to his look. Well, he didn't know where he went wrong with Eric, but he was sure glad he had one successful son.

Eric led him into the living room and motioned for him to sit down and offered him some coffee. The large picture windows displayed a beautiful view of the San Francisco Bay. There were sailboats bobbing in the distance and seagulls gliding through the beautiful clear blue sky. Tony stood up from the brown leather chair that he was sitting in and extended his hand to Bill and said, "Remember me, I'm Tony. It's been a while. We met at a couple of Giants games. "

"Yeah, that's right. Where's Stephen?" Bill asked.

Tony answered, "He's in the bathroom and should be out soon." Trying to make conversation, he asked, "How are the Giants doing anyway?"

"Not as well as last year. Right now they have won seventy-eight and lost seventy-one. At least they aren't doing as bad as a couple of years ago. After the season is over, they are doing a big retrofitting project on the stadium because of earthquake standards, and hopefully they will have it done before next season starts. I think that the inspectors are being overcautious, wanting all that work done, and probably getting a kickback from some of the big contracting companies. I really don't think it's necessary."

Just as Eric brought a carafe of coffee and cups and sat them on the beautiful glass-topped coffee table, Stephen entered the room. His father glanced at him and then did a double take. Was this really his son? He was pale, gaunt, and his blue seersucker robe hung loosely over his thin frame. Bill couldn't believe how much his son had changed in the last few months. He shook his hand and they both sat down.

Bill looked at Stephen and said, "You look like hell, son. What is wrong with you?"

Stephen took a deep breath and said, "Dad, I have AIDS."

"Oh, my God," he gasped, "How could you have gotten that? I mean, you haven't had any blood transfusions."

"No, Dad, I didn't get it from blood transfusions. I got it because I am gay and I wasn't careful."

"Now, wait just a minute. You are not saying you are a homo, are you? You can't be! I mean you have always been so manly, so athletic; I mean you were a Marine officer, for God's sake."

Stephen answered vehemently, "Yeah, Dad, I am a 'homo,' and if you knew me, you wouldn't even need to ask me. My whole life you have tried to shape me into who you wanted me to be and I tried to do everything I could to fight who I really was, and I'm not going to live a lie anymore."

Bill looked over at Tony and said sharply, "This is a family matter and I think you should leave while we are discussing this."

Stephen went over to Tony, took his hand and said, "This is my family. Tony is my partner, and he is not leaving because he lives here, and I love him."

Bill's hands shook as he put his coffee cup down. Was this a bad dream? Eric sat quietly and for the first time that he could remember had some compassion for his dad. Yeah, he was an asshole, but this was such tough news to hear, and all in one conversation.

After a long period of silence Bill asked grimly, "What's the prognosis?"

"I was diagnosed with the HIV virus two years ago. Up until recently, I was doing pretty well, taking a lot of supplements, being very careful with my diet. However, in the last few months I have been losing a lot of weight, and two weeks ago, I was diagnosed with pneumocystis pneumonia. It is hard to say how much time I have, because each person is different. I plan to resign from my job this week, and I am getting my affairs in order. We'll either sell this place or rent it out, and we want to move to a little place near the ocean. The good news is that I have been fortunate in the investments that I have made, and so we are financially secure."

"There has got to be something they can do for you," Bill insisted.

"There's no cure, Dad. They can try to treat the symptoms, but my immune system is so compromised, I will continue to get sicker."

"What are you going to tell them at work? Maybe you could tell them you have cancer or something, I mean they really don't need to know."

Stephen responded angrily, "That's what you are most worried about, Dad? What people will think of me being gay and having AIDS, and the reflection it will have on you! It's all about you, and it always has been! I will not lie anymore and I want to only be around people who can accept me as I am. Stress is one of the things that can contribute to my illness and that I have some control over, so if you can't be supportive, I think it's best that we really limit our contact. I know that this has been a lot to take in, so why don't you take some time and let me know where you stand."

Bill nodded and said, "Yeah, okay, well, I better get going and let you get some rest."

Eric stood up and said, "I'll walk out with you, Dad, I need to get back up to Willits and pick up the kids from Katie's apartment."

When Eric went to Stephen and gave him a hug, he noticed that his eyes had welled up with tears and that they had started trickling down his face. Eric hugged Tony, who burst into tears. Bill awkwardly shook Stephen's hand and nodded his goodbye to Tony.

Eric and Bill rode down the elevator silently, and when they arrived at the ground floor, Eric said, "Let's try to do whatever we can to help Stephen. I know it's tough, but we are going to get through it." He gave his Dad a hug and when they parted, saw, for the first time ever, a tear running down his father's cheek.

Eric unlocked his car and started driving north over the Golden Gate Bridge, and thought, "This is definitely the worst year of my life." Separating from Katie and adjusting to life without her had been so painful. They had worked out a split custody agreement, and the boys seemed to be adjusting okay. Katie had gone back to school and was commuting to Sonoma State two days a week. She seemed to be really enjoying her classes and her new life in town and actually looked happier than he had seen her in a long time. She was no longer seeing Ted, but Eric was still reeling from her betrayal, and didn't know if he would ever be able to put it behind him.

CHAPTER 71

October 16, 1989

Katie had just picked up Max from his third grade classroom, and he was wild with excitement in his orange and black Giants hat. "My teacher said that I am so lucky to get to go to the World Series tomorrow. The kids think I'm really lucky not to go to school tomorrow. Mrs. Jones says that she'll watch it on TV and look for me. Do you think she'll see me?"

Katie laughed, "Well, there will be a lot of people, but she might." Driving through town, she pointed out the beautiful orange, yellow, and crimson leaves falling onto the sidewalk. She turned into the middle school parking lot and Sam, now an eighth grader, was standing out in front of the office. He was wearing his Giants hat and t-shirt, and though he was probably even more excited than his younger brother, he was trying to be cool about it as he climbed into the car.

"How was school, Sam?"

He shrugged, distracted by the group of girls who were looking at him as they drove away.

"Did you both pick up your work for the rest of the day and your homework?" They groaned that they had, but really didn't see the necessity.

"You know that was part of the bargain. I packed some snacks for you, so help yourself. I want you to work on your schoolwork now because it will be a busy day, and you will be getting home late."

"So Dad is going to pick us up from Nonno's tomorrow?" asked Max.

"That's right. We are going to meet Nonno at Tommy's Joynt for lunch in San Francisco. He is going to take you from there to Candlestick where you will meet your Grandpa Bill. After the game, Nonno will take you back to his house and your dad will pick you up there and drive you back home. It will be really late, but you guys can sleep in the car on the way home."

"Aw, Mom, I think we should spend the night at Nonno's and not worry about school on Wednesday," said Sam.

Katie decided to ignore Sam's comment. She was hoping that Eric would get them to school on Wednesday, but she was going to leave that in his court.

Max said, "I wish you were coming to the game, Mom."

"Yeah, that would be fun, but there aren't enough tickets, and I want you and Sam to get to experience this World Series with your grandpas. You know, I got to go the last time the Giants played in the World Series and so did your dad. So we thought it would be great for you to go this time."

"Yeah, thanks, Mom. My friends, especially the ones I play Little League with, all think it is really cool that I get to go to this game. Where are you going after you drop us off?"

"Well, after lunch with you guys, I have a little shopping to do, and then I will head to Oakland. My good friend and college roommate Rosemary from Chicago is in the Bay Area on business. She is staying with her sister in Oakland. I am going to have dinner with them and spend the night and will leave in the morning in time to get to my class at Sonoma State at 10:00. It will save me going all the way home and then coming back. It's been a long time since I have seen her, so I am really looking forward to it."

It had been a challenging last couple of years, and her biggest concern had been how her separation from Eric had affected boys. She knew it had been hard on them, having to go between the two households. They had begged them to get back together, but seemed to have adjusted now to the new "normal." Eric seemed to be doing well in his career as a registered nurse, working at a nearby hospital, and sharing custody with her. Though sharing custody at the beginning of the separation had been somewhat contentious, they had been able to work through it with the help of a mediator.

Katie still felt guilty about her affair with Ted, and hoped that Eric would find it in his heart to forgive her someday. She didn't think that either of the boys knew about it and was thankful that Eric hadn't found it necessary to tell them about it. Katie hoped that she and Eric could become friends eventually, but he was still very cool with her, which she understood because he was hurt. However, she was grateful that they could co-parent civilly, and she would settle for that.

Right now her focus was on finishing her education and taking care of her sons, and she really wasn't interested in the complications that dating would inevitably bring. She had been able to secure some grants and scholarships and, along with her Dad's support, she was able to take a full load at Sonoma State University. She was making good progress toward her goal of completing her degree in social work in three more semesters. She absolutely loved her college classes and found it so intellectually stimulating to be in college again. There were times when Katie had wished that she had stayed in school when she was young and made other choices, but then she remembered that there were many good times and lessons she had learned through those years as well. Now was a different season of her life, and she had made peace that her past had brought her to where she was now.

Her heart was heavy about her brother-in-law Stephen, and she wished there was more that she could do to help. Stephen had sold his penthouse apartment in San Francisco and the previous year had bought a little house in Mendocino with a view of the ocean. He and Tony seemed to really like the community and the slower paced life.

Stephen was now in hospice care, and was being cared for by Tony and in-home care providers. Eric went there when he was able to, to care for his brother and give Tony a break. The plan was that when the end was near, Eric would stay with them full-time and care for him. Katie was touched by Eric's devotion to his brother, and it reminded her of what a genuinely kind man her sons' father was.

She glanced in the rearview mirror and saw that Max was asleep with his head cocked backward and his mouth wide open; his cap had fallen off, and his straight blonde hair was sticking straight up in the front. Sam had his Walkman cassette player earphones on and was keeping time to the music of Weird Al Yankovic. Katie turned the radio on and listened to local news. All of Northern California was buzzing about their Oakland and San Francisco teams playing each other in the World Series and had coined the matchup teams the "Battle of the Bay."

CHAPTER 72

October 17, 1989

5:15 p.m.

Gino talked to the security guards, who were down by the field, told them about his missing grandsons, and described them. One of them radioed the others on patrol at the exit, and they said they would be on the lookout for kids separated from their families and would keep them with them until claimed, but hadn't seen any kids by that description. Although their other grandfather Bill had ordered Gino to stay near their seats in case the boys came back, Gino thought to himself, "That's stupid; they would never head back here. They were at the bathrooms when the earthquake hit or heading back to the seats. Although the crowd has been orderly, there was always a chance for panic and stampede, and the last thing someone would want to do is go against the crowd. Sam is a smart kid, he would know that."

Gino started toward the exit, and when he reached the gate, he saw Ralph O'Connor, a policeman who he had worked with many years before. He approached him, and Ralph called out, "Pulli, can you believe this crazy situation? Gotta say the crowd is pretty mellow considering the situation. It scared the crap out of me." Gino went on to tell him about the missing boys and described them. Ralph radioed a couple of his fellow officers and assured him that he would be on the lookout. "It's getting dark, if you don't find them in the next fifteen minutes, come back and let me know."

Gino then saw Bill, wandering through the crowd looking for the boys. Gino suddenly had a realization and called, "Bill, I think I know where they are, follow me." They headed toward Gino's car a few blocks away, and sure enough, there were the boys sitting on the hood of the car. When the boys saw their grandfathers coming, they ran toward them, giving them hugs, and crying into their shoulders. Bill accepted the hugs and kisses, and the trauma of the earthquake was overshadowed by the relief and joy they felt seeing each other in the dusk of that eventful evening. Sam said with a quivering lip, "We were just coming out of the bathroom when the earthquake hit. I shoved Max under a doorway in the bathroom, because I had always heard that was the safest place, and when it stopped shaking and all the people were headed to the exit, I thought we better just go with the flow, and then it was so crowded near the exits, and there were so many of them, I thought it would be best to come to the car and wait for you here. I knew you would come here eventually."

Max was still crying and said, "When the earthquake first hit I thought it was like you said, Nonno, that the place was rocking and rolling because of the World Series. Yeah, I was really scared, but Sam said I'd be okay and that you guys would find us."

"Good thinking, Sam," Bill said proudly.

As Gino unlocked the doors of the car and motioned for them to get in, he said, "Yeah, well done, I'm proud of both of you boys. You used good judgment, Sam, and it sounds like you cooperated with your brother, Max. Now we need to figure out our next step. I want to get you boys out of the city. No telling what could happen next. My friend Ralph is on patrol near where we exited. I am going back to talk to him and find out more information about what bridges and roads are accessible. He will have the latest information. Okay, Bill, you stay here with the boys. I will be back as soon as possible."

Gino jogged down the crowded street and found Ralph, who

was in his patrol car, listening intently to his police radio. When the broadcast was over he started to put his siren on, and then noticed Gino standing at his window. "We found the boys! Now I'm trying to figure out how to get them to San Rafael. Can you help me?"

"Jump in, Gino. Where are the kids?" Gino told him, and with the siren on, they headed to Gino's car. Ralph said, "A big fire has broken out in the Marina District and I'm heading there. I suggest you leave your car here. I'll take you and the kids down that way, and you can get on a ferry to Larkspur."

"Thanks, Ralph," Gino said as they got to Bill and the boys. He yelled at the kids to jump in the police car and then asked Bill, "Want to come home with us?"

Bill answered, "No thanks, I'll go get my car and head down the Peninsula toward home."

At that, they all waved to Bill, and with lights flashing and sirens wailing, headed through the city, weaving in and out of traffic. Gino asked Ralph how the bridges had been holding up through the earthquake. Ralph said, "The Golden Gate Bridge seems to have weathered the earthquake all right, but part of the Bay Bridge has come apart and the Cypress Viaduct has collapsed. They think hundreds of people may have died. There are people trapped in their cars and—"

Before he could finish, chilling fear hit Gino, and he thought, "Katie was supposed to meet Rosemary in Oakland around 5:30, and that means she could have been going over the bridge or on the viaduct at the time of the earthquake. Oh, my God, please, you answered my prayers regarding the boys, now please, I plead that she is safe."

Ralph slowed the squad car and Gino yelled, "Thanks a million!" He and the boys jumped out and watched the flashing lights head toward the Marina District. They had to walk about four blocks to the ferry. He passed a long line of people at a phone booth, and considered stopping to try to make calls, but it was obvious that the circuits were busy. His priority was to get the boys home, and he needed to get to the ferry. When they arrived at the ferry terminal, there was a very long line, but he was told that they had put extra boats in service and that the line should go pretty quickly.

A woman in line in front of them had a small transistor radio and Gino strained to hear the news. The announcer was talking about the Bay Bridge collapse, and reported that earlier reports that hundreds could have died on the Bay Bridge were wrong—they were now receiving reports that the traffic on the bridge was a lot lighter than average because people had either gone home early to watch the World Series or stayed after work to watch it at bars or at viewing parties, so the estimate was much lower for the number of potential casualties. Gino was glad to hear that, but the fact remained that Katie may have been one of them.

After waiting for about an hour and a half in line, Gino and the boys boarded the ferry. He realized that he had left his old plaid picnic bag, thermos, and stadium blanket at the game. Well, that was the least of his problems, and he had been holding on to those way too long anyway. They squeezed into a table near the snack bar, and Gino ordered them hot dogs, chips, and hot chocolate. As the boys sat eating their food, Sam said, "How are we going to get from Larkspur Landing to your house, Nonno?"

"I haven't figured that one out yet."

A man dressed in a business suit at the next table overheard them and said, "Where do you live?"

"In San Rafael," Gino answered.

"Well, my name is Phil and I live in Novato and go right through San Rafael; I can give you a lift," the man offered.

Gino gratefully replied, "Thanks so much."

Max started to tell Phil all about their adventures getting separated at Candlestick and then their ride in the police car. Phil told them that he had been working on the forty-sixth floor of the Transamerica building when the earthquake struck; it was crazy how the top of the building swayed. "The architects who designed it really knew what they were doing, thank God. The electricity went out, so we had to walk down all forty-six floors in the dark." It had been quite an evening for all of them.

When they arrived in Larkspur, Phil led them to his late model silver Mercedes-Benz and they all climbed in. The traffic on Highway 101 was congested, but was not as bad as they had anticipated. Within thirty minutes, they were driving up to the Pulli house, thanked Phil, and jumped out of the car. Eric barged through the front door and swept both of the boys in his arms. They clung to their father for a long time, and when they were ready to let go, Eric came over and hugged Gino. "Thanks for keeping my boys safe," he said, and as the men embraced, they cried. The boys had already run into the house looking for their mom.

"Have you heard from Katie?" Gino asked with a trembling voice.

Eric answered somberly, "No, and I have been worried sick. I know that the circuits are busy right now, so even if she's trying to call us, I don't think she can get through. I was going to try to call Rosemary's sister, but I have no idea what her married name is, do you?"

"I don't know either. Did you hear about the Bay Bridge?" Gino asked, and Eric nodded.

The boys came back out to the porch and Sam asked, "Where's Mom? Is she okay?"

Eric said, "She was over in Oakland, so it will probably just take her longer to get back here. Why don't we go back inside? Why don't you get ready for bed, we are going to stay here tonight."

"Yippee! We don't have to go to school tomorrow!" Max exclaimed. They got into the twin beds in the spare room that was very familiar to them. Sam got out his book to read and turned on the little reading light above his bed.

Max said, "Would you rub my back, Dad? Would you have Mom come and tuck us in when she gets home?"

"Sure, I will," Eric responded.

As he sat there rubbing Max's back, he started thinking about Katie. He was so worried about her, and more than anything he wanted her to be all right. Initially, he had blamed the failure of their marriage on Katie and her being unfaithful to him, but recently he had really been seeing the big picture more clearly. She had been so young and innocent when they got together; she had never even had another boyfriend. She had essentially given up college and even her relationship with her dad for some time to be with him. She had supported his Conscientious Objector journey, had gone along with their alternative lifestyle, and was even initially supportive of his Rock Medicine work. Hadn't she said in later years that she felt isolated, unhappy, and had wanted to move into town? Wasn't he gone long hours putting work, college, the kids, his volunteer work, before spending time with her? Hadn't she asked him to go to counseling and he had said it was unnecessary? Had he really stopped and asked her along the way what she wanted, or did he just assume that she had the same goals as he did? These questions all ran through his mind, and the feeling that he finally was having this epiphany, but that it may be too late, was excruciating. He didn't know if they could ever get back together as a couple, but he made the vow that if she had lived through this, he would apologize for his part in their break-up and work toward being friends as she had wanted.

Max and Sam had both fallen asleep, so Eric went out to the living room where Gino was listening to the news. He had barely sat down when the phone rang, and both men sprang up with their hearts in their throats. Gino was breathless as he answered the phone, "Hello," and then said, "Hello, Katherine. We thought maybe it was Katie. Yeah, the boys and I got home okay from the game. It was an ordeal, but we're fine, Eric is here, too. We're still waiting to hear from Katie, she was over in Oakland we think. Yeah, I know about the bridge. Yeah, we're praying she wasn't on it, too. Okay, we'll let you know when she gets here, if we can get through. Love you, too, sis."

"The good news is that the circuits are opening up, so if Katie is trying to call, maybe we'll hear from her soon. I want to get a hold of the Oakland Police Department and see if they have any information, but I don't want to tie up the phone in case she calls. Maybe I should go to the neighbors to—"

Just then, they heard a car pull up in the driveway, they both rushed to the front door, and Gino flew the front door open. "Thank God! It's Katie!!!"

She jumped out of the car and ran toward the house, crying hysterically, "Are the boys okay?"

Gino ran toward her, replying, "Yes, yes, they are fine. They are in the house sound asleep." He hugged her tightly and said, "Honey, I was so worried about you, and I felt so helpless. I prayed so hard that everyone would be okay and that God would send angels to protect you. I'm so grateful that my prayers were answered." He cried tears of relief as he held his precious daughter and kissed her on the forehead as he did when she was a little girl, and pulled out his handkerchief to dry her tears.

When Gino finally let go of Katie, she saw that Eric was standing behind him. He came up to her awkwardly, giving her a hug for the first time since their separation. "It's really good to see you, Katie."

As they walked inside Eric said, "Max and Sam are exhausted, they had quite an adventure with Nonno getting back home. I'll let them fill you in. Of course, they are as happy as clams that they don't have to go to school tomorrow. We just told them that it was taking you a while to get back from Oakland. We have been so worried about you. We were worried that you may have been on the Bay Bridge or the Cypress Viaduct when it hit."

"It was a total miracle. I was just coming off the viaduct when the earthquake hit. If I had been a couple minutes later, I—" Katie stopped herself. "I went all the way around to the north side of the Bay and through Vallejo. The traffic was terrible, and that is what took me so long."

"I need to see the boys," she said as she headed down the hall.

"I told them you would come tuck them in," Eric answered.

They walked into the bedroom, and Katie tucked them in and

kissed each of them tenderly on their foreheads while Eric watched her. He took her hand and said, "Katie, I want you to know that I am sorry for the part I played in the break-up. I can see that I really didn't make your needs a priority. I want to be friends, and if you are interested, maybe more?"

She smiled and said, "Thank you, Eric, I feel so badly about how I hurt you, and I was afraid that you would never forgive me. Let's take it one step at a time. Right now I want to relish this moment of us all being here, safe, together, with our wonderful children. Lots to be grateful for, huh, and you have to admit we made some beautiful children together."

"Smart, too," Eric answered and gave her a big hug.

The phone rang again and Gino pulled the familiar yellow receiver from the wall. "Pulli Residence," he said with a light heart. "Oh, Rosemary, thanks for calling. Katie just got home. Yep, everyone is fine."